BLOOD MOON RISING

TOOTH & CLAW
BOOK 2

AMELIA FAULKNER

Ravensword
Press

First electronic publication: April 2015.
First paperback publication: March 2025.
https://ravenswordpress.com

Blood Moon Rising is set in the UK, and as such uses British English throughout.

CONTENTS

GLOSSARY

Areet: All right. E.g. *Y'areet there, petal?* or *It's areet, in't it?*

Aye: Yes. *Aye, it was me.*

Barmpot: Fool. This tends to be used as a term of mild frustration or exasperation. It isn't too derogatory, but it's not all that fond either. *The fella's a total barmpot!*

Cadge: Borrow. *Can I cadge a tenner? I'll pay it back…*

Daft apeth: Fool. This is a term of fondness or endearment while still expressing how silly you think someone's being. *You don't have to pay me back ten quid, you daft apeth.*

Earwig: Eavesdrop. This can either be in, on, or as-is: *I was earwigging in on Albert t'other day* or *Oi, stop earwigging, it's rude!*

Gradely: Good. Excellent, even, especially combined with reet: *Aye, it were reet gradely!*

Happen: Reckon. *I'll 'appen as it'll take a few days.*

In't: In the, or isn't. *I'll be over in't morning* or *It in't time for dinner yet!*

Owt: Anything. *I didn't bring owt with me. Were I s'posed to?*

Reet: Right. Very. *I'll 'appen as it were reet gradely!*

Petal: Term of endearment. *Y'areet there petal?*

Tosser: Wanker. From 'tossing off', i.e. wanking. *Aye, 'e's a reet tosser, he is.*

Wazzock: Idiot. Mildly derogatory. *Then the wazzock dropped 'is trousers an' we all had a good laugh!*

PROLOGUE

CHARLES' desk was polished to perfection. The low light in his office glimmered across it, bringing out red and golden highlights from the imported cherry wood. It was already an antique when he had purchased it a hundred or so years ago; rescued from the French Revolution like a child borne from a house fire.

The room itself was cavernously tall for London. All the rooms in the house were tall. He'd been overawed by them during their construction when he was a child, and that awe had propelled him toward a purchase once he married. The house had evaded cholera and The Stink. It had withstood the mass exodus of London's fashionable elite and the influx of the lower classes. It managed to escape demolition after the Great War and the Blitz of the Second World War. It was a survivor.

Like its owner.

He'd never produced offspring. His wife died of tuberculosis weeks after they had moved in together, a handful of months before the cure was found. The house he bought to raise a family in became a tomb for the life they never lived.

The world continued on, uncaring. Lives were destroyed, buildings wrecked, and time marched forward without pause and without mercy.

He regarded the desk. It was older than him. It had seen the inside of a royal palace. Yet here it was, to serve his purpose. And his purpose was to thrive, not merely to exist.

He drew just enough breath to slide a single word of command past his lips, and raised his head to do so.

"Speak."

The vampire across the room from Charles hadn't been invited further in, and knew better than to approach. He stood with the closed door at his back, his shoulders high and his head bowed low in obedience. The vast room made him look especially small. He was one of these young idiots, the post-war generation of undead: too cretinous to have any ambition and too thrilled by eternal life to do anything with it.

He was, on reflection, Charles' favourite kind of vampire.

"Constable Hughes delivered his verdict to the Council." The vampire didn't fidget or so much as glance in Charles' direction. "He finds Ellis O'Neill not guilty of the murder of Tomasz Jasiński."

Charles curled his lip. His anger rose like bile, bitter and unpalatable, but it would not do to lose his temper. Instead he lifted a hand from the desk and used it to feign an adjustment of his tie.

O'Neill should have died.

Charles did not go to all the trouble of sending two people in to kill a supposedly helpless blind man only for both attempts on the cripple's life to fail so spectacularly. He even armed Jasiński with a bloody silver knife and *still* O'Neill survived.

Hughes' verdict was utter nonsense. O'Neill had killed the fool Jonas and gotten away with it, but that was Charles' error; he shouldn't have sent a vampire. O'Neill claimed defence of his territory and the matter passed into obscurity. Sending a mortal had been a far stronger proposition, yet now Jasiński lay rotting after a strikingly vulgar death.

It was enough to make one quite irate.

Charles looked toward his visitor. "Does Hughes speculate as to the cause of Jasiński's demise?"

"No. Or if he does, not openly to the Council."

"You may go." Then he added his power to his next words and said "Tell no-one that you were here."

"Yes, sir."

He watched the worm wriggle its way out of his den and looked to the newspaper beneath his hand. The advertisement was small, but offended him all the more for its subtlety, as though it were mocking his failure.

Charles could, in theory, walk up to Mayfair and murder O'Neill himself. It would be a tawdry affair, but not against the Council's laws. Getting one's hands dirty was uncouth, though, and rather tedious.

More to the point, O'Neill was shaping up to be quite the deadly opponent. Young, blind, ostensibly helpless with no allies and very little knowledge of either the history or future of his own kind, he had messily dispatched two assailants already, and Charles had no idea how he had done it. According to his sources - and what had influenced his choice in selecting an artist as a weapon - O'Neill's power was some sort of psychometric reading. So long as an item held some significance to a previous owner, O'Neill could gain some sort of vision of it by laying his hands on the item's surface.

That was hardly a lethal ability. Charles required more

information before he could make another move, or doing so could well tip his hand.

He considered the paper.

Required: Full-Time Sales Assistant.
The O'Neill Gallery seeks a Full Time Sales Assistant for immediate appointment at our Mayfair location.
The right candidate will be personable and friendly, with an avid interest in contemporary art.
No experience necessary. Full training will be given.

He had treated O'Neill far too casually and thus had underestimated him. From here on in he would tread with more care, and the first step in any successful campaign was to collect intelligence.

How fortunate, then, that O'Neill sought new people to enter into his domain. Charles merely needed to make sure that O'Neill's new employee was observant.

Obedient would not be a problem.

ONE

IF ELLIS WEREN'T ALREADY UNDEAD he was sure he'd be grey-haired by now.

Poor Jay was run off his feet fielding all the phone calls Ellis couldn't answer. The latest was from Edison, the older of Ellis' brothers. "I'm sorry, Mr. O'Neill. He isn't here at the moment-"

Ellis winced as Jay lied into the handset. He could hear Edison's shouting from across the room.

"When is he ever there? I've tried mornings but nobody bloody answers! I've tried afternoons and all I get is you, telling me he isn't there until the evening. Well, now it's the damn evening! Where is he?"

"Mr. O'Neill - er, Ellis - is hosting a private showing this evening. If you care to leave a message-"

"I swear to god if I have to come down to London to speak to him I damn well will!"

Ellis tugged his glasses off so that he could rub the bridge of his nose. He closed his eyes to avoid having to cope with dim light seeping into his world.

"Why don't you do that, Mr. O'Neill?" Jay chirped with an undercurrent of glee. "I'm sure Ellis can be just as busy whether you're here or there."

"You little shitweasel! When I-"

"Have a lovely evening, sir!" Jay dropped the handset back onto the cradle with a light crash. "He's a keeper!"

Ellis snorted. "If by keeper you mean arsehole."

"You know me, sweetie. I like to keep a good arsehole on hand."

Jay's tone was positively filthy, and Ellis couldn't help but twitch out a flicker of a smile. He nudged his glasses back into place. "You're a constant horror in my life, Jay. I hope not to hear any more about your husband's rear end."

"At least until tomorrow," Jay chimed in. His chair creaked. "What're we gonna do though?" he asked, tone fading toward serious.

"I haven't a clue."

He knew why Edison was trying to get in touch. Dad wanted his money back and was making Edison do all the leg work. The trouble was that electronic equipment didn't register Ellis' presence so he couldn't speak to Edison over the phone, which left Jay in charge of that department. And Ellis didn't have a million pounds lying about the place to pay back the loan and get Edison to piss off.

That wasn't the only caller Jay had to fend off either. Guide Dogs for the Blind had been ringing incessantly to schedule a welfare checkup for Tiberius, but not only did they phone, they wanted to see Ellis with Tiberius during the day and preferably out on a walk together to observe dog and owner as a holistic unit. There was only so long Jay could fob them off before they simply arrived one day to collect Tiberius and take him away.

Ellis frowned and dipped a hand down to the side of his

chair. He sought Tiberius' head and fussed it, more to soothe himself than the German Shepherd.

They had been inundated with C.V.s for the sales assistant job, too. On the tail end of a recession they had received applications from people who weren't remotely suitable yet who were desperate enough to call the gallery every day to ask about the status of their application. He had to admire their dedication, even if they felt that the requirement for an interest in art was only necessary for *other* candidates.

If all the fuss over Ellis' mundane existence weren't enough, he then had Constable Hughes to worry about. Hughes had dropped by to question him over the death of Peter Barnes - who turned out to have been a Polish painter named Tomasz Jasiński - simply because Jasiński had been mauled to death in Ellis' territory and Ellis owned a dog. Fearful that Tiberius could be put down for attacking someone, Ellis had denied everything only to realise all too late that Hughes only cared whether or not Ellis had acted in self defence. Instead Ellis had lied to a Constable, pretended he hadn't been anywhere near the scene of the crime, and now Hughes was suspicious of the unexplained wounds on Jasiński's corpse.

Which brought Ellis neatly to Randall.

Kind, sweet Randall. First date, dinner and frottage; second date, manslaughter.

No wonder Randall wouldn't commit to a third date.

Ellis trapped his lower lip and gnawed on it without any real force. He couldn't put into words his feelings for the vibrant werewolf. Everything was so jumbled up, so complicated, but just the thought of him made Ellis' mind whirl with hope and his body quiver in need. He loved the warmth radiating from Randall's satin skin and the way that softness was underlined by hard, stocky muscle. He was captivated by the texture of Randall's close-cropped, wiry hair. Randall's lips were soft and full, and always eager. He smelled of fresh earth and woodland after the rain, and his blood was-

Ellis lifted his regrown hand from Tiberius' head. Good as new. Randall's blood had healed what anyone in their right mind would call a major injury, and it had done so within minutes.

He hadn't had to feed since then, either. Almost a whole month without so much as a twinge of hunger. He felt warm. Sated.

Alive.

That was what made it all so complicated. Separating his lust for Randall's blood from his love for the man himself seemed to become more difficult as time passed and memories mingled together. Maybe it'd be easier if Randall hadn't then turned into London's most elusive bachelor.

Or maybe Ellis had fallen too hard, too fast, and he'd pushed Randall away.

He couldn't help it, he really couldn't. His passions had always been swift to rise up, whether for art or men, but Randall had proved himself to be something else entirely. A whole new level of desirable Ellis hadn't ever experienced. He craved Randall so intensely that his thoughts always turned to the werewolf if he had even a moment's peace and quiet.

Like right now. He was doing it again. And he didn't care.

But Randall? Who knew what Randall thought, what he wanted, what he needed. He was evading Ellis' questions, avoiding any further dates. He stopped by the gallery two or three times a week, he responded to texts easily enough, but would he come back to Ellis' flat or go out to dinner with him? Would he heck.

It shouldn't have been a surprise. Within a fortnight of meeting Ellis, Randall's world had been flipped on its head.

He'd gone to bed with a vampire. He'd admitted that he was a werewolf. Then together they'd fought with and killed a man who had been armed with a weapon capable of destroying them both. And if that hadn't been enough to dampen Randall's feelings they'd gone back to Ellis' and had rough, desperate sex, and Ellis had fed from him.

If Ellis had intended to keep Randall in his life he was going about it all wrong.

"Penny," Jay said.

"Er." Ellis' thoughts raced to try and pinpoint where exactly in the conversation he'd stopped paying attention.

Jay's chair squeaked. Its feet dragged across the carpet. Then Jay's footfalls softly crushed fibres beneath his shoes as he walked to the kettle. "You were away with the fairies. Randall?"

"You calling Randall a fairy?" It came out flatter than Ellis had aimed for, and he felt in his pocket for his portable braille keyboard as though he'd been contemplating sending a text all along.

"I wouldn't dream of it. I'm the biggest fairy of them all." Jay chuckled as he filled the kettle. "Nobody takes my crown." The tap was turned off, the kettle slotted onto its base, and the switch clicked on. "It's high time you made him tell you what's going on."

"It's not as though I haven't tried." Ellis ran his fingers across the display, then began to text Randall. Yet again. "I think he's getting cold feet."

"If he breaks your heart, I will slag him off on Yelp. I've told him this already."

Ellis could imagine the cross look on Jay's face right about now. He'd seen it a few times, back when he still could see, and it wouldn't exactly strike fear into anyone's heart. But it was cute, and Jay was well aware of how cute he was. Jay's constant awareness of any and all nearby reflective surfaces was part of what made him so essential after Ellis had been turned.

His lips twitched themselves into an amused smirk in spite of himself. His fingers pushed at keys as he entered a text to send to Randall.

Dinner. One hour. I have a reservation.

He didn't have a reservation, of course, but it wasn't hard to get one.

"There. I've put my bossy pants on," he said as he nudged the keyboard away across his desk.

"He strikes me as a man who likes your bossy pants." Jay clinked mugs and spoons together as he continued to make tea. "You want a cup?"

"No, thanks."

"Still feeling nice and warm, eh? What's it been? A month?" Jay let out a low whistle. "I haven't seen you go for so long without any nibbles. That is-" He gasped. "You haven't, have you?"

Ellis snorted. "It's not like feeding is cheating on him somehow!"

Except he felt that it would be. So he didn't do it. But there wasn't any way he could let Jay know how potent Randall's blood was. That would lead into murky waters, and likely toward Jay figuring out that Randall wasn't strictly human.

It was bad enough that the Council would kill Jay if they found out what he knew about vampires. If Randall's people had the same kind of rules Jay would be at risk from two dangerous sources instead of just the one.

"Oh my god! Ellis! You can't go around canoodling strangers when you've got a boyfriend!" Jay poured water into his mug and stirred it. Ellis could even hear him give the tea bag a gentle squeeze and the two drips that fell from it into the tea before Jay tossed the teabag into the bin.

"The jury seems like it's out on whether or not I still *have* a boyf-" Ellis' phone buzzed in his pocket, and he grabbed the keyboard. He splayed his fingertips across the miniature braille display below the keys as they mechanically chunked away to output the text message he'd received.

Meet you at the gallery?

He flashed a grin. His fingers slid to the keys.

Yes.

Ok, Randall replied.

"Result!" Ellis straightened up, and waved a hand with artificial largess. "Bossy pants doin' the business."

Jay's footsteps, his heartbeat, came toward Ellis. His desk gave the faintest of creaks, likely inaudible to Jay, as his assistant sat on it. "Uh huh. But stop dodging me. You aren't seriously still going around necking people in pubs, right?"

Ellis' triumph flickered and dimmed. He sighed.

He couldn't lie to Jay. Hell, if he could, Jay wouldn't know he was a vampire, and Ellis himself would probably have been killed or caught any one of a hundred times over the past year.

"No. I'm not."

"Yeah. You didn't strike me as the type." Jay blew on his tea. "You aren't biting Randall while he's here, right? I mean, you're more discreet than that."

The conversation would get there sooner or later. Jay was a persistent bugger.

"I'm not. I haven't needed to eat since I last fed from Randall."

Jay's pulse perked, just slightly. He gulped down hot tea, then hissed.

Ellis waited.

"I thought..." Jay stopped.

"Yeah. Me too. But his blood's different. He's different. But I can't tell you why. I mean-" Ellis chewed the inside of his cheek "I *know* why. But it's not my secret to tell."

"Oooh." Jay put his tea down on the desk. "Okay. That's way more reasonable."

Ellis winced. "You don't mind? I mean, I can't bald-faced lie to you, Jay. Not you. But I can't tell you what he is, either. That wouldn't be fair to Randall."

Jay's hand covered Ellis'. Alive, and slightly warmer than his own flesh. Even the touch didn't stir any hunger.

"Sweetie," Jay murmured, serious for once. "I totally understand."

Ellis raised his eyebrows. "You do?"

"Uh huh. I wouldn't tell anyone about you. It'd be super shitty of me to expect you to tell anyone about Randall." Jay squeezed his hand, then hopped off the desk, feet landing lightly against the carpet. "But if he dares-"

Ellis laughed. "I know, I know. Bad reviews, the whole works."

"You're damn right!"

TWO

RANDALL TRIED to put on a smile as he studied himself in the bathroom mirror, but it wasn't coming to him. Freshly cleaned teeth and a recent shave weren't enough to hide the dark circles under his eyes.

He wouldn't fool a small child, let alone Ellis. Hell, the vampire would probably hear his cowardice in his heartbeat or something like that. The bloke was bloody perceptive for a blind man.

Couldn't hide forever, though. And a dinner date might give him the breather he desperately needed.

It wasn't easy to hide from a pack of werewolves; less so when that pack was your own. But what else could he do? Briar had made it abundantly clear that if Ellis was a vampire Randall was to destroy him, and what had Randall done?

Yeah. He'd held down Barnes so that Ellis could stab the painter with his own knife, then run back to Ellis' apartment and ridden the vampire's cock like it was going out of fashion.

If he'd just let Barnes kill Ellis he wouldn't be avoiding his own pack like the plague now, but the idea of Ellis dying shredded his heart and brought tears to his eyes.

Why hadn't he found the balls to tell Ellis how he felt? With actual words, not insinuation and a lame cop-out.

He was a bloody coward, and the knowledge made him miserable. He didn't want to lose Ellis, but he didn't dare see much of him either. What the hell was wrong with him?

Was it the bite?

His body quivered at the mere memory of it. Pinned between Ellis' cock and his fangs, he'd been helpless, weak, utterly at another predator's mercy, and he'd come harder than he could remember.

There wasn't a mark after. Not even a bruise. He hadn't expected one, but it was still weird to know that Ellis' teeth had penetrated his skin and taken something so vital and precious from inside his body and left no evidence in their wake. Was that a vampire trick or his own high-speed healing in action?

The evidence was in Ellis' body, not his own. Somehow, carried on his blood, his fast healing restored Ellis' own flesh from all the damage Barnes had done to it. It was uncanny.

His reflection seemed to mock him with its dark-eyed glower, so he turned his back on it. He had a date, and he was *not* going to bail on Ellis yet again.

Randall flicked the bathroom light off as he left and grabbed a dark purple shirt from his wardrobe. He only had a handful of proper shirts and they didn't see much use. Hell, he'd bought two of them since he first met Ellis. It didn't seem right to date in a t-shirt.

Tonight. Tonight he'd say it. He'd grow a pair and tell Ellis how he felt. It was three words, for crying out loud. How hard could it be? He'd say them, then they'd go back to Ellis' place and fuck like bunnies, and Randall would stay the night and wake up in his boyfriend's arms. No more flying visits to the gallery, no more fobbing Ellis off with shitty excuses. And he wasn't going to wait for the full moon so that he got out-of-his-head horny and stopped thinking with his brain.

That was an excuse though, wasn't it? Yet more rubbish he fed himself to paste over the fact that he was hiding out and hoping the whole mess would disappear.

Coward.

Loud knocks on the door of his flat punctured his self-loathing and twisted it into fear. Who would bang on his door this time of night? One of the neighbours come to complain about the barking from an earlier client's dog, maybe?

The knocking turned into banging, then a shout layered over the thuds.

"Randall! I know you're in! Answer the fucking door!"

Sweat prickled to the surface of his skin.

Briar.

"Oi! Randall!"

Shit. If this carried on the neighbours *would* complain.

"Okay! Okay! I'm coming!" It dried in his throat and squeaked out. He hurried to the door to fumble with the lock, and another slam of a meaty fist against the wood almost knocked the door right into his face.

Briar loomed in the doorway, filling it for a second. Then he pushed the door open all the way and strode into the flat.

Randall squeezed up against the wall. His gaze swept out into the corridor, but Preeti wasn't with her husband.

Double shit.

Randall closed the door and followed Briar into the living room, where the Alpha of his pack filled the tiny area with his presence. The flat wasn't huge by any stretch of the imagination, but with Briar in it there suddenly seemed to be no space left for anyone else.

"Where's Preeti?" Randall whispered.

"With the pack. Where you should fucking be." Briar loomed over him, sapphire eyes bright with anger.

Randall shrank back from him. Briar's gift was what made him Alpha: the ability to rein in his temper and feed his calm out to the rest of his pack. To see Briar's fury was a rare and terrifying thing, and meant that he'd made a choice to *not* hold back. Added to that was the fact that he was six foot five of tanned muscle versus Randall's five foot eight. There was a whole head's difference between them, which left Randall eye-level with Briar's pectorals at the best of times.

"I-" Randall's voice wasn't even a whisper. His mouth was dry.

Briar gave a slow, deep sigh and rolled his shoulders. His muscles unwound slowly, and the brightness leeched out of his gaze.

Randall swallowed and waited while Briar crushed his rage until it was little more than irritation.

"We need you, Rand," Briar grumbled. "I know you're all loved up, but we're your family."

Randall rocked his jaw. He couldn't meet Briar's gaze, so instead he stared down at his own feet when he said, "Um."

Briar paced like a tiger in an undersized cage. "There's shit going on, Rand, and you keep bailing on us."

Randall's cheeks grew so hot it felt like he'd developed a fever in three seconds flat. "Well maybe if Nazim-" he spat.

"You're Omega," Briar snapped, shutting him down before he'd even begun. "That's your job."

Randall balled his fists until the nails dug into his palms.

"And speaking of your job," Briar continued without pause, "have you worked out what exactly this fella you're taking it up the chuff from is yet?"

The wind was all but punched out of Randall's sails. His shoulders slumped and his fists unfurled. "No."

"But you know enough to insist he's not a vampire." Briar's eyes glinted in the low light from the energy-saving bulb over his head. "How can you be so sure about that without knowing what he *is*?"

"It's complicated," Randall mumbled. It sounded lame and he knew it.

"Then explain it proper slowly."

Randall resisted the urge to check the time. If he ended up late for his date Ellis would understand.

Hopefully.

"I'm waiting," Briar prompted.

Randall hissed. His shoulders hunched again, acting of their own accord.

Briar snorted and curled his lip, baring his teeth. "Did you ever wonder how we haven't found any new cubs in years?"

"Uh-" Randall blinked, thrown off-balance. Was this relevant? Was Briar suggesting that vampires ate cubs now? How had they leaped here from Ellis? "I, uh-"

"We search. Sometimes we even catch a scent. But then nothing. And then there are all these packs crowding in on our territory. I think they're stealing our cubs. And the more they steal the bigger they get, while we stagnate, barely able to hold ourselves together because our fucking Omega rarely shows his miserable face!" Briar had launched into a full-volume tirade by the end, and his cheeks were ruddy with fury. The light had returned to his eyes, too.

"I'm sorry," Randall blurted. The words sprang out like his mouth had already switched sides without waiting for the rest of him to follow.

"They're testing our boundaries. Some days their scent is

all over Whitechapel, Tower Hamlets, you name it! They *pissed* in Mile End Park!"

Randall fidgeted. Once he might have cared about the pack's turf being so flagrantly challenged, but now it hardly seemed to matter. "Okay."

"Okay?" Briar shot forward so fast that his chest slammed into Randall's and his spit sprayed Randall's forehead.

Randall fell back, caught his heel on the corner of a rug, and fell back onto the broken old couch. It nearly swallowed him whole.

"Nothing about this is fucking okay!" Briar's bulk seemed to blot out the light from the bulb, casting his features into shadow. "We need you, Rand. I need you! Before this shitting mess turns into a bloodbath. You're the pacifist, the body language guy, the negotiator! *You're* the one who can fix this, if only you would stop being such a pussy and show your fucking face once in a blue moon!"

Randall was curled into the sofa as though it could save him if Briar finally lost his rag and he didn't dare move enough to right himself. "I'm sorry. I didn't mean-"

"No," Briar agreed. His voice softened, and he turned away from Randall. "I know. You're younger than most of us, and you're in love. Or at least you think you are. It doesn't matter. Either way you're compromised if you think this bloke is more important than us. And that mistake could cost lives."

Randall took deep breaths and dared to sit up straight. He moved slowly, lest any sudden shift re-ignite Briar's rage.

Christ, he was already a mess and he hadn't even left the flat.

"I think maybe your lack of experience is clouding your judgement. The more time you spend away from the pack the worse it'll get." Briar glanced over a shoulder toward him. "You're already out of balance. You know you've got to stay near your Alpha, Rand. I can't help you if you keep avoiding me."

"I'm not-"

Briar nodded. "Okay. Yeah. Here's what we'll do." He turned to face Randall again, folding his arms together across the vastness of his chest. "We'll go see this boyfriend of yours and work out what he is. Once that's squared away you'll be able to concentrate on your duties more clearly. Where does he live?"

Randall's heart thudded against his ribs. His eyes felt dry, but he didn't dare blink. He felt a pressing urge to run to the bathroom and lock himself inside.

"Where, Rand."

"Patrol," Randall croaked.

Briar squinted for a moment, like he was trying to work out if he knew a place called Patrol. "What?"

Randall tried to swallow, but he was all out of saliva. "I'll join you. On patrol. Now. Tonight. I need to speak to these other shifters, defuse the situation. You're right. There's a full moon soon. It needs fixing fast, before it all goes pear shaped."

Briar stared at Randall, weighing his words.

"Good," he said. "Get something on your feet."

Randall fought his way out of the couch and scurried to the doorway to grab his boots. He crouched down and pulled his laces tight. The boots didn't go with the trousers he had on, or the purple shirt, but he doubted Briar would let him change back into casuals. The Alpha wasn't one for waiting around once his mind was set. Hell, if Briar was determined to find these other shifters they'd probably be out all night every bloody night until it happened.

Randall grit his teeth and rubbed at his eyes, then stood. He grabbed a jacket from the hooks by the door and dragged it on, his back to his Alpha, and dropped his keys into his pocket. Then he took out his phone and sent Ellis a text. Another lame excuse. Another push away from the one person who knew what he was and still gave a shit about him.

I'm sorry. Something's come up. Tomorrow, maybe?

"Get on with it," Briar rumbled, stalking toward the door.

Randall pocketed his phone. He wasn't going to see Ellis tonight, and he wasn't going to get to say the words he needed to say.

A little piece of him felt like it had died.

THREE

BY THE TIME they reached St. Mary's, Randall was dragging his feet and looking down every single side street and alleyway on the off-chance that they offered a last-minute escape.

They didn't.

Briar unlocked the unmarked door in its cubbyhole just off the High Street and held it open for Randall to precede him. It was as though the disused tube station was a prison and Briar was his jailer. But what choice did he really have?

He descended the stairs into the gloom and could hear the patter of claws, along with the yips and growls of rough play.

Randall hesitated. His fingers gripped the old hand rail so hard that he could feel the sharp edges of rust dig into his skin. There was no point to his hesitation, though. It wouldn't save him. They were wolves. They could already smell him.

Briar's hand on his spine propelled him forward, and Randall stumbled down the last few steps. He picked his way through the disused foyer and on to where the pack met, in the antique shell of a platform last used as an air raid shelter in the war.

They were all here. Preeti, Nazim, Lara, and Jim. Preeti's coyote-like form darted toward Randall and she nipped playfully at his leg, but her ears and tail were both up. She was enticing him for play, nothing more, and Randall smiled as best he could to her.

Then Nazim came, and his teeth weren't gentle.

"Enough!" Briar stepped around Randall and raised his chin.

It was like magic. Magic that Randall wished wasn't necessary. The assembled wolves skulked away from him and began the grotesque transformation back to their human shapes. When only one changed, it was something you could get used to, but with four shifting at once the sound of tearing muscle and grinding cartilage churned Randall's stomach. Then it was done, over as quickly as it had begun.

"You too busy with your new boyfriend to spend time with your family, huh?" Nazim hopped on one foot while he pulled his briefs on, which took the sting out of his words somewhat.

"He better be treating you right," Lara grumbled. She didn't bother with clothes. She stood there with her pasty white fists on her even pastier little hips and stared right at him.

"He must be," Preeti said, eyeballing Randall. She flashed him a fond smile. "'Cause Rand knows I'd rip the guy's throat out if I had to."

That was probably supposed to be heart-warming, but the image of Preeti sinking her teeth into Ellis' throat made Randall bristle.

"Easy, tiger," Briar rumbled, resting a hand on his shoulder.

And in an instant he was calm again. Everyone was.

Randall was overcome with the suspicion that Briar's

earlier fury was a calculated thing, more tightly controlled than Randall had been led to believe.

Randall gritted his teeth.

Briar had manipulated him. Briar was Alpha. He had full control over his own temperament. If he chose to loosen the leash on it for effect it would take little more than a tug to pull it back again.

Some family this was.

"Clothes," Briar said. Then he gestured to Preeti and Lara, adding, "Noses."

The women underwent the change without argument, dropping down to all fours and landing lightly on their toes.

It was better to patrol with as few wolves as possible. London was a city which bristled with CCTV, and both Preeti and Lara's wolf shapes looked more like lean, hungry dogs than the more recognisable Eurasian wolf. There was something about the ears that made them less likely to draw attention, and their tails were not as bushy.

Nazim and Jim finished dragging their clothes on, and Jim shoulder-checked Randall on the way to the stairs. The glare that accompanied Jim's contact was filled with disappointment, but not disdain.

They all bought into this bollocks idea that Randall was supposed to be their Omega, no matter how many times Randall argued against it. Might made right. It was the favoured argument of playground bullies all over the world. He'd tolerated it for more than a decade because it was an argument he couldn't win. He needed Briar, just like they all did, or they'd tear themselves apart under the full moon. That was why they patrolled. It was why they worked so hard to save cubs before they first experienced the change. Briar and Preeti had saved him from himself when he was a teenager and he would always be grateful, but he should be with Ellis right now, and he wasn't.

Randall sighed and followed them obediently up the stairs.

BOTH PREETI'S and Lara's ears perked forward at the same time.

Randall almost wished they'd found nothing; that they could all go home and no other cub's life would get sucked into this ragtag pack of miscreants, whether it would be to join Randall in his position as bottom of the pile or contribute to keeping him down there. He could go to Ellis tomorrow night and say what needed to be said, and Ellis could soothe him, take away the hurt and fear, calm his heart and his thoughts the way that only Ellis truly could.

Randall's response to Ellis' words, his presence, was as welcome as it was impossible. The vampire had some way of deflating the moon's effect on him as surely as if he were an Alpha himself. Maybe after this patrol Randall could slip away and never come back.

He glanced up as Preeti and Lara led them on. They were well into Limehouse now, travelling down some block-paved side street lined with modern flats and anodyne houses. They passed a line of parked cars - mostly smaller models better suited to inner-city life - and walls which backed a handful of gardens. Preeti darted up some steps and they all followed.

The buildings fell away as they all stepped into a small park. It was surrounded by trees to cut out the road noise and give the illusion of peace in a fairly bustling part of the city, and for the most part it would have worked if the place hadn't had a group of teenagers lolling about on the swings while they worked their way through a crate of cheap supermarket beer. It wasn't too difficult for him to see which one of them was the cub. A girl on one of the swings sat with her toes dug into the ground beneath it, and the tilt of her head was reasonably submissive, with her gaze never meeting that of her companions. It wasn't enough on its own to mark her out as a wolf shifter, but coupled with Preeti and Lara's noses Randall was around ninety percent sure it would be her.

His gut fluttered. If the girl was naturally deferential she'd easily join him at the bottom of Briar's pack's structure.

He wanted to be wrong. He hoped that she was just a shy girl and that one of her louder more extroverted friends was the source of the scent. Without his wolf's nose he couldn't even detect it, let alone work out where the trail led.

Preeti rumbled in her chest and her ears flicked as her gaze fixed on the girl Randall had earmarked.

Shit.

Briar strode toward the teens. "You," he boomed to the girl. He jabbed a thick finger toward her. "We need to talk."

The teens turned toward Briar as one, then a few gazes swept over the rest of the pack. Randall did his best to look inoffensive.

Then they erupted into a discordant array of voices. Some backed off. One boy stepped forward.

But none of them were speaking English.

Randall strained to listen. Nazim's head was tilted, too. All Randall really had under his belt was some French from school over fifteen years ago, but Nazim spoke Urdu fluently. Between them they stood a chance of recognising three of London's three hundred languages.

"Fuck," Nazim grunted. He shook his head.

Randall shook his head too, and stepped forward, his hands raised to try and show the teenagers that they meant no harm. The problem was that Briar almost always looked like he meant harm, all through the sheer size of him.

"Anyone speak English?" he said, stopping by Briar's elbow.

The teens exchanged glances, then one of them huffed. "Might do."

He had one of the most local accents Randall had ever heard. Identical to his own. The little shit. Randall couldn't help but grin slightly.

"Great. We're not here to start anything-"

The teen eyeballed Briar. A couple of others did, too, so there were at least two more English-speakers in the crowd.

"-we just want to talk to her for a few minutes." He nodded to the girl on the swing.

She couldn't have been older than fourteen. About the right age for the change to come along, and with the moon waxing in the sky overhead it would probably come damn soon.

"If you think we're leaving without her, you can fuck right off, mate."

One of the other lads began chattering away in whatever other language it was, and the rest of the teens began to bristle. The girl on the swing looked downright terrified - justifiably so, Randall reckoned.

"It won't take long," Randall said. "And you guys can keep an eye out right over there." He pointed toward trees. "We won't lay a finger on her."

"What, you think we're thick or something? Fuck off!"

Briar growled low in his throat.

The teens took a step back.

Preeti and Lara bristled and released low growls of their own before they yipped in unison. It was a warning.

About what? Not a group of human children, surely. Randall looked around, gaze scanning the trees quickly.

A group of adults entered the park through the same steps Briar's pack had used. They had three wolves with them - small, lithe things with short fur and dark backs. It was hard to tell more in the poorly-lit park with his human eyes, but the outlines looked like Indian wolves to him. It wasn't especially useful information, though. With the werewolf gene being recessive, the subspecies of wolf could come from just about anywhere in a werewolf's genetic history so far as Randall could work out.

The back and forth between the new shifters and the teenagers was immediate and indecipherable. Randall watched the interplay between them. The teens were more polite to the newcomers, and had that sullen look of kids caught with their fingers in the cookie jar. Most likely the beer, Randall surmised, but it could also be the lateness of the hour. Either way, the fact that the teens cared at all about being told off told him that at least some of one group knew some of the other. Friends of family, perhaps, or members of the same community. Either way the teens milled around before dispersing, casting looks back toward the girl they were leaving behind who, for her part, stared at the ground and gripped the swing's chains with whitened knuckles.

When it was just shifters and a cub together in a park, the dance began. The other pack was larger and, for the most part, younger. There was a spread from teens to early twenties among them, although the Alpha was somewhere around his mid-twenties.

It wasn't hard to pick an Alpha from a crowd, that was for sure. He was just shy of six feet tall and slender like a dancer. He moved with poise and confidence, and his dark eyes held a relaxed, attentive look to them. The poor light made it difficult to gauge his skin tone, but Randall guessed it to be slightly lighter than his own.

Briar's pack was outnumbered a good two to one. Jesus, no wonder Briar was getting nervous about them encroaching into his turf. He didn't have the manpower to stop them if they really wanted to make a go of it.

Both packs spread apart, trying to gain the upper hand, trying to intimidate the other into submitting first.

"I don't suppose anyone speaks English?" Randall offered, showing his palms again.

"Tell them to get off my fucking territory," Briar snarled.

"Yeah, uh, I don't actually speak anything but really basic French," Randall muttered.

"Well, what are *they* speaking?"

"I don't know."

"Nazim?" Briar bellowed.

Nazim shook his head. "Dunno."

Briar curled his lip. His fingers flexed.

Some of the other pack's shifters snorted. One gave Briar an excellent look at his middle finger. The wolves bristled at each other, their fur rippling and their ears folded back.

"You!" Briar pointed at their Alpha and took steps toward him. "You take your pack, and you leave. Now."

Their Alpha simply smiled and beckoned the girl on the swing toward him.

She sat rooted to the spot. Poor girl looked ready to pee herself.

All in all, Randall thought, tonight was proving to be proper shit.

FOUR

THIS COULD GO SOUTH ALL TOO EASILY, and nobody on either side seemed to care.

Randall sucked in a deep breath, then stepped forward, placing himself dead centre between Briar and the other pack's Alpha. He lifted his chin and held his hands loosely at his sides.

"Easy, everyone," he said. He raised his voice, but kept himself calm. "Let's not rush things." It didn't really matter what words he used; he needed his body language and his tone of voice to convey more meaning than the words he chose.

Like training dogs. Just stay calm. Be assertive. Let them take their cues from your mood.

"Get out of the fucking way," Briar snarled.

Randall kept his back to Briar. He didn't dare look him in the eyes. "Briar, you are our Alpha. You need to calm your pack."

Wolves growled at each other like soldiers across a no man's land, so Randall walked in between them until he was strolling back and forth along the invisible boundary, speaking softly, looking at each member of both packs in equal measure.

"That's right. Just relax. Nobody is getting hurt tonight, okay?"

"The cub-"

"Clearly doesn't speak a word of English." Randall cut Briar off in the same even tone. "We can't help her. They can. She has to go with them."

"She's on *our*-"

"What matters is what's best for *her*. Not for you, or me, or anyone else here." Randall risked a glance toward Briar, but didn't make eye contact. "Whatever the language is here, they can communicate with her, and we all know she's going to need a lot of communication in the coming days. Let her go, Briar. You know it's the right thing to do."

"That doesn't solve this problem." Briar gestured to the opposing pack.

"No. But we should leave first."

"Why?"

Randall puffed out his cheeks. "Because it's easier for them to speak to her while she's in a place where she feels safe. They can explain things to her here and she won't feel like they're kidnapping her. Her night's going to be terrifying enough. She doesn't need us to add to it."

Briar narrowed his eyes. Then he spat on the ground and snarled, one final parting shot to the other Alpha, who simply sneered back at him.

"Fine," Briar rumbled. "We go."

Jim and Lara moved first. They broke away toward the stairs, giving the other pack a wide berth. Then Nazim followed, taking his first steps backward before he turned away.

Briar gestured for Randall to go, but Randall shook his head. "Wrong energy. You go first."

Preeti flicked her tail in agreement, and looked up to Briar with a soft chuff to invite him along with her. Then she tailed Nazim.

Briar flexed his fingers before he headed after his wife, and Randall bowed deeply to the other Alpha before he followed his own.

They walked over a mile in silence. Nobody dared speak. Preeti and Lara kept their eyes forward, their tails low. Back toward Whitechapel with their failure at their backs.

Nazim was the first to peel away. "I'm going home," he grumbled.

"G'night," Briar answered.

"Good job back there." Nazim nodded to Randall. "Stopped a fight, if not worse."

"Thanks." Randall gave a fleeting smile.

Jim and Lara were the next to go, veering west once the pack reached Stepney Green. Lara nudged Randall's calf with her nose, and Jim gave him a one-armed hug before they left.

Only a hundred yards or so to Randall's flats. He could see the building up ahead, lit in the sickly wash of the street lights. Five stories of premium 1970's cheap-arse housing estate, each flat's naff little balcony home to an assortment of crap. Some people tried to cram a bit of patio furniture out there, like watching the road was worth anything. Others stored bicycles or fitness equipment. Randall mostly used his own for airing laundry in the summer.

Briar gripped his shoulder, and Randall jolted to a halt.

"Thanks, Rand."

Randall bit back the wave of irritation that surged through him. It must've been in his eyes though, if the way Briar blinked at him was anything to go by.

"I mean it. This is what we need you for. Your level head, your way with people. You calmed that whole thing right down. It would've been a shitfest without you."

Randall curled his lip and jolted his shoulder free of Briar's hand. "If you all need me so bloody much, why the hell do you let this Omega bollocks carry on the way it does?"

Briar rolled his eyes. Actually rolled them!

Randall growled.

"We've had this out a hundred times," Briar muttered.

"Then maybe at a hundred and one it'll sink in. This isn't right." Randall's face felt hot. "Wolf packs don't have Omegas, Briar. This is human shit. You've assembled a bunch of rowdy misfits and you keep them focused by letting them bully me. It's not on!"

"Oh, come off it." Briar snorted. "It isn't bullying-"

"That's *exactly* what it is. Thirteen fucking years, Briar! If anyone treated Preeti the way you let them treat me you would've torn them a new hole!"

"Preeti's not the Omega, though."

"You're an arsehole."

Randall moved to step past him, but Briar's tree-trunk of an arm blocked his path.

"You're walking a fine line," Briar hissed.

"You are gonna lose me if this doesn't stop," Randall snapped back. "You're like some feudal king who keeps taking his country to war to prevent rebellion in his own ranks. You focus all the aggression on me so you don't have to learn to be a better bloody leader. I don't have to put up with it anymore."

"You can't leave," Briar said. "What're you going to do every full moon? Lock yourself in a basement? You don't *have* a basement, Rand. Stop being so childish."

"It isn't childish to stand up for yourself." Randall smiled bitterly. "It's the exact opposite."

They stood inches from each other, staring directly into one another's eyes, for what felt like ten minutes. It couldn't have been anywhere near that long, but Randall wasn't backing down and neither was Briar.

"We need a long-term solution," Briar growled. He lowered his arm.

"Yeah. We do."

"They'll think just because they won this round they've got the upper hand."

Randall sucked air through his teeth. His eyes widened. Yet again Briar just swept the whole thing under the rug and changed the subject like Randall's input was irrelevant.

"I can't believe anyone lives in London these days without speaking English," Briar groused. He rammed his fists into his pockets and glowered at Randall as though it was the shorter man's fault somehow. "It's not like we can just hire a translator, either. If we can't negotiate it'll come down to violence."

"It doesn't always have to-"

"Not everyone's right next to their Alpha when stuff happens." Briar eyeballed Randall. "What if Nazim bumps into one or two of theirs over the next few days when neither Alpha's around? You know he's a pushy little shit. All it takes is for them to be just as up themselves and it'll be out of control in no time."

"Then don't let him go out without you." Randall crossed his arms and looked down to Preeti. She was staying well out of the conversation, sitting by the kerb and paying attention to their surroundings.

"Yeah. I think you and I both know how daft that idea is." Briar sighed, and his stance shifted, weight coming to rest over one hip. It was a more relaxed posture, one which spoke of his confidence in himself and his certainty in his ideas.

As ever, Briar couldn't possibly consider the thought that he might be wrong about something. Randall ran a hand over his hair, trying to work out not only how to proceed, but also whether or not he could really be bothered any more. The thought of Nazim getting himself into trouble with this other pack didn't bother Randall on anything more than a purely abstract level. He should care, shouldn't he? He should care about the wellbeing of his so-called family? But instead he was more worried for the safety of the other pack, or anyone caught in the crossfire.

Or Preeti. He looked toward her again. Preeti who had saved him all those years ago, and who had always had time for him. Whenever she joined in with the others, her attitude was purely playful. She was the only one of them who treated him like a brother, like the family they all claimed that they were. Probably because Preeti was the only one of them who didn't have a family of her own to begin with. She'd run away from home as a child and fled down to London all the way from Leeds. She never spoke about why she ran, but Randall figured it had to be pretty bad to drive her a couple of hundred miles south when she was barely a teenager.

He scritched his scalp in frustration, then began to dig out his keys from the pocket of his jeans. "You want my help, but you don't want to help me," he murmured, turning back to Briar. "You're Alpha by gift, not by any kind of democracy or choice. Everyone in the pack tolerates your leadership because they need your gift to survive, not because you're good at what you do." Randall shook his head. "You don't deserve Preeti. She's too good for-"

The blow came so fast Randall didn't see it. He didn't even feel it at first. His head spun and his body twisted after it, and the next thing he knew he was on the pavement as a rush of pain flooded through his skull. One small voice somewhere in the jumbled chaos ticked off likely injuries: broken jaw, dislocated shoulder, road rash. It was all fleeting though. His skin repaired the quickest and was already whole when the pain in his head dulled to an ache. His body was shifting on a small scale, automatically knitting itself back together until all he was left with was the memory of pavement rushing toward him.

"You have a long, hard think about what you say next." Briar towered over him, his face cast into shadow by the streetlight overhead.

Randall rolled onto his front. His keys were only a couple of feet away, so he moved toward them and scooped them from the ground.

He did have a long, hard think. He pushed himself off the floor and stood, trembling with adrenaline as he brushed dirt off his scuffed jacket. He thought about how this could ultimately end if he didn't back down; not right now, but in the coming years. He couldn't live like this forever. He was an adult, and his understanding of animal behaviour only fed his unwillingness to tolerate this treatment.

"I'm really fucking regretting calling off my date," Randall spat. Then he pushed past Briar and headed for the door of his block of flats, putting them both behind him.

FIVE

ELLIS SKIM-READ the C.V. as he listened to its owner effuse about the pre-Raphaelites. She seemed to have a particular appreciation for the work of Sir John Everett Millais, but Ellis held a degree in Fine Art, and listening to her waffle on was a hell of a lot like being back at university, but with far less booze.

Her words were punctuated by the *clunk chunk clack* of the display's pins rocking up and down in their mounts to form each syllable as required. She'd been distracted by it earlier and her voice had paused often, but now she was in full flow.

He heard Jay's joints click as the other man stretched. Ellis hoped he'd done so discreetly.

"I think his aesthetics were most encapsulated in *Autumn Leaves*," she continued. If Jay hadn't been discreet, she hadn't noticed anyway. "And indeed the twilight he captured was one of the forerunners of-"

Ellis cleared his throat. "The ad specifically stated that we need someone with a grounding and interest in contemporary art, Miss Ryan."

Her pulse quickened. He heard her swallow. "Yes," she squeaked out. "But I feel that to understand contemporary art requires a full background in previous periods-"

"What's your opinion on Transgressive art?" he murmured.

"Er-"

"Joan Cornellà, for example."

"Well, I'm, er." He heard her wriggle in her seat. "Not completely up to speed on, uh, *every* artist."

"Of course not. Another movement then, aye? How about the Young British Artists, or the Stuckists? The flow from Stuckism to Remodernism?"

"Oh!" Relief. Ryan easily gushed into Britart, touching on Emin and Hirst with confidence and familiarity.

Not a total loss, then. But Ellis would need someone capable of getting to the point more quickly than this or he could end up with customers leaving the gallery out of sheer boredom.

The moment she had to pause, whether for breath or to arrange her thoughts, Ellis interjected "All right. And what's your availability like?"

"I can start right now if you want me to."

Ellis chuckled. "Maybe not at nine in the evening, aye? Let poor Jay go home at some point. Thanks for your time, Miss Ryan." He stood and offered his hand across the desk. Hers was clammy and hot when she shook it. "Jay'll be in touch by the end of the week either way."

"Okay. Thank you."

Ellis sat and waited for Jay to escort the young woman out of the gallery. He wiped his palm off on his trousers, then wished he hadn't. Now there was a slight trace of the odour of sweat on him that would linger until his clothes went into the wash.

He drummed his fingers on his desk while Jay came back up the stairs, then murmured "Close the door."

"Okay." Jay did so until the latch gave a soft click. "Wow. You were horrible!"

"I was not!" Ellis huffed. "Anyway, you were the one to pass her through to the second round. What were you thinking? She's all about Romanticism to Modern, not Contemporary."

"I picked the candidates who were best with people." The chair opposite Ellis' desk, so recently vacated by Ryan, squeaked under Jay's weight. "And who were the smartest, and neatest, and cleanest. Oh you should have seen some of them! Horrible!"

Ellis scrolled through Ryan's C.V. again, trying to match it to the woman he'd spent half an hour listening to. "Who would you take on?"

Jay laughed. "I don't know. Oh my god. You know, I have been to so many interviews and always worried about getting picked. I thought that was bad enough. But this side of the table? The big metaphorical table, I mean. I don't know. It feels like this huge responsibility! One person gets a job, who knows what happens to the other. God, what if they *never* find work? I couldn't live with myself!"

"Maybe I should've asked Han for his help after all." Ellis shook his head. "He did offer."

"Hey. We can do this." Jay sniffed. "I got them down to two, didn't I?"

"Did you make it rain in here and pick the ones which didn't land on the floor?" Ellis grinned.

"She's a perfectly nice young lady."

"With really clammy hands."

"With properly clammy hands, yeah," Jay agreed. "Can we make her wear gloves to work? Is that legal?"

"I don't think so." Ellis pushed hair back from his forehead. "Eh. We're being catty. It must be late. Shouldn't you get home?"

"You can't blame me for all of this. Anyway. Han gave me some pointers."

"On hiring?" Ellis' lips twitched.

"Yup. But really it just comes down to hiring the superior candidate."

Ellis scratched his stubble. Damn stupid scruff of not-quite-beard, not-clean-shaven that had been stuck with him like glue since he'd been turned. He had tried shaving it off but it was always back within hours, yet it never grew any further. His last living days had been filled with booze and self-pity, so a shave hadn't been high on his to-do list back then and now he was saddled with the fluff forever. "I thought she were reet boring," he finally said.

"Mebbeh tha's reet spot on, eee by gum, aye," Jay said, putting on his terrible mock-Yorkshire accent.

"'Ey. Pack it in."

Jay chortled. "Spoilsport. Fine. Ryan's boring, but Pearce isn't a thrill a minute either."

"I thought you picked the ones who were good with people?"

"Sweetie, you should've seen the others. One was an unrepentant liar, and two couldn't even name five artists off the top of their head regardless of period or style. One lad rocked up in combat trousers and a t-shirt with more than the strictly required number of holes. It's like they don't *want* to be hired." Jay's usually kind, lively demeanour faltered at the recollection.

Ellis' smile faded. "You've been working too hard," he said. "That's my fault. But we'll take on one of these two, get them trained up, and things will calm down, all right?"

"It's fine. We'll get there. Anyway, I'm not going to let either one of them field your brother's incessant calls. You can't ignore him forever, sweetie."

"I know."

"But you have my total sympathy. Edison is an arse." At least Jay's voice was lively again. "How are we going to deal with him?"

Ellis had absolutely no idea.

Edison was his eldest brother. Elijah sat in the middle, and Ellis was the youngest; the black sheep. God knew what had gone through his parents' heads when they came up with those names, but Ellis at least felt like he was the luckiest of the three in that particular regard. Both Edison and Elijah followed daddy dearest's footsteps and became solicitors back home in York, but Ellis had to be the one to run off to study art then pinch a wad of dad's money and consistently fail to repay it.

It wasn't really any wonder that Edison had taken to calling all hours. Their father presumably didn't want to speak to his artsy-fartsy pansy-boy of a son anymore than was wholly necessary, and Edison was a reasonable choice of middleman.

"I don't know," he murmured. "But if I don't figure it out it won't be phone calls any more, it'll be paperwork."

"You think your dad would take his own son to court?" Jay sounded appalled.

"Probably. But the phone's out of the question, and I can't respond to any summons. I could try to head home and ask for an abeyance but dad will insist on meeting at a sensible hour and that's before we even go so far as to look into whether there are vampires up there or what laws they govern themselves by."

"You people seriously need a forum or something. It's like the Dark Ages."

Ellis laughed. "I don't want to *talk* to any of them, Jay. Bad enough that I have to go present myself like a prize turnip every year. Socialising? Come off it. What do you think they'd talk about on a forum?"

"A vampire book club," Jay decreed.

"Oh yeah. I can see it now. This week's book is The Life of Pi. Discuss."

"Ha. Anyway. I think there's a very obvious solution to Edison that you're just avoiding."

Ellis leaned in and raised his eyebrows. "And what's that?"

"Just give your dad back his million quid."

They burst into raucous laughter at the same time. Ellis wheezed as he tried to get enough air in to keep going, and Jay devolved into some kind of choking snort.

The door to the gallery below opened, the slight but recognisable groan of its hinges a sound that cut through Ellis' hysterics. He stopped abruptly and tilted his head.

Footsteps on the hard wood floor. The door squeaked as it swung closed.

Jay's laugh petered out. "What is it?"

Ellis pressed his lips together tightly. He heard the newcomer walk deeper into the gallery, footsteps light and slow.

What he didn't hear was a heartbeat.

He raised a finger to his lips, then affected a voice which he hoped conveyed that he and Jay had been mid-flow. "Thanks for that. If you want to head home, I can wrap up here."

"Sure," Jay said without hesitating. He was a bloody quick thinker. It was one of the traits Ellis valued most highly about him. "Want me to-"

"Hello?" A voice called out from the gallery. "Is anyone here?"

Ellis pursed his lips. It was a woman's voice, and he didn't know any female vampires. She could potentially be a Constable or a Vassal here on Council business, but she could just as likely be here to attack him. Either way she'd catch anything he said to Jay, and would already have heard Jay and Tiberius' hearts. If he told Jay a damn thing it would give away Jay's possession of illicit knowledge, and if she were indeed here on behalf of the Council he and Jay would be on the chopping block before sunrise.

He nodded quickly to Jay and tugged his portable keyboard out of his pocket.

"Coming!" Jay called out cheerily. His chair squeaked and brushed over the carpet, and Jay's pulse moved toward the office door. He opened it, and added "I won't be a moment. Why don't you have a look around, and we'll see if we can't find something of interest to you."

Ellis typed as fast as he could and sent the text to Jay. They usually had more time to work with, but with him and Jay caught in the same room he was on the back foot. He'd have hurry.

I don't know her. Leave. Pretend this text is from Han.

He sent it and heard the buzz from Jay's pocket just as the vampire began to climb the stairs.

"No need," she called. "I'm here to see Mr. O'Neill."

Ellis could hear Jay's heart hammer away, and his assistant's fear threatened to betray them both.

SIX

ELLIS ROSE from behind his desk and stepped around it. The fingers of his left hand traced the edge of it to guide him. He had to get Jay out of here, but the vampire was coming up the stairs fast, and Jay had stepped back into the office. Ellis supposed that it was to make way for their visitor, but it was bloody inconvenient.

He hurried toward Jay, using the sounds of his assistant's living body as guidance, and slid a hand down his arm until he could hook his fingers around Jay's elbow.

"I'm O'Neill," he said toward the doorway.

It felt like some perverse kind of hostage situation. Ellis silently urged Jay to read the bloody text message, but he had no way of knowing whether Jay had done so.

"Ellis O'Neill?" she said.

Shit. She was at the top of the stairs now. Coming closer. He heard a minuscule click. Was that Jay's phone, or something else?

"Aye, Ellis." He offered his free hand toward her.

She entered the office and her cold fingers slid around his. "Good to meet you. And who is this delicious young man?"

Ellis' lips pulled back almost involuntarily. Was she threatening Jay, or was it a figure of speech? Without the aural cues of a living creature it was difficult to know for sure.

"Oh I am so sorry!" Jay laughed and moved under Ellis' grip. "My husband texted me: I was miles away. I know, I *know*, I am so rude!" He took his arm away from Ellis' hand. "I would stay, but he's offering to do the sort of things we absolutely should *not* discuss!" He leaned in and placed a light, hot kiss against Ellis' cheek. "Take care, sweetie. I'll see you tomorrow!"

And like that, the situation was over. Jay was free and darting out of the office, leaving Ellis with the other vampire.

They both stood, deathly silent. Waiting.

Jay's footsteps receded, and then the front door opened and closed again.

Ellis gave a slight nod, then turned his back on the trespasser. He strode to his chair and sat.

So far, so good. She hadn't killed him yet.

He gestured across his desk. "Please, take a seat."

The desk would be his best defence. If she was willing to sit on the other side of it, the barrier gave him time to react should she choose to move against him. He would hear her chair, her clothing, and potentially any jewellery she wore if she launched an attack after she sat down. The only risk was whatever power she wielded and whether it would give her some way of negating the fraction of a warning he expected.

He was hardly a fighter, of course. A degree in fine art, a job at a desk, and a dog selected and trained for his utter lack of inclination toward violence did not all combine to create some kind of vampire ninja. For most vampires their undead strength and stamina were enough to elevate them to a more survivable state against the majority of living creatures out there, but a vampire who had some rudimentary combat training before they were turned would probably stand head and shoulders above any others.

So far Ellis' only fight with another vampire had been with a man as useless in combat as himself. Ellis had survived by cheating his arse off, and he'd do it again if this woman leaped at him, except now he knew that his sole tactic actually worked; last time it had been a complete gamble.

"Thank you," she replied. There it was: the creak of the seat. She would have heard it too, but with any luck she didn't view it as important. "My name is Barbara Applegate, but it's just Barb for short. I'm not here to start anything." She laughed weakly.

Was she nervous, or faking it?

"Well, I kind of am here to start something, but it's not... Okay. I'll start again. I'm sorry for entering your territory without prior arrangement. I didn't know how to go about contacting you. I heard you were blind, so I didn't think a letter would do it, and phones are out of the question."

"And it's not the kind of letter you can have transposed into braille on your behalf," Ellis murmured, offering her a gentle smile which he hoped would calm her.

"Oh yeah, that'd go down well with the Council, wouldn't it?" She barked what he decided was probably her laugh. It was a short, sharp thing, cynical and hard, contrasting with her flustered words. "Anyway. You and I need to talk."

"About?"

Her fingernails tapped on the desk. He waited.

"I don't want to take your territory and I don't want to fight you. I've never met you before, I don't have a problem with you. You've never fucked with my chi. You keep yourself nice and tidy over here. But I will be forced to protect myself and others if you don't agree to keep quiet about what I'm going to say."

Ellis smiled slowly. "What if what you say is objectionable?"

"That's the risk, ain't it? But I dunno. I've heard things about you, O'Neill. You're the youngest vampire in the city and that makes you the hottest gossip, but nobody's got a bad word to say."

"That's because nobody's actually met me."

She emitted her snap of a laugh again. "It's hard for us to meet, don't you think? So many annual visits to the Council, yet none of us cross paths on our way there or back. No man is an island, yet every vampire seems to be."

"So what is it you want to discuss?" he asked softly.

Her nails tapped again. Habit, perhaps. "My turf is Soho. Just the other side of Regent Street. I'm your eastern neighbour. I've been there more than ten years, yet you and I have never met. Why is that?"

"I don't really go into Soho," Ellis said cautiously.

"No," she agreed, "because Mayfair is your stomping ground. And you don't leave it, because the Council's laws don't let you. They don't let any of us stray outside our own borders unless it's for our annual check-in. We have a Council that none of us voted for, and we obey the laws they carved out in the Stone Age without question. Because the ones who turned us told us that was how it was. Because the punishment for breaking just about any one of those laws is our death. But the Council? They're allowed to travel wherever they want and they don't have to ask permission or give you a letter from their mum. The Constables can go anywhere and claim it's on Council business, but any one of them could lie about it and we'd never know."

"Uh huh…" Ellis kept his response as neutral as possible.

"I don't see," Barb went on, "why the whole city should run this way. Age is no guarantee of good leadership yet the Council's the five eldest vampires in the city, thrown together regardless of skill or quality. If they all died tonight, there wouldn't be any voting. The next five oldest would step up to the plate and we'd all accept it. It's total balls. Why should any of us give a shit about the Council or its rules?"

Ellis furrowed his brows. "I don't know?" he offered.

"No, me either. But I'll tell you this for nothing: I think those laws exist to keep us in our place."

"What place, exactly?"

"Bottom of the pile. Think about it. If we aren't allowed to wander out of our own little pigeon holes, we can't make friends. Or allies. We can't spread news. All our information comes through official channels. They control everything about us, from who we interact with to what data we receive. If we wander into someone else's patch we run the risk of being murdered by the vampire we've intruded on before we even have the chance to introduce ourselves. Even you've killed an intruder, haven't you?"

His frown deepened. "Aye. I wasn't aware this was circulated news."

"It wasn't. Just gossip."

"If we aren't allowed to leave our little patches of land," Ellis countered, "who are you hearing gossip from?"

Barb chuckled. "Yeah, well. Like I said. I don't care much for these so-called laws. I'm much more in favour of democracy. I think we should get to know each other and work together, and we should vote on issues which affect us all. This isn't the Fifties anymore. Our system of government is holding us back. We should be working together, not sitting around like obedient little dogs. No offence," she added.

"I don't think he's taken any," Ellis murmured. "He's good like that."

"I've never seen a guide dog before. I thought they were usually Labradors?"

Ellis reached down to pet Tiberius' head. "Not always. It has to be a big dog, though. That or you have to be a really short blind person."

Barb's laugh was longer this time, and less cynical. "There's a mental image I'll treasure forever."

Ellis grinned and returned his hand to his lap. "I'm guessing then that you didn't risk the wrath of the art dealer just to vent your spleen at me about the Council?"

"Truth." Barb slowly cracked her knuckles. "I've heard gossip because I'm not the only vampire in town who has these deeply controversial ideas."

He lifted an eyebrow. "If the Elders hear this kind of talk, I reckon they won't be too amused."

"Gotta hand it to you there, I think you might be on to something. There's a few of us who aren't too settled with the status quo. We might have broken a few rules and snuck around talking to each other. There might even be some kind of cross-territory communications network going on."

Jay's comment about a forum sprang to mind, and Ellis laughed briefly. "Is it online?"

"Ha! No. Don't be silly." The chair squeaked, and her clothes rustled against each other. Had she stood? When she spoke again, though, her voice came from the same place; she had only adjusted her position. "Are you really blind, or is it just a ruse?"

Ellis smirked humorlessly. "Tell you what, I wish it were a bloody ruse. But no. It isn't."

"But you've got a mobile phone, right?"

"Aye." Ellis had a feel for where this was going. How could

he possibly have any use for a mobile if he couldn't read text messages? "I've got some kit that converts texts into braille."

"Wicked!"

Ellis schooled his expression to keep it neutral as one single word gave Barb away as a child of the Eighties. No wonder living under the Council rubbed her up the wrong way, if she'd grown up in the decade that tore down the Berlin Wall.

"You wanted something," he said.

"Yeah." Then her voice came closer, and she said "I want you to join us."

Ellis' smile froze. "What?"

"Long live the revolution?"

SEVEN

RANDALL DIDN'T WAKE until almost noon. Sleep hadn't come quickly or easily, and once he was up he still couldn't calm down.

Thank god he didn't have clients today. He was a wreck.

He paced his apartment, then it reminded him too much of Briar so he left to wander the local market. But it was too busy, too many people pushing and shoving, too much shouting from the stallholders, and it all grated on his nerves so he went home again.

What time did Ellis wake up?

Randall didn't really know. He didn't want to text in case the vampire had a set hour for waking up. He didn't want to spoil Ellis' sleep.

He'd text later.

So he cleaned his flat. He reorganised his books. He checked his emails and wasted time online and fidgeted through channels on the television while trying and failing to play games.

His chest ached. His stomach roiled. He felt sick. He

missed lunch, and when dinner time came around he missed that too.

He needed Ellis.

Randall had nobody to talk to about the chaos rampaging through his thoughts. His mum and his brother might carry the recessive gene but they weren't shifters themselves, so talking to them about his pack woes was off the table. Only Ellis knew what he was and could listen to his problems.

He took out his phone, but couldn't bring himself to write a text message.

What would he say? *Hey. I love you, but I keep pushing you away. Please let me come over and unload on you, then leave again without telling you how I feel.*

Randall tossed his phone onto his couch and growled at it.

I love you.

Why was it so fucking hard to say? Would admitting it out loud make it any less true? Of course not. Would it make Ellis happy to hear it? Probably! The vampire was more than comfortable with his own feelings and desires and had no trouble telling either of them to Randall.

Randall had seen Ellis be attacked. He'd been right there, inches from the fight, and watched in horror as Ellis struggled against a man dead-set on killing him. He'd been terrified in that moment that he would lose Ellis forever, but it seemed like now that the urgency was gone there was no pressing need to say the words.

He'd meant to say them last night. He'd got himself at least in a position where he was willing to *try* to say them.

Fucking Briar.

Randall snatched his phone up, then ditched it again.

Those words would make it real, wouldn't they? And what if that was the problem? What if Randall didn't want it to be real?

Nightfall. He'd wait until nightfall. He wouldn't be able to see Ellis before then anyway, so there was no point contacting him until the sun set.

Right?

NIGHT CAME, and Randall texted Ellis, but there was no response.

Another three texts and still no answer.

He was probably at work, right? With a customer?

He wouldn't be ignoring Randall after Randall bailed on their date.

He *wouldn't*.

Would he?

RANDALL HATED THE DISTRICT LINE. It was rickety and rocky, and the brakes would screech at utterly random moments like the train was in distress. It was enough to put a man on edge, and Randall was already tense.

He texted Ellis while the tube was still above ground, but he still hadn't received any reply before the tracks sloped down and the darkness swallowed his carriage.

Signal became a patchy and unpredictable beast. He fiddled about with his phone, trying to occupy himself with his diary or a game, but when the train screamed to a halt at each station he stared out of the windows to check whether it was Westminster yet. Thank god he didn't have to switch to another train; the idea of fighting crowds set his teeth on edge.

Westminster tube station was vast. While it only served three lines, it handled a massive footfall every day, all passing through an open escalator hall that was like some Bond villain's underground lair. Mostly grey and chrome, it sported a lattice of thick struts in the walls which showed the ancient stone on which the Houses of Parliament sat. Randall sprinted up the middle of three escalators and slapped his wallet against the Oyster reader once he reached the barrier.

Signal at last.

No texts. What if it was Barnes all over again? What if Ellis had been attacked, and Randall was already too late?

He scrolled to find Jay's number, then called it.

"Randall?" Jay answered quickly. "I'm not with Ellis at the moment, if that's who you're after?"

"Oh." Randall felt a rush of guilt. "Sorry. Have you seen him though? He's not answering my texts."

"He's okay. We've been doing interviews, but he's in another meeting now."

There was some kind of tension in Jay's voice.

"With who?" Randall's throat constricted.

Was this it? Ellis had finally given up on Randall, hadn't he? Was he seeing someone else? Right now?

"I don't know," Jay said, lowering his voice. "I can't talk, I'm on a bus."

Randall was about to ask what that had to do with anything, then swallowed his words.

Jay couldn't tell him who Ellis was meeting, because he might be overheard.

"Okay. Okay. I'm on my way there."

"Be careful, okay?"

Randall laughed bitterly. "I'm always careful."

"I mean it, sweetie. He all but pushed me out the door. You promise me you'll be careful."

Randall chewed his thumbnail a moment, then said, "I promise."

WESTMINSTER WAS one of those places which was mostly deserted after dark. He sprinted past the Houses of Parliament, Big Ben's pale clock face floating overhead like a baleful eye. Once he was on the relatively narrow Birdcage Walk there was next to no foot traffic at all, and he reached St. James' Park in what must have been some kind of record time.

Maybe he should've just hopped onto the Jubilee Line up to Green Park rather than run a mile and a half across London, but ultimately it'd take around the same amount of time and at least this way he felt like he was doing something. Sitting idly on a platform waiting for a train this time of night could take anything up to ten minutes. It was better to run.

He reached the bridge that Ellis had been so worried about last month.

Was that what Ellis' meeting was about tonight? *Had* they strayed onto some other vampire's territory that night? Was Ellis in trouble for their bungling investigations?

He pushed on through the park with renewed vigour and ran straight across The Mall with only the briefest of looks to check for cars.

Randall snarled under his breath. He would have arrived at the gallery by now if he could run on four paws. What was the use in being a shifter if the city he lived in wouldn't ever allow him to shift? It was like a dirty secret, only done in private homes or underground, locked away from the prying eyes of anonymous cameras, and here he was preserving that secret when the man he loved could be under attack.

He skidded to a halt at Piccadilly. A couple of buses dawdled along it, and the five second wait for them to pass was like torture. He caught a lungful of diesel fumes when he bolted out behind them and coughed his way over to the other side of the road, toward the vertical garden of the Athenæum Hotel. It sat on the corner of Piccadilly and Down Street, and the edge of it was greenery from the ground all the way to the roof.

Randal shot past the plant-encrusted corner and along Down Street, where white stone suddenly gave way to red brick. He was so close to the gallery now. Ellis would take a convoluted route which led down little Mews' and alleyways as he worked to avoid reflective surfaces and cameras alike, but Randall had no such restriction, and he redoubled his efforts to zigzag his way through the residential maze of Mayfair.

Should he have just waited for the tube?

Berkeley Square Gardens. Davies Street. Randall's mind blanked, falling into a near-Zen state as his boots pounded the pavement.

Brook's Mews.

He ran down the narrow, dark street toward its lonely streetlamp. He couldn't see light from the gallery's windows, but they were probably shuttered closed.

Randall used the door to stop himself, slamming into it with his shoulder, then he yanked it open and came face to face with a woman with short, spiky blonde hair and a full set of biker leathers but no helmet.

"Oh!" He panted and wiped sweat from his forehead. He probably looked like some crazy serial killer. "Sorry."

She looked him up and down with eyes like chips of polar ice. The only eyes he'd seen even remotely like those were Ellis'.

He sniffed, hoping it came off like he was just trying to breathe and not sniff strangers in doorways, but all he could pick up was a whiff of perfume, harsh and cheap. It tickled his nose, and his eyes watered with the urge to sneeze.

"No worries," she said, casting a grin his way. "But, you know, if I could use this door it'd be pretty neat."

"Oh." Randall took a step back, door handle still firmly in hand. "Sorry," he added. "After you."

"You're a gent. Thanks." She waggled her eyebrows at him almost comically as she swept past. "If Mayfair's where they're keeping all the totty I'll have to come here more often!"

"Uh. Oh." Randall just nodded. He didn't have time to deflect flirting. Especially not from a vampire.

He watched her saunter off down the Mews, then rushed inside and took the stairs to Ellis' office two at a time.

EIGHT

ELLIS HEARD Randall's voice as the werewolf encountered Barb, then his boots as they clanged up stairs. His heart was thundering at one hell of a pace, and his breath was laboured. It seemed much more likely that Randall had been running, not injured, but Ellis frowned nonetheless and took a slow breath through his nose.

He couldn't smell blood. Only the remains of Barb's perfume.

Randall crashed into his office like a herd of elephants. "Ellis! Are you okay?"

"I am, aye. Are you?"

"Yeah, yeah, I'm fine."

Ellis could hear the lie a mile away. It was too dismissive, too hurried to be true.

"Who was she?" Randall continued, coming closer. He stopped somewhere near the chair facing Ellis' desk, then stepped aside like he might be working out which side of the desk he wanted to be on.

Ellis lifted a finger to his own lips. "Come here."

Randall took the lifeline and hurried to Ellis' side, and Ellis felt for the werewolf's body. He encountered hard, muscled thigh with denim moulded to it, and felt his way up. Sweat-drenched t-shirt. Ellis ran his hand quickly up Randall's front until he reached the t-shirt's collar, then he gripped it and dragged Randall down for a kiss.

Randall's breath was hot, his lips slick and salty. Ellis took the man's breath into his lungs and held it there while his tongue pushed over Randall's and ensnared it.

The shifter leaned into the kiss and his weight rested against Ellis' chair. His breathing slowed in stages until a small whimper escaped him.

"There," Ellis murmured. He sucked Randall's lower lip before he released the t-shirt and had a momentary pang of loss at his inability to see the damp cotton sculpted to Randall's pectorals. "Now. What's got you running in here like the world's on fire, eh?"

"Who-"

"Later." Ellis let his hand drift down across Randall's hard body until he could find a belt loop. He hooked a fingertip through it. "You didn't make yourself all hot and sweaty just for me. What's wrong?"

"I've been texting and you didn't answer," Randall gasped.

"I'm sorry. Jay and I were interviewing candidates, and then I had an unexpected visitor." Ellis pulled on the belt loop lightly. "Where have you been?"

Randall's breath hitched. The upset hadn't left him, it seemed, even after a kiss. "I just, I don't... I didn't want to leave you in the lurch last night, but I couldn't get here and I'm sorry, I don't know what to-"

Ellis pursed his lips and stood. He used his calf to nudge

his chair back so that he could turn and face Randall, and pressed his chest against the shorter man's body. Ellis dipped his head slowly so that he wouldn't hit Randall in the face with his glasses, and found the shifter's mouth once more.

Randall sagged. His body, so firm and powerful, began to wilt. He parted his lips as though it were an act of surrender, and Ellis plundered his mouth more fiercely. He wrapped his arms around Randall's waist and pinned him as he luxuriated in their closeness, the scent of Randall's musk, the heat radiating off his skin and the hardness in his jeans.

Ellis' lips twitched, and he lifted his head away. "Now," he murmured. "Try again. What's wrong?"

Randall swallowed down a whine. "There's another pack," he whispered.

Ellis began to run his palms tenderly up Randall's spine to soothe him further. "Of werewolves?"

"Yeah." Randall gripped Ellis' hips. "They keep coming into our territory, and we think they're poaching our cubs. That's what they did last night when we found them."

"Poached how?" Ellis wasn't sure whether his mental image was the right one. "Like, taking? Not to eat, right?"

"No! Christ!"

Ellis smiled faintly and placed a soft kiss to Randall's cheek. "Then how?"

"Like, coming in and taking them off to join their pack."

"Oh." Ellis suspected it was probably more complicated than an exchange of phone numbers and an invitation to some woodlands under the full moon. "And what is a cub?" He grinned. "I assume a young werewolf, but you don't say 'child'."

Randall huffed. Good. His panic was dissipating at last. "Before we change for the first time we're pretty much human.

No more resilient, no particular scent, nothing untoward about us. Then after we go through puberty we'll start to have properly vivid dreams about being a wolf. For some people it's hunting, others it's just walking around. Preeti says hers was a dream about Briar and that's how she knew he was her mate when she met him." Randall's body moved with a slow shrug. "Anyway, once the dreams start our scent changes. That's when we're a cub: before our first shift, but after others can tell what we are."

Ellis leaned in and drew a lazy breath along the side of Randall's neck. The unique aroma of woodlands and spice filled his senses. "You do have a rather distinctive odour," he murmured.

Randall's body tightened, and his length dug a little harder against Ellis' hip. "Yeah," he squeaked.

"Mm." Ellis pressed his lips to the skin just below Randall's ear. "So you found a pack on your territory, and they were with one of these cubs. Was anyone hurt?"

Randall's body flinched. It was a tiny movement, but one Ellis felt keenly. "No."

Another lie. That made for two in five minutes.

Ellis stroked Randall's back, causing the shifter to tremble as cooling t-shirt pressed into still-hot flesh. "What are you hiding, petal?" he finally asked.

Randall's heart sped up again. "It's-" He broke off, and his grip on Ellis' hips loosened.

Ellis waited. His fingers roamed gently.

"Our Alpha." The words whooshed out of Randall with the weight of a burden relinquished. "Briar."

"He was hurt?"

"No." It sounded as though Randall half wished that he had been. "He's so angry about this pack on our turf and poaching cubs from us that it almost escalated to violence last night. I had to step in and calm everything down, but he treats me like shit and in all honesty I'm pretty glad we don't find these cubs before some other pack rescues them. Nobody should have to put up with this bollocks, especially not a young kid."

Ellis' lips pulled back, almost of their own accord. "Treats you like shit how?" he whispered. It was the only way to keep the sudden anger from his voice.

"Like he insists I'm the Omega, so he lets the pack pick on me and stuff, and he encourages it. Then when he thinks everyone's had enough he steps in like he's protecting me, and acts like I should be grateful."

Ellis hissed softly. He had the insane urge to cross the whole city just to try and tear this Briar's throat out, and suppressing it took a surprising amount of willpower. He wanted to grab Randall and demand to know where he could find Briar right now. His hands clenched into fists and he held Randall against him as though the shifter were at risk of falling without support. "It sounds," he snarled once he found his voice, "like they're bullying you."

Randall scoffed. "Yeah. Pretty much."

"Then leave!"

"I can't."

Ellis' heart broke at the despair in Randall's voice. "Why not?"

"Because we need Alphas. Without them everyone around us is in danger during the full moon. We can't control ourselves, our tempers, but an Alpha can. They've got some gift that lets them calm the rest of us down. If we don't have an Alpha the smallest thing can set us off. That's why we try to find cubs so fast, 'cause most of them will be at home when it first happens and they'll just kill whoever's closest." Randall sighed. "Preeti found me when I was a cub and she convinced me to go with her, and it probably saved my mum and my brother's lives. She made sure I wasn't home when it happened. I think it's the screaming that sets us off. We'll change right there in front of our loved ones and they'll scream, and then we just see them as prey and-" Randall's body trembled. "Briar killed his parents, and his little sister. He slaughtered them all and ate bits of them. It's why he's so dead-set on finding cubs now. Nobody got to him before it happened and he lost everything. Preeti was already homeless by the time she was a cub, but if Briar hadn't found her she could've killed anyone. She could've been in a shopping centre or a tube station, could've been caught on camera and killed innocent people." He pressed his forehead against Ellis' shoulder.

Ellis' fingers unfurled with some reluctance, and went back to stroking Randall's spine. "I don't understand," he said cautiously. "Weren't you with me during a full moon last month?"

Randall hesitated. "Yeah."

"I don't seem to have been killed and eaten…"

Randall laughed weakly. "Yeah, you noticed that?"

"Aye, I did."

"You've got this… I don't know what it is." Randall's body moved as he began to bear his own weight at last. "You say something and the anger evaporates, like you're somehow an Alpha. Like you're taking a pin to a balloon. It all pops and deflates."

Ellis' lips twitched. "So you *don't* need Briar. Is that what you're telling me?"

Randall was quiet, so Ellis withdrew his hands and laid them against the werewolf's chest instead. He waited, listening to his lover's pulse, feeling the breath flow through him.

"Look, petal." Ellis straightened up. "Sounds to me like what you've got is an abusive relationship with someone who thinks that because they have power over you, the way they choose to apply it is all justifiable. I know the sort, believe me. But the only way to remove that power from them is to walk away. It isn't easy, especially not when they've worked so hard to convince you that you need them, that you can't live or be happy without them, but when you can't live or be happy *with* them what is there really to lose by letting them have a good, close look at a couple of your fingers?"

"He wants me to kill you," Randall blurted.

Ellis froze.

"I mean, if he knew what you were. Which he doesn't. But he suspects. And he thinks vampires are fleas and that too many fleas on a dog kill the dog so he thinks vampires are fleas on a city and they should be eradicated like we'd deal with parasites."

"Right," Ellis said faintly. He took a step back and found the chair, then sat with care to avoid misjudging its location and falling flat on his arse. "It's a bit of a leap for him to think I'm a vampire, isn't it? He hasn't even met me."

Randall's breath picked up.

Ellis tried to quash the sickening feeling that he'd been betrayed.

"I didn't know what you were," Randall whimpered. "I'd just met you, and I fancied the hell out of you, but I didn't know. You don't have any scent and I couldn't work out why, so I asked Preeti if she had any idea what you might be."

"And she worked it out?"

"No. She thought you might be some other kind of shifter. Then I saw you didn't have a reflection."

"And you told Preeti." Ellis sank into his chair, wishing he could make the whole situation go away. "And she told Briar."

Because she loves him. Because telling your secrets to those you love is just human nature. The same urge which had forced Ellis' hand to admit what he was to Randall and - hopefully - the reason Randall had told him he was a shifter.

Because holding onto a lie in the face of love wasn't an option.

"I didn't know," Randall breathed. "I'm so sorry. He said if it turned out you were a vampire I had to kill you."

Ellis' fingers gripped the arms of his chair. "Is that why you've been avoiding me?"

"No. Maybe. I don't know."

Ellis gave a faint nod. "Well, then we just need to make sure he doesn't find out, eh?"

Randall made a sound that didn't sound especially committed.

"Randall. It's all right. It is. You do what's best for you, do you hear me?" He leaned out of the chair's safe embrace and reached toward Randall, trying to find his hand. Once he had it, he held it tight. "I can't tell you what to do. I just want you to be happy." He tried a small smile, and added "This other pack must have an Alpha, right? Why not just join up with them?"

Randall's fingers squeezed back. "'Cause I wouldn't understand a word he said. I don't know if it'd work if I dunno what he's saying."

Ellis' smile faded. "What? But I thought-" He frowned. "I thought you said you talked them down?"

"Body language. Tone of voice. None of them speak a word of English. We can't negotiate with them, and they're pushing further and further into our territory." Randall swallowed. "If we can't talk to them, there's going to be war."

Randall's words hung between them, and Ellis had to

wonder what else he'd told Preeti. It was starting to sound a whole lot like Randall had come here to ask for a translator.

He wouldn't. Would he?

There was only a finite amount of betrayal Ellis could take in a single night, so he wasn't sure he wanted to know the answer to that question.

NINE

RANDALL WATCHED Ellis go from comforting, through concerned, and land in outright hurt all within the space of a few minutes. All because of what Randall said.

He hated himself.

God, why hadn't he come here sooner? Why was it always excuses or quick visits, like Ellis was somehow responsible for Randall's cold feet? Even now he'd only come because Ellis had stopped answering his texts. Had he really been worried for Ellis' safety, or was it something else? Something worse?

Maybe he'd run halfway across town because he was afraid Ellis had lost interest in him.

But Ellis hadn't. He'd been working all evening, and now Randall had thrown all this shit into his lap and Ellis had withdrawn, features tense and pinched. The vampire's mood seemed to have soured the moment Randall told him that he couldn't speak whatever language was necessary to negotiate with the other pack.

He hadn't meant to come here for Ellis' help with that. Not

consciously. But maybe the knowledge that Ellis had some power with languages was eating away at his subconscious.

It'd be bloody useful, he had to admit, but Ellis had sworn him to secrecy over it.

"So, um." Randall cleared his throat. "I don't suppose you…"

Ellis' body stiffened. Classic fight or flight preparation, but Randall couldn't begin to guess which way Ellis would go if he continued.

"No," Ellis said coldly.

Randall moved back nervously, stepping away from Ellis' desk. "People could die," he said, uncertainty causing his throat to constrict and his voice to fluctuate. "Just having someone there who could interpret for us could be all it takes to stop this escalating-"

"I said *no*," Ellis hissed, his features contorting in rage.

Randall fidgeted with the hem of his t-shirt. God, it was still horribly cold and damp. He grimaced at it. Sweat was a lot less appealing once it started to cool down. Not that Ellis could see it, so maybe Randall was worrying about nothing.

He pushed his thoughts back on track, and said, "You could save lives!"

"No means no." Ellis' words were flat, and the anger behind them made them clipped and quiet. "Don't ask again."

Randall wrapped his arms around himself, and tried to work out what was so upsetting about this. Everything he said seemed to hurt Ellis in some way, yet Ellis refused to explain why and Randall failed to understand what could be so bad about being a polyglot.

He hadn't seen Ellis angry before. Not like this. He thought he might be able to cope with it if Ellis were yelling at him, but this was something else. Something more like his mum's anger. The kind of anger that came when you mingled love with disappointment.

What wasn't Ellis telling him? Why was this such a huge secret?

"It's not like speaking Polish can get anyone killed, right?"

He thought he could defuse things with a half-hearted joke, but the look on Ellis' face didn't change.

"Yes," the vampire breathed. "It can. If I only ever ask one thing of you, Randall, it's this: Don't *ever* ask me to do this again. Don't ever mention it again. Don't even *think* about talking about this again. Is that clear?"

A wave of hurt threatened to drown Randall. All he could do was nod, even though he knew Ellis couldn't see the gesture. He'd been shut down so effectively that it stung like a slap to the face from the man who moments earlier had said he just wanted Randall to be happy.

How could he tell Ellis that averting a war would make him happy if Ellis wouldn't let him get those words out?

He'd watched Ellis speak Polish with Barnes. Ellis didn't hesitate, and he had spoken rapidly, with the confidence of fluency. It wasn't a natural second language for someone from Yorkshire, so it made sense to Randall that Ellis had learned more than one other language in his time in London, and as a polyglot he might at least be able to *recognise* the language being used. Maybe he had a natural talent for it, or maybe he studied his arse off, but either way if he spoke whatever language this other pack used it could save them all a lot of trouble.

Could it be that Ellis didn't trust him?

Randall winced. Maybe it was a big ask to begin with. They'd only been kind-of seeing each other for a few weeks now. They'd started out under Briar's orders to kill Ellis, which Randall had disobeyed. They'd gone on to kill Barnes together, but Briar was pushing hard now to know what Ellis was, and it wasn't like the Alpha would forget all about it one day if Randall ignored it long enough. Ellis told Randall that he loved him, but had Randall ever reciprocated?

He *did* love him. He knew he did. Every morning that he woke up without Ellis was like a knife to the gut, and every night that he patrolled without seeing Ellis made him ache like a part of him was missing. He dropped by when he could, but he couldn't stay when Ellis was working. It'd be like Ellis following him around when he was training dogs or discussing an animal's requirements with its owner. The art crowd would probably look down their noses at him anyway. He didn't know a thing about paintings or statues or whatever. He reckoned Ellis' friends and customers would get a big kick out of the idiot boyfriend who hadn't ever set foot inside the National Gallery and who usually had dog fluff stuck to his jeans.

Now that he was running through it all in his head, though, it sounded like a dustbowl of excuses; patches to cover his own cowardice with.

So yeah. Maybe Ellis didn't trust him. And maybe he had damn good reason not to.

"Perfectly clear," he whispered. His eyes stung and he blinked quickly, but that made them worse.

Ellis frowned. Randall wished he could see Ellis' eyes, but those bloody sunglasses kept them hidden. Ellis had told him that he didn't like light because it was enough to try and convince him to attempt to see things, but his vision was incredibly limited and such attempts were usually frustrating and exhausting. Better to never see at all than have his impairment all but rubbed in his face at every opportunity, although Randall had to admit that it made reading Ellis' expression all the more difficult. He ached to go back to Ellis' side, to take those glasses away and kiss him.

It wouldn't make any difference. Randall had royally screwed up now. He'd destroyed Ellis' trust in him before it had even had a chance to fully form. From here on out it could only get worse.

Well done. You find someone who really makes you happy, and you shove them away.

He grimaced and stood quickly. Ellis' head tilted to follow the sound.

Randall inhaled, but held his breath. What could he possibly say now? What words could ever make this situation right?

None. None, and he'd fucked the chance to say the three that really mattered. They'd be hollow lies to Ellis' ears now. Why the hell had he called off last night in favour of Briar's bollocks? And instead of telling Ellis how he felt he'd received a fist to the face.

That was gratitude for you.

"Randall?" Ellis said quietly.

"What?" Randall snapped. He regretted it immediately. He hadn't intended the word to sound so aggressive, but it was out now.

Ellis' lips pressed together into a thin line. He ran slender fingers through his soft, wavy hair and let it fall forward once he was done. "Never mind. Is there anything else I can help you with?"

So that was it. Randall shook his head and turned for the door. "No."

"Right, well. Stop by tomorrow, eh? I'll be free, and we can talk a few things over, areet?"

Randall rubbed his eyes. He doubted Ellis really meant it. There wasn't any way the vampire wanted him back after this utter fucking shambles of a conversation, surely. This was nothing more than a polite goodbye, the way that people would agree to meet up then cancel later. He'd text tomorrow to see if Ellis was free and Ellis would have more meetings, or clients, or something.

Better to get fobbed off for a few weeks than dumped to his face, though. Randall wasn't sure he could handle that.

"Yeah," he said. He didn't look back. "Okay. Anyway, I better shoot off."

"Take care."

"You too."

Randall had to force himself to walk out of the office and down the stairs. He wanted to run, but Ellis would hear that.

Mayfair wasn't his neck of the woods. It wasn't even his *kind* of area. This was a postcode for London's wealthy, whether they were local or visitors. The hotels were the sort that had people to take your luggage from your chauffeured car up to your suite on your behalf. Restaurants held Michelin stars. The art galleries were plentiful, and the works they sold *started* at five figures. Randall was as out of place here as Ellis would be over in Stepney.

What the hell had he been thinking? They didn't have anything in common! Hell, Ellis probably thought Randall *was* common. He might be from up North, but his dad had been minted enough to send him off to London with enough money for a posh flat and an even posher business to run. And here was Randall, the working class boy from the broken home, reckoning he was in love with the man up on the pedestal.

It wasn't going to happen, no matter how much Ellis insisted he loved Randall.

Once he was sure he had to be beyond the range of Ellis' hearing, Randall broke into a run.

Only then did he let the tears fall.

TEN

ELLIS AWOKE to darkness and the ever-present sounds of the life both inside and outside his building. The distant rumble of traffic was sometimes punctuated by a nearer vehicle, but cars didn't often come down the little residential street he lived on.

That sound alone meant that it was daytime. He could pretend for a few hours that he wasn't confined to his apartment by the tyranny of the sun's rays. He was merely indoors because he had nowhere to be right now. Yes. That was it.

He heard Tiberius' heart and his breathing. Both sounded healthy, thank god.

He rolled onto his side and reached for his watch on the bedside table. He shook it first, in case taking it off and setting it down last night had nudged the ball bearings out of place, then he ran his fingers across the surface.

Two in the afternoon. That seemed a reasonable time to get out of bed.

Tiberius scrambled to his feet at the sound of movement

and stuck his cold, wet nose into Ellis' face. His tongue rasped over Ellis' skin, and his tail thudded against the carpet.

Ellis laughed a little and ruffled the dog's head between the ears. "Good boy. Back up, go on. Get back. Good boy."

As Tiberius backed away from the bed, Ellis fought his way out of the sheets and sat up, then fastened the watch around his wrist.

It was nice having someone here when he woke up. And as much as he loved Tiberius, it'd be far nicer to have Randall here too.

Ellis' shoulders sagged a little. The shifter's timing could use a little work, that was for sure. God alone knew how long Barb might have been lingering around outside the gallery, yet all Randall wanted to do was talk about things he shouldn't know and which could get Ellis killed. For all Barb's talk of revolution, Ellis didn't know her from any other stranger who walked in off the street.

Randall had sounded like Ellis was insulting his beloved mum or something. They'd have to clear it up tonight. For now, though, Ellis had several hours of being a prisoner in his own home to look forward to.

He grabbed his glasses and slid them on before heading out of his bedroom. It was a habit now. The longer he went without seeing a glimmer of light the more normal it became and the more he could concentrate on getting on with his existence.

Ellis strode to the kitchen and checked Tiberius' cache of food, then dished him up breakfast and gave him permission to eat. He emptied the water bowl, cleaned it, refilled it and returned it to the floor. Then he left Tiberius to his food and disappeared into the bathroom to clean himself up.

He wasn't really sure whether he needed to shower for

hygiene reasons. He couldn't catch any diseases, he didn't sweat, his hair didn't grow unless he'd cut it. Still, it felt wrong to turn into a shower-dodger on account of being undead, so he stuck with that habit every bit as much as he did his others.

Habit and routine were part of any blind person's life. A little unpredictability here and there was fine, but overall everything had to be in its place and the best way to make sure of it was repetition. Maybe he was trying to cling to some remnant of humanity by showering and brushing his teeth, but fuck it. Better than letting himself go to ruin.

Tiberius' loo time wouldn't be until much later, so Ellis settled in the living room once he was dressed, popped the television on to counteract the sound of a woman two doors down having an argument over the phone, and booted his computer.

This was when he would get most of his work done for the day. Attending the gallery of an evening was more of a formality, although it was nice to touch base with Jay and get out among the living. The *other* living. Tiberius didn't really count; he was a pretty lousy conversationalist. Ellis' afternoons were spent chasing invoices, paying bills, emailing customers and artists alike, and dousing the occasional fire of a lost consignment or transit-damaged work. In between all of this he'd loiter on forums or chat with Jay over Skype. The one thing he didn't do was order Tiberius' food; Jay handled all of that. It was easier for Jay to have it delivered to the gallery than for Ellis to try and find a shop that sold pet food in Mayfair which wasn't stuffed to the gills with CCTV.

He sifted through his inbox and handled what little awaited there while unfeasible storylines unfurled from his TV. Running a business from home really wasn't so bad, but it took some gumption to get dedicated and not be distracted by every little beep his computer made.

When he reached the top of his inbox, his fingers hesitated. Had he read that right?

He tried again, more slowly this time. The display thunked away as it refreshed the email's subject line and sender.

Anna Serkis. Checking in.

Tiberius' handler at the Guide Dogs for the Blind office. He'd been avoiding her for weeks.

Ellis winced and opened it.

Hi Ellis, Just wondering how Tiberius is doing. He's overdue for his annual, and I'm in London this afternoon so I'll stop by and we can get everything squared away. See you at 4PM!

His hand darted to his wrist.

Five to four.

"Shit." He pushed away from his desk and stood, but it was a futile gesture. She'd be here in five-

BZZZZZZZZZ!

"Shit!" *What kind of bastard turns up five minutes early?*

Four in the afternoon, with a woman who probably wanted him to take his dog out for a stroll so that she could observe them together. *Shit shit shit.*

The buzzer razzed again as though it were mocking his panic, and he all but ran to the intercom. He lifted it and thumbed the button to unlock the front door before she had the chance to speak, and he held it down for several seconds before he hung up again.

God, he hadn't just let Randall's Alpha in, had he?

It hadn't even occurred to him. Maybe Anna was going to turn up in five minutes and it'd already be too late.

Calm down, you great Jessie. Calm the fuck down. You can handle this!

He screwed his eyes shut, pulled his glasses off, and

rubbed the bridge of his nose. When he eased them back into place and opened his eyes, he headed for his front door and listened.

Heels on the antique marble flooring. *Tap tap tap.* A heart beating a little harder for climbing the stairs. He somehow doubted that Randall's Alpha wore such dainty heels, but perhaps it was this Preeti instead.

She rapped on his door, and he took a deep breath, trying to detect any of that woodsy shifter scent through the door.

Not a jot. Just Chanel No. 5.

He plastered a smile across his features as he pulled the door open. "Anne!"

"Ellis! Sorry it was such short notice! Glad you could make it, though."

He grinned and stepped back to allow her inside. "Oh, it's fine. There's only so much daytime TV I can take. You're doing me a favour. Come in."

Anne's chuckle was warm, and she breezed past him before halting quickly. "If I'm doing you a favour you could at least be a bit more available, eh?" Her Welsh accent was soft, likely from the south of Wales rather than the north, and her voice was slightly nasal, as though she had a blockage.

"Sorry. Running a business is pretty hectic, especially when you've only got one member of staff who isn't yourself." He shut the door and chuckled faintly. "We're smack in the middle of hiring someone, actually. I probably would've been more available in a couple of weeks. But it's all good. Why don't you come on through?" He reached for the light switch and added "Lights'll be on in a sec, if you want to close your eyes."

"Ah, that'd be wonderful, thank you."

"No worries." He flicked the switch and stepped around her, hand briefly touching her arm to guide himself past her body without making it too awkward. "What can I be doing for you this afternoon, then?"

"Well. Tiberius' vet check-ups are coming through nicely so there's nothing to worry about there. And he's a healthy boy, which is good to see." She followed him, her heels muted by carpet. "Hello, Tiberius! Not working at the moment? Who's a good boy, aren't you!"

He heard the swish of Tiberius' huge, fluffy tail and the patter of his feet as he crossed the lounge to greet Anna. "No," Ellis agreed. "No harness at home. I've got the place laid out the way I want it, so there's no need to get him into work mode until we need to go out. Can I get you a cuppa?"

"Coffee would be lovely, thank you. Black. Not too strong."

Ellis smirked slightly and headed into the kitchen. "He's a good lad," he called back to her as he aligned the kettle under the tap and ran the water slowly. He dipped a finger into the filter's reservoir and shut the tap off once the water reached his fingertip. "No problems."

Absolutely no problems, and no dog trainer ever got called in. He waited for the trickle of the filter to end, then refilled the reservoir. It took a couple of goes to get enough water for two, and it'd look odd if he made her a drink without fetching himself one.

Thank Christ she didn't want milk. He didn't keep any around. Tipping it away once it went rancid was an experience he never intended to endure.

"None?" He heard her move around out in the living room. God, she was going to be one of those people who nosed around his shelves and touched his things, wasn't she? He heard a faint clatter, then the noise from the television cut out. She'd already put her hands on the remote, then.

Now he'd have to check the flat once she'd gone to put everything back in its place. He expected casual visitors to do this kind of thing, but not a Guide Dogs handler. Still, he could be leaping to conclusions. Perhaps she'd placed the remote down exactly where she'd found it and had muted the television so they could talk. That'd make more sense, wouldn't it? No human had his level of hearing, after all.

He shook his head. "Nope," he called back to her. "He's excellent. I couldn't live without him." *And have killed to protect him.* He grimaced and brushed the thought aside while he lined up mugs and dropped a tea bag into one, then a teaspoon of coffee granules into the other. Buggered if he knew how strong "too strong" was. All coffee was too strong as far as he was concerned. He'd never acquired the taste while he was alive, and now that his senses were sharp as a button the idea of putting it in his mouth seemed extra-unappealing. Besides, tea was a proper drink for a Yorkshireman, even one who'd have to regurgitate it later.

He waited for the water to boil, then grabbed the little plastic liquid level indicator from its shelf and hung it over the edge of his tea mug first. It beeped at him once his mug was full, and he ran it under the tap before setting it on the rim of the coffee mug.

Anna was still moving around out in the lounge. Maybe she was waiting for an invitation to sit. Ellis grabbed the mugs and moved through, setting the coffee down on the table.

Her breathing came from his right, over toward the windows.

Ellis tensed. She wouldn't.

Would she?

He'd put the lights on specifically for her. There was no need to mess with a man's curtains.

"Have a seat," he said, trying his damndest not to panic.

"Oh, thank you!" She sounded grateful. "I'll just let a bit

more light in. My RP makes seeing in low light a royal pain in the arse."

"N-"

Ellis' voice died in his throat, cut off by the scrape of metal curtain rings along the steel rail.

"Goodness, are these blackout curtains? They're heavy, aren't they?" Plastic rasped over plastic as she opened the blinds, too.

It was all Ellis could do to hang on to his mug of tea. He backed away from the windows, but it was too late.

There was sunlight in his flat.

"There. That's a little bit better." Anna paused. "Are you all right?"

His brain was stuck in a holding pattern. Wasn't he supposed to be dead by now? Properly dead? Or did he have to be out in the sunlight directly? Maybe that was it, maybe he had to walk outside for the problems to begin. Glass bounced some small amount of UV rays away, didn't it? What were the odds of those little rays being the sole dangerous component of sunlight?

"Mr. O'Neill?"

"I'm fine," he choked. He gulped a mouthful of near-boiling tea, and winced as it burned all the way down. His body healed the slight damage within a second, taking the pain away, and he felt his way toward his armchair. He sank slowly into it. "Uh. Sorry. I was miles away. I just... remembered a... work thing..." *Smooth. Sounds convincing.* He fixed a smile into place and added "What's the weather like?"

"Oh just a couple of clouds, nothing too bad. I don't think it'll rain, though it was whipping up a cold wind while I was on my way over."

Ellis silently thanked the British obsession with the weather.

"Now, I have some paperwork with me," Anna said. He heard the creak of his couch as she sat, then the clasp of a briefcase and swish of paper. "It shouldn't take too long."

"Of course," Ellis said, his mouth on auto-pilot. "Go right ahead."

As he answered her questions, part of him couldn't let go of the fact that he was supposed to be a pile of ash by now.

What the hell was going on?

ELEVEN

ELLIS STOOD BY THE WINDOW. His fingers pressed against the cold glass. Dim light edged around his glasses and made his world dull and grey.

Anna had gone through her checklists and left soon after. She'd thanked him for the coffee and said she'd check in again in a year, but might not be his handler for long after that at the rate her eyesight was failing. They'd commiserated together on the irony of her disease, and she'd expressed a level of acceptance and practicality that he wished he'd had back when he was at her stage.

He should have burned to a crisp. Or caught fire, or turned to ash. He didn't really know which it was. Jonas swore up and down that sunlight was death, yet here Ellis stood, not dead. His skin itched like he'd been caught out at midday without sun block, but that was pale-arse Yorkshire skin for you. He'd never been able to take more than ten minutes of the kind of exposure other people ran off to sunbathe in.

He moved away from the window but the itching

remained. *Was* it sunburn? It felt like it, or at least the beginnings of it.

Ellis hurried back to his desk and slid into his seat. His fingers ran across the display until he tabbed to the Skype window he had open with Jay, and he pressed out a quick message.

Jay. Are you there?

Jay's response was immediate. *Yep!*

Can you come over to mine?

What about the Gallery?

Ellis pursed his lips. *If it's empty, lock up.*

Be there in ten minutes, Jay responded.

Ellis busied himself by getting rid of the tea he'd drunk and brushing his teeth. Then he collected the empty mugs and washed them by hand. The hot water against his skin turned an itch into a horrible burning sensation.

Exactly like sunburn.

He grimaced and ran cold water, hoping it would take the sting out of his flesh.

Why wasn't it healing?

The doorbell buzzed, and he tore himself away from his thoughts to let Jay up, and soon his assistant was at the door.

"Hey! Came as fast as I cou-" Jay gasped and hurried past Ellis. "Oh my god! What happened?"

Ellis shut the door and followed him. "Woman from the Guide Dogs came over, and before I knew it she'd opened the curtains."

He heard the blinds. Jay had hurried to close them. "That bitch! Are you okay?"

"She didn't mean any harm."

"She could have killed you!"

"But she didn't." Ellis frowned and moved to Jay's side, then reached past him to re-open the blinds. "Look."

Jay's pulse raced. His breathing was stilted in panic, then he exhaled in a rush. "I don't get it."

"You an' me both." Ellis squeezed Jay's arm. "It's still sunny out, right?"

"Yeah. It's not going to last all that long, but there's still light out there."

Ellis nodded. "So maybe we should pop out."

He felt Jay tense. "Have you gone mental?"

"Look. What if the whole thing about sunlight is rubbish? What if Jonas lied? What if he believed this and never dared test it?"

"I'm pretty sure I wouldn't test getting shot to see whether it was as lethal as it sounds," Jay agreed.

"Aye, that's exactly it. What if it's..." He hesitated.

What if this was one of the Council's stories to frighten and control the population? Barb might be onto something with her crazy-sounding ideas, but she hadn't mentioned this.

Maybe it was Ellis who was immune for some reason, or maybe he'd been hiding out this past year for nothing and other vampires were swanning around the city in daylight and having themselves a right old laugh at the blind recluse who hid away in darkness.

"What if it's what, sweetie?" Jay gasped, then added "Oh god, don't pull that face! It might stick with you!"

Ellis blinked and realised that he'd sunk into an angry fug. He rubbed his cheeks. The itching had died down at least. "Sorry 'bout that. How much daylight do you reckon we've got left?"

"Probably only half an hour, an hour at most."

"Then let's go take Tiberius for a walk."

ELLIS WRAPPED himself up in a thick wool coat, and he stuffed gloves and a scarf into his pockets in case they were caught out too far from shade all of a sudden. Tiberius was to his left, working now that his harness was on, and sounding much more relaxed after he'd done his business somewhere far behind them.

The itch had slowly returned, but the air outside was cool and mitigated some of the discomfort. Ellis hadn't keeled over when they stepped out of his building, and he still hadn't dropped dead now the sun was going down. His world was going dark once more, which was much how he preferred things, and his anger had deflated into a sullen grumpiness which Jay had gently mocked.

"I think that's pretty much it for the sun," Jay observed.

Ellis lifted his face toward the sky. It made no difference. "I suppose my face is still attached?"

Jay snorted. "Just about. Although stop a second."

Ellis told Tiberius to halt, then faced Jay. "What is it?"

He felt Jay's warmth come closer, and his hunger stirred faintly. He hadn't felt it in so long that he'd almost forgotten what it was like to have that niggling little sensation that life could be made a bit better if he'd have a little snack.

"You do look like you've caught the sun a bit," Jay murmured. "You've got that pink just-singed look to you." Jay took his right hand and turned it between his fingers. "Back of your hand, too. Palm looks okay."

"How singed?"

"Oh, not like freshly cooked lobster or anything." Jay released his hand. "You know, more that delicate English rose caught out in midday kind of flush."

"It does feel a bit burned," Ellis said. "Maybe that's all there is to it?"

Jay sighed. "I hate to admit it, but I think the only way

we're going to find out is more tests, and under more varied conditions."

"Sounds like science," Ellis grumbled.

"Does, doesn't it?" Jay sniffed. "I'm awful at science. Han's the genius, not me."

Ellis chuckled at that. "Don't put yourself down. I couldn't get by without you, and nor could he. You're the linchpin of our lives."

"I am the sun around which everyone orbits," Jay declared with a laugh. "Shall we get back to work? You never know, we probably had thirty tourists all desperate to buy the most expensive art they could find knock on the door while we've been tanning ourselves."

Ellis nodded and turned Tiberius around. "Tell you what's reet odd about it."

"What's that?"

"It doesn't heal up all that fast." Ellis lifted fingers to his own face and nudged at his cheek. It felt sore, and he grimaced. "It really is like proper sunburn."

"Maybe that got blown all out of proportion?" Jay suggested. "Or maybe it's prolonged exposure that's fatal. Who knows, maybe it's Randall's blood. You still haven't eaten, have you? Could be linked to that somehow."

"I'm starting to get a bit peckish," Ellis murmured as they sauntered along the path. "Not proper hungry like, but certainly could go for a snack."

Jay gave a lewd snort. "Time to give him a little nibble, then!"

"God, where'd Han ever find you?" Ellis grinned, but he had to stop when stretching his face so widely caused it to sting.

"Technically I found him. He was all 'Oh if only I could organise my shit! I better hire someone to do it for me!' and I was like 'Hey baby, I hear you like people who know how to use a calendar!' and it was all roses and dinners on cruise ships."

Ellis laughed at that. "You make Han's interview process sound far more interesting than mine."

"Oh sweetie, that's how I went through your first round of hiring! I threw out all the ones who didn't bring me flowers!" Jay huffed, then added "Oh, by the way, I sent out the offer letter to Ryan this morning. Just waiting to hear back."

Balls. Ellis had completely forgotten about the interviews after Barb had dropped her bombshell on his desk. "Ryan, eh?"

"I think she's a better learner, and it'll be a good start for her."

Ellis smirked. "I'm not running a charity, Jay."

"Oh, hush. She can move on to a more suitable gallery in a year or two, and she'll always be able to recommend you whenever customers ask where to find Contemporary art. She's a solid long-term investment."

Ellis' eyebrows shot up. "That's genius."

"That's Han," Jay chuckled.

Ellis pursed his lips as they walked toward the park exit. "Are you suggesting that Han placed you with me to get insider information about upcoming events? He could have just signed up for the mailing list, you know."

"Ah but without me there was nobody to *run* your mailing list!" Jay patted Ellis' shoulder lightly. "You seeing Randall later?"

Ellis slid his free hand into the pocket of his coat, squeezing past the gloves which were wadded up in there. "Ostensibly."

He heard Jay suck air through his teeth. "What's that supposed to mean?"

"I don't know." He sighed. "He's told a friend about me."

"Like…" Jay trailed off. "You're shitting me!"

"I'm not." Ellis' shoulders hunched up briefly. God, this was a right can of worms. Jay had no idea what Randall was, and now it looked as though Randall had told some random human about vampires. Which, all things considered, may well have been better than what had actually happened.

He shouldn't have mentioned it. It could only lead on to admitting what Randall was, and Ellis couldn't do it.

"I'm going to scratch his eyes out!"

"Don't." Ellis tipped his head toward the taller man. "He's supposed to come by later so we can talk things out. He'll probably be less likely to talk if you've torn out his eyeballs."

"Probably," Jay agreed.

"Besides. He made a mistake. He was talking to a friend about this fella he'd met who he'd noticed odd stuff about, you know?" Ellis gave a small smile. "Before we got together. Stuff like 'You know, this guy I fancy the look of doesn't seem to have a reflection.' I think really what's going to count is how we move forward, eh? So let me see whether he's got the gumption to show, and what we're going to do about it, then worry about cat-scratches to the face."

"Uh huh. So!" Jay's speech became decisive. "Who was that woman? A vampire, right?"

Oh." Ellis shook his head. "Aye."

"So what did she want?"

"You know how you knowing what I am could get us both killed?"

"Sure, yep."

"Well, knowing what she came to me about could get all three of us killed, I'm thinking."

"Juicy!" Jay squealed with sarcasm. "Still, better to know than die of ignorance."

Ellis's lips twitched, and he tipped his head forward. "She claims to be part of some revolution or resistance sort of thing. They want to do away with the current system and replace it with a democracy."

Jay puffed out air. "Correct me if I'm wrong, because politics is totally not my thing except it kinda is, but generally speaking totalitarian regimes don't gladly step aside to help form democratic governments. I mean, that's just my personal understanding of these things."

"No I think that pretty much sums it up."

He could almost hear the cogs in Jay's mind cranking along as they left the park and crossed Piccadilly.

"There's no good way for this to move forward," Jay concluded.

"Yeah. I'm glad I'm not the only one to think so." Ellis shook his head. "It's a reet proper shitstorm brewing on the horizon is what it is."

They tromped the rest of the way to the gallery in sullen, companionable silence, which gave Ellis plenty of time to fret.

TWELVE

BRIAR SEEMED to want to patrol all day, every day, but even shifters needed their sleep. Sadly it meant that by the afternoon Randall was already out on bloody patrol again, along with everyone else in his pack who could get the afternoon off work. That meant everyone except Nazim and Lara, both of whom had the undoubted joy of a full day's work leading into an evening and night of patrolling to look forward to. Yeah, this close to the full moon that wouldn't cause *any* problems.

Jim brushed up against him as they crossed the street, and Randall curled his lip, growling low in his throat. He didn't want any of them to touch him. They could rot in hell after what Briar did last night.

Jim looked startled and gave him some space.

Preeti was in front, her nose leading them along. The one person in this shitty pack Randall still gave a damn about and he couldn't even talk to her.

They walked along like a gang, and most people got the hell out of their way without a second look. Those who didn't risked a stare that could melt ice, and even the most lippy teenager usually thought twice about getting smart with them, especially with the overbearing mass of Briar in their midst.

Randall's attention wasn't on the job at hand, though. Ignoring the fact that he just didn't give a flying shit about what Briar wanted anymore, his mind was replaying his argument with Ellis on some kind of masochistic loop, and the unanswered questions were nagging away at his brain like a determined woodpecker. What was so dangerous about Ellis speaking Polish? Would Briar allow Randall to leave the patrol later so he could meet up with Ellis? Could the vampire ever trust him again?

He trudged along after the other shifters as they wove their way toward wherever. Randall didn't care where, though the occasional brightly-coloured tower block suggested they were heading for Tower Hamlets again, and he ground his teeth. Briar wanted to keep poking this bear, didn't he? Why couldn't he leave it well enough alone?

Randall checked his phone. It was coming up on half four in the afternoon, he had emails from clients he needed to schedule appointments with, and there weren't any texts from Ellis. His stomach percolated, which made Preeti's ears flick toward the sound for a second, and her tail lifted in amusement.

"It's all right for you," he muttered. "You can eat crap off the street."

She wagged her tail and grinned, then turned her attention back to her work.

Briar lagged behind until he was parallel with Randall. "What's up?"

"What do you think is up?" Randall growled.

"I don't know. That's why I asked."

Randall glanced up, and squinted into the sun to be able to

see Briar. "You honestly think you can punch me in the face and I'll have forgotten all about it by the day after?"

Jim's step faltered and he looked back over his shoulder. Briar showed his teeth and pointed forward, so Jim's head obeyed and he hurried to catch up with Preeti.

"I did what had to be done," Briar said softly.

"You're a cunt, Briar. We'll get through this moon, then you and me are done."

"Don't you ever take that tone with me again, Rand. Final warning." Briar spoke lowly, his voice a bass rumble of menace.

Randall snorted. He felt light-headed. "Or what? You'll crack my jaw again? Maybe break a few other bones while you're at it? Yeah, I'm not using me arms right now, you could 'ave a go at them if you fancied it. Yer a big man, aren't you? You think you can just-*hkkk!*"

Briar's fist clamped around his throat and he all but lifted Randall from the ground. The muscles of his arm bulged like angry snakes, and Randall's toes scraped over the pavement as they tried to find leverage. "Enough," he whispered.

Randall struggled for breath. He clawed at Briar's fingers and his body writhed in an uncontrolled and desperate need to escape. His pulse rushed in his ears and his eyes felt as though they might burst. His chest was on fire.

Preeti snarled.

Briar threw Randall to the ground. "It's this boyfriend of his," he grumped at Preeti. "Ever since they met he's been acting out."

Randall curled into a ball. He coughed and wheezed while his throat healed itself as fast as it could manage. The black receded from the edges of his vision. Rage wound itself tightly in his gut. He used it to propel himself to his feet, but retained barely enough common sense not to push it any further than that.

"Let's get back on the job," Briar snapped.

Preeti gave him a disapproving stare and turned her back to him, while Jim studiously pretended to be fascinated by the metalwork fence he'd stopped next to.

Randall shoved past Briar and jogged ahead to catch up with Preeti, then walked alongside her. He fumed in silence, and she cast the occasional look up toward him, her amber eyes sad and her tail held low.

They walked like that until the seagulls of the Thames screeched nearby, and Preeti's nose twitched. She ran her tongue over it to wet it and improve its sensitivity, and soon her hackles had risen and her tail fluffed out.

"We should go," Randall whispered.

She glanced up to him, then over her shoulder to Briar.

"Cub?" Briar said.

Preeti flicked her head and yipped a light *yes*. But her ears swivelled too, and her fur rippled with tension.

"Not alone," Briar said.

No, she agreed.

Much of a wolf's ability to communicate was nonverbal. Sound was more useful over long distances, but for close range scent and body language were far more important, and as they couldn't smell too well at the moment they were limited to reading Preeti's movements and expression to infer her meaning. Still, it was natural to Randall now. Understanding a wolf was like learning another language, and dogs used much the same language to communicate with their owners and with each other. When he wasn't with his pack Randall used the skills they had taught him in his working life.

The fact that he owed them so much rankled with him. It never used to be a problem, but now-

"Rand," Briar growled. "Pay attention."

He jerked to a halt and looked up.

There were a group of people dead ahead, looking every bit as much of a gang as Briar's pack did. Randall recognised a couple of them from Cemetery Park, and they had the young cub in their midst. Five of them to Briar's four, all told, and none of them were in their wolf bodies right now. They didn't have their Alpha with them, either.

Randall drew his shoulders back and nodded to them, but his gaze slid down to the pavement. They might be okay out and about without their Alpha this near the full moon if they hadn't stumbled into another pack, but now that they had, the chances of violence had significantly increased and Randall was buggered if he was going to do anything to provoke them.

Briar looked like he had other ideas. Of *course* he did. Why should Randall have expected any better from him? The man-mountain stepped forward, all aggression and caveman dominance, and the other pack immediately spread out across the pavement, pushing the cub behind themselves to protect her.

"Don't do this," Randall croaked.

"You!" Briar pointed to the shifters ahead of him. "You get your arses off my fucking turf. *Right* now."

Glances were exchanged between the men and women of the other pack, then they muttered to each other.

"I said now!"

"They don't speak English," Randall hissed.

"They don't need to. I can say it in a way they'll understand."

Randall stood transfixed in horror as Briar launched himself forward and buried his fist in a woman's stomach. The air rushed out of her, and she slid to the pavement, wheezing for breath.

Within seconds the street devolved into a disaster zone. Preeti and Jim had to press forward, and the other pack rushed in to either attack or rebut them. Fists careened into bodies. Blood sprayed through the air, whether from busted lips or bitten flesh Randall couldn't really tell.

On the other side of it all, the cub stood, as frozen as he was. He waved frantically to her and yelled "Go! Get somewhere safe! Run!"

But she stared at him, then back at the milieu, her mouth hanging open.

"Fuck," Randall whispered.

He'd have to get in there, if only to stop his own pack hurting someone who couldn't heal herself yet.

He shrugged his jacket off and laid it over the fence railing to stop his phone getting broken in the mess, then waded into the fray. He had no real plan other than to try and stop people from hurting each other too badly.

The problem with shifters was that they could take it and dish it out all day long if they had to.

"Guys," he yelled. "Guys! For god's sake, break it up! Walk away!"

He saw Preeti's teeth sink into one bloke's thigh. Blood gushed from the wound and spewed across the pavement, rendering it slippery. Soon enough Jim's feet lurched across it, and he dragged a woman to the ground with him, where they both got covered in red while trying to claw each other's eyes out. Briar's forearm sent one of the men flying back, and the cub spurred into action, hurrying forward to see if he was injured. Tears were glistening down her cheeks by now.

Randall took a kick to the balls and howled in pain. He folded to his knees, but his assailant was as relentless as she was anonymous, and she kicked him in the face next. His nose lurched to the side, and his body fell the rest of the way.

He was getting sick of his face being on the floor.

Someone booted him in the kidneys then trod on his thigh. The fight scrambled on all around him as his wounds healed. He tried to get up, but a punch knocked him right down, so he rolled away from the fight before he tried again.

All he saw was a mass of bodies and blood. Jesus, how was there so much blood? It couldn't be Preeti's teeth doing all this damage, could it?

Then he saw it: the knife in Jim's bloodied fingers, its blade slick with arterial scarlet.

Randall felt sick. If Jim stuck that in someone once too often they'd lose their shit and change shape right out here in the street.

"Preeti," he yelled. "Jim's got a knife! Stop him!"

She turned and launched herself at Jim, but was sideswiped by a foot and Jim lunged away from her. He swung the blade, and it found the cub's flesh.

The girl gasped in shock.

Jim plucked the blade out and swung it for the woman who came at him yelling words none of them could understand.

The cub finally screamed. She clamped her hands over her stomach as her blood began to ooze free of her body.

"You fucking idiot!" Randall roared. "She can't take it! You don't stab a fucking child, you arsehole!"

The fight broke apart. The other pack clustered around their injured cub, snarling and swearing at Jim.

Jim stared at his blade, the bright red now dulled with darker stains.

"I didn't mean-" he began. Then his face contorted, and he spat "What the fuck was she even doing in the middle of all this shit? Why didn't she run?"

"Don't you fucking *dare!*" Randall stepped back and snatched his jacket from the railings. "Don't you even *try* to say it's her fault you stuck a fucking knife in her! Why the hell are you carrying anyway?"

Preeti was snarling at Jim. Her muzzle was drenched in blood. It stained her teeth, her fur, even her whiskers.

"I am getting the fuck out of here before the police rock up, and you better think about doing the same."

"Randall," Briar warned.

"No. Fuck off. You fucking started this, and now she's going to hospital for your fucking ego. You can fuck right off."

He slung his coat on to try to hide the worst of the blood on his t-shirt, and hurried away from them, leaving their swearing and snarling behind him. He half hoped that they'd get arrested, but since the only hope of that was eyewitnesses phoning 999 the odds were probably pretty slim, and if Jim had any brains he'd toss that knife in the damn river, fast.

"Fucking idiots," he seethed as he huddled in his jacket and strode quickly toward Stepney. He stuck to small streets and alleyways as best as he could, but people were everywhere this time of day. Rush hour was picking up. People were leaving work and heading home. He was forced to duck into doorways every few yards rather than run into people.

He wished he'd been able to understand a damn word the other pack had said. Maybe the whole thing could have been negotiated down rather than propelled into blood and anger.

Ellis was holding out on him, and it looked like whatever Ellis' secret was, his refusal to share it would start to cost lives.

Something had to give way, soon.

THIRTEEN

RANDALL GOT HOME, shed his clothes, and stuffed the bloodstained garments into the washing machine before he disappeared into the shower.

The water didn't soothe him. The loud hum from the power shower grated on his nerves. The drops of water were fat and hit like little knives, and the run-off was swirled with pink across the white ceramic of the shower basin. He washed his hair until his scalp felt raw and the water ran clear. Every time he closed his eyes he saw Jim's knife in the young cub's stomach.

His skin rippled and he didn't care. The fury built inside him and he had no interest in fighting it. His body tore itself into a new shape and healed every bit as quickly until his massive bulk didn't quite fit in the shower enclosure any more. The only way he was going to solve anything was to put his fist through the sheet of glass between him and the rest of the bathroom, so he did.

It cracked and then splintered. Shards of it burst outward while others gouged into his furred forearm. His body rejected the injury even as he did himself more damage by withdrawing his arm.

More blood. The water ran bright red, and then faded to pink again. His fur became waterlogged. The noise of the shower pissed him off, so he raked at it with claws the length of a man's fingers.

All he'd succeeded at was transforming his bathroom into some kind of disaster zone. The remains of the shower head spewed water in an arc over the top of the enclosure and drenched his towel rail.

Randall let out a howl of frustration which died horribly in his throat when the realisation of what he'd done penetrated his moon-ridden brain.

Shit! He was in his halfway shape in his own sodding bathroom.

He shrank back as quickly as he could. His fur withdrew, and the blood which had been trapped in it sloughed off his bare, human skin. The discomfort of shifting shapes passed quickly and he stared in dismay at the shower.

Jesus, he hated it when Briar was right. He *couldn't* live without an Alpha.

He slid what remained of his shower door to the side so that he could get out, but doing so was fraught with danger. Glass had a horrible habit of becoming invisible in clear water, and the floor of his bathroom was now covered in both. He had no choice but to step out and let his body heal up whenever he trod on a shard.

There was a rapid knocking on the door of his flat, and he froze.

"Rand? It's me! Can I come in?" Preeti's voice drifted through the air.

"Uh." Randall nodded to himself, then hurried out of the wreck and jogged to the door. He checked the spy hole, but

Preeti looked to be alone. She was wearing her usual overalls, so she must have run back to St. Mary's to grab her clothes first.

He opened the door and she let out a low whistle. "I know I've seen it all before, but maybe it's not the best way to open the door, eh?" She grinned up at him.

"Ha ha. My bathroom's a wreck. You dunno how to turn the water off, do you?"

"I am best engineer!" She hopped into the flat and made her way straight to the kitchen.

Randall closed the door and frowned. "Er. Bathroom's that way."

"But your inside stop valve is probably under yer sink."

"Oh." Randall felt like an idiot, and he spurred himself toward the kitchen. "Where's Briar?"

"Should be at St. Mary's by now, waiting for everyone else." Preeti had already half disappeared beneath his sink, her tiny frame barely sticking out from it. "Yeah, here it is!"

He heard metallic squeaks and Preeti's grunts, then she reversed out from under the sink and bounced to her feet, her face flushed. "There we go! Put some clothes on. My mum'd have a field day if she knew I'd run out on an arranged marriage just to hang out with naked blokes all day every day."

"Wow." Randall stared at her. "You really had a wedding lined up?"

"Oh yeah. Never even met 'im. Just as well I didn't, eh?" She grinned and slapped him on the shoulder. "Fuck off and stop being naked, you pervert."

That nudged him into action, and he mumbled a quick apology before scurrying away to his bedroom. He could still hear water in the bathroom, but when he turned to ask Preeti she pointed to the bedroom and mouthed "Go!"

He snagged a fresh towel from the airing cupboard and got

himself to the point where he could at least get a t-shirt and shorts on, then he returned to the living room.

"Takes a few minutes for the system to drain," Preeti explained. "Stopped now. Your bathroom's a fucking mess! What'd you do? Hulk out in there?"

Randall rubbed a palm over his hair in embarrassment.

"Oh my god! You did!" Preeti's eyes were wide, then she laughed it off. "Never mind. Pick up a new shower unit and enclosure some time, and I'll come over and repair it. I'm all kinds of handy, me!"

It was Randall's turn for wide eyes. "You'd do that? I mean, after earlier?"

She sighed and flopped into the couch. "You're basically my little brother, Rand. I love you. I'm never going to abandon you just because Briar's being a prick."

Randall lowered himself to the cushion beside her. He watched her, and she returned his gaze. She was confident and calm where he was filled with doubt.

"You admit he's being a prick, then," he said slowly.

She scratched her cheek with short, neat nails. "I'm his wife, not his mum." Then she sighed. "It's autumn."

"Uh huh…"

Preeti tutted as though she were having to educate a child. "There's always the danger of a Blood Moon this time of year. We've been on this ride a few years, Randall. Even he can't resist the pull of the moon when it's red."

"He's done all right most of the time." Randall frowned at her.

"Uh huh. But this year's a supermoon at the same time. That thing's gonna be the closest to Earth it's been in ages *and* all while it's Blood Moon time." She sighed. "I mean, his dickishness is why I'm pretty much convinced this year's going to be a rough one. Usually he's on top of things, but the full moon hasn't even arrived and he's already losing his rag. And now here you are hulking out in your own shower." She leaned in and hugged him tight. "We can get through it, Randall. I know we can. But if you can't keep it together in the shower how are you gonna cope out on the street, eh? I don't want anyone hurt and that includes you."

"Then what about Briar lamping me in the face, eh? He broke my fucking jaw, and don't you dare say I deserved that."

"Of course you didn't. Nobody does." Her words soothed him faintly and took the edge off his rearing anger. "I love you both. It was horrible. I couldn't do anything about it in public, not in that shape. I gave him a piece of my fucking mind when we got home, though. Not that that's worth much." She sighed.

He rested his forehead against the side of her head. "It's worth plenty," he said quietly. "None of the rest of them would have said a word."

"I'm sorry. If I'd ever known how it'd all turn out for you, I..." She held her breath, then exhaled in a puff. "I probably would've still gone up to you at that party. I know what killing his family did to Briar, and I couldn't let it happen to anyone if I could prevent it."

Randall grimaced.

Preeti hadn't ever mentioned why she had run away from home. As a twelve-year-old girl she'd braved the journey from Leeds to London and lived on the street until Briar found her, Randall knew that much. She'd always insisted that she'd just "run away, like kids do" and he had no reason to dig any deeper. But Briar had been very honest with him about his own problems once she took Randall to him. Between them they were desperate to save other cubs from the horror Briar had endured when - at the age of fifteen - he had slaughtered his parents and his little sister in the family home.

Randall sympathised. He really did. He was haunted by Briar's story and what it could have meant for his own mother and his older brother. The shifter gene seemed to be recessive, so none of them had been born to werewolf parents or had a shifter for a sibling. Each and every one was alone, and without a pack to find them and take them somewhere to change in safety everything could go fatally wrong. But not for the shifter, no: wrong for anyone caught near him when it happened.

Briar's story was a stark warning, and he wasn't alone. Nazim too had killed during his change: he'd left a nightclub and got into a fight with a mugger, and the next thing he knew he'd disembowelled the guy in an alleyway. Nazim acted like he didn't care, but Randall could read it in his posture on the rare occasions he talked about it. Nazim hated that he'd killed. He might be a bully, he might be an arrogant little shit, but he never wanted to be a killer.

He sighed and leaned back, reaching for her hand and giving it a squeeze. "Would it really be so bad to lose some territory?"

"Uh-"

"I'm serious. What do we even do with it?" He turned to face her. "It's about time we modernised instead of sticking to this weird Seventies idea of what a wolf pack should be like. It's all wrong. We're not wolves. We don't really know *what* we are. Everything we know we've had to learn the hard way, and the rest we've pretty much made up on the spot. We wander the streets and piss in parks like we're homeless. It isn't getting us anywhere. This pack can wander in out of Essex or wherever and they're two, three times our numbers and if they fucking want in we aren't ever going to be able to stop them. Not unless we can damn well talk to them."

"Briar wants us to hold," Preeti said simply. "So we hold."

"Why?" Randall cried.

"Because he's our Alpha. Because whether or not we're getting it right, we only have each other."

He pushed up from the couch and padded away to the bedroom to grab some socks and jeans. "Fuck it," he growled. "This isn't working. I'm just getting pissed off again." He hopped from one leg to the other while he tugged the jeans on.

"What are you doing?" She appeared in the doorway, her delicate eyebrows creased together.

"I'm going out."

"Briar wants-"

"I don't give a sodding shit what Briar wants! He lost any right he ever had to tell me what to do the moment he punched me, and he lost any chance he ever had of me forgiving him for that the moment he decided to start a fight with a cub present. She could be *dead*, Preeti, and that's his fault! Nobody else's!"

They gazed at each other through the open doorway. Preeti's arms wrapped around herself. Randall panted with outrage.

"I'll tell him you're not coming," she finally said.

Randall nodded. "Thanks. You're my big sis. You know that. I'll always have your back."

She smiled and hopped in to kiss his cheek. "I know. Promise me you'll stay out of trouble tonight. And don't visit your mum, okay?"

"I promise." He nodded.

"I will kick your arse if you break that promise." She gestured toward the bathroom as she backed off, and added, "Come 'round to mine if you need a shower before yours is fixed, okay?"

"Yeah. Thanks."

Preeti let herself out while Randall pulled his boots on. If he wanted to go out he had to get well away from their turf or Briar would take it as an insult.

He couldn't think of anywhere that much further away than Mayfair.

FOURTEEN

THE GALLERY WAS QUIET, and Ellis couldn't help shake the feeling that if it hadn't been shut for a couple of hours they could have customers in by now. The logical voice in his head tried to argue the point that most customers came from events and openings, not from walk-ins, but it was frequently drowned out by the other voices: the ones that wanted the rent paid, for example.

His sunburn had begun to heal. His skin felt less tight, and the itching had all but stopped now.

"Ooh," Jay said. It was very much an 'ooh' that meant *go on, ask me what I'm oohing about!*

Ellis pursed his lips to try and contain his smile. "What is it?"

"She's accepted the offer!" Jay chuckled. "I feel almost mean! Isn't she supposed to try and negotiate for more money?"

"Well I'm glad she didn't. I haven't got any more money." Ellis leaned back. "Don't you put ideas into her head. When's she going to start?"

"I'll see if she can come in tomorrow for orientation. She said she was available immediately, so let's see how immediately she meant." Jay's keyboard clicked with his swift, sure typing. "There we go. So, where's Randall?"

"No idea. Where's Han? I haven't seen him in a couple of weeks."

"Oh, nice deflection!" Jay laughed. "He's fine. Sleeping a lot lately. I think I'm wearing him out!"

"I don't need to know." Ellis smirked.

"Nope. Text Randall. See where he is."

"No. I'm not going to badger him. He agreed to come tonight. If he can't stand by his promises then..." Ellis sighed. "Then I don't know."

"Well it sounds to me like he has The Fear. Don't go calling the whole thing off for cold feet. Give him some space. He'll come around." Jay sounded like a jaded old queer propping up the bar; he'd put on a wise-woman voice toward the end and it took away any chance he had of being taken seriously, but then Jay wasn't often one for handling things with gravitas.

Ellis gave an absent nod, but before he could answer he heard the gallery's door open. Footsteps entered, along with a pounding heart and heavy breathing.

"Could be him now," he said cautiously. "Whoever it is sounds like they just ran a marathon."

The sounds came up the stairs, quickly.

"Quick," Jay whispered. "Let's pretend we're working!"

Ellis snorted as his office door was shoved open.

"Hey, Randall!" Jay peeped. "Oh, wow! Is that the time? I have a husband to get home to you know!" His chair rubbed over the carpet. "Great to see you again!"

Randall growled.

"Uh." Jay sounded uncertain. "Okay. You two totally have a thing to work out right there. Catch you tomorrow, boss!"

"Good night," Ellis murmured.

Jay hurried away down the stairs. Randall came toward his desk.

Ellis lifted his chin. If the werewolf had finally chosen to do his Alpha's bidding, there wasn't really a whole lot Ellis could do about it.

"I have fucking had it up to *here*," Randall snarled as he leaned over Ellis' desk, "with Briar."

Well, that wasn't exactly what Ellis had expected to hear. He blinked. "What happened?" He caught the faintest hint of blood on the air when he inhaled to speak, and his hunger reared its ugly head like a cobra scenting a mouse. "Are you bleeding?"

"No," Randall snapped. "I'm not. But I swear to fucking god Briar will be if I ever see him again!"

Ellis bit the inside of his cheek while he worked to stay quiet. Randall was furious and his heart still pounded even now that he was in Ellis' face. The whiff of blood was faint, but Ellis' senses were primed to find that one scent above all others. Perhaps he'd been injured earlier and washed the blood off without soap. The speed Randall could heal at was mind-boggling; it rivalled Ellis' own ability, potentially even outstripped it, so for there to be no current injury didn't mean there hadn't been one only minutes ago.

"When's the full moon?" he asked as evenly as he could.

"Tomorrow," Randall snapped.

"Right then." Ellis eased his chair back from both the desk and the killing machine leaning across it, and reached for Tiberius' harness. "I suggest that we take this elsewhere."

"Why?"

Ellis shut down his computer, checked he had his keys in his pocket, then headed for the door. "Because I have several hundred thousand pounds worth of art stored in this building and I can't even begin to imagine the insurance nightmare if you destroy any of it."

THEY MADE IT TO ELLIS' flat in record time. Ellis led the way and crossed the street to avoid people, hoping to avoid Randall starting on any of them. He didn't want to find out what could happen if someone bumped shoulders with the werewolf while he was in this state.

Ellis knew damn well he was taking his life into his own hands. What else could he do? The poor thing was angrier than Ellis thought possible for one man to be, and for a man as gentle and kind as Randall? It broke Ellis' heart to know that something had upset him so badly, but there'd be no talking to him like this. Ellis didn't have the greatest amount of experience with the werewolf temperament, but he knew one way to get Randall to unwind. It had to be worth a try, before the shifter turned into a wolf and went on a rampage.

He got them upstairs and said nothing while he removed Tiberius' harness and checked his water bowl.

"Now what?" Randall snapped.

Ellis took a breath. He had to be precise. If there were an ounce of doubt or strain in his voice it could all end here and now. He turned toward Randall and eased his glasses off. Neither of them had turned the light on, so the view remained pleasantly unchanged. "Now," he said calmly, "you take your clothes off."

Randall's breathing rasped in surprise. "What?"

"You heard me." Ellis set his glasses down on the coffee table, and nudged his shoes off. "I'm not about to wait around. Get your clothes off or by god I'll take them off you myself."

He heard Randall's heavy breath give way to a weak, almost inaudible moan.

Ellis peeled his jacket and shirt off quickly and ditched them onto the sofa. He shimmied out of his trousers and flung them to hopefully land somewhere near the rest of his clothes, but he didn't stop to check. Instead he stepped into Randall's radiated warmth and pressed against his body. He didn't place his hands anywhere on the shifter's person; he held them down at his own sides, robbing Randall of his touch, and leaned in to breathe softly along the side of his neck. He drew slow and deep draughts to pull cool air over Randall's sensitive skin, then exhaled down between his jaw and collarbone without once allowing his lips to make contact. If Randall wanted any more than that he'd have to make the next move himself.

Ellis could measure the time passing in the beat of Randall's heart. They stood connected only by their centres while Ellis teased with his presence and his unnecessary breaths and a minute crawled past, followed by another.

Three minutes in and Randall caved. His moans found strength, his hands came to Ellis' hips, and he whimpered as his fingers found bare skin. The dam broke, and Randall poured out from behind it as though he'd been caged for weeks on end. His fingers dug into Ellis' flesh and pulled the vampire's groin against his own. His lips found Ellis' shoulder and nuzzled ferociously into it. His tongue was hot and wet and desperate as it planted itself against skin.

Ellis' lips twitched. He let Randall paw at him a few moments, then breathed into his ear "You can take your clothes off now, petal."

Third time, it seemed, was the charm. Randall made a flustered whine but took a couple of steps back and began to undress in a flurry of flapping cotton and rustled denim. Ellis grabbed the opportunity to nudge his own boxers down and get rid of them, and Randall was on him before he'd straightened up again. Hands. Tongue. Bare, sweat-coated chest, nipples like buttons. Cock hard and eager, trapped against Ellis' thigh.

Something had upset Randall; that much was abundantly clear. He'd been close to blood, close enough to get some of it on himself somewhere. He was furious at his Alpha, too. Whatever Briar had done, Ellis desperately wanted to take Randall in his arms and whisper that everything was going to be all right, but he couldn't. Not with the moon driving the poor man insane.

He didn't understand the relationship shifters had with the moon. He hadn't had the chance to ask Randall about it, and now would be completely the wrong time to try. But he did know what could take the moon's influence down a peg or two and it didn't involve kind words or a loving embrace. There would be time enough for those later.

Ellis slid his hand between their bodies and grasped Randall's length. He held on firmly until he was sure he had Randall's attention and then stroked from base to tip.

Randall bucked in his hold. His breath shuddered and intermingled with desperate keening.

"Shh," Ellis murmured. He ran his teeth lightly across Randall's shoulder, just light enough to let him know they were there. He drew his hips away to make room and delved his other hand between them so that he could stroke hand over fist, one palm then the other, until Randall's cock was fully hardened. "That's it, darling. I'll look after you. Just relax."

"Fuck me," Randall growled. He thrust against Ellis' hands and leaned in to rub his cheek against Ellis' chest. "Please, don't make me wait. Not like last time. Just fuck me-"

"You better go get the lube then, hadn't you?" Ellis withdrew his hands, which made Randall whine loudly. "Go on. You know where it is."

Randall's heat left his side. Ellis could hear him fumbling his way across the living room, and he followed a few steps behind. As appealing as bending Randall over the sofa was, who knew how quickly his temper could flare up again if he caught his leg on the corner of the coffee table or something equally painful. The bed would have to do for now.

Randall clattered around in the drawer of the bedside table. The little grunt of triumph he released after a few seconds' rummaging made Ellis grin in the dark, and he had to push his humour aside before he could speak.

"Got it?"

"Yeah."

"Good. Better get yourself nice and ready then, hadn't you?" He stepped up behind him and slid one hand around Randall's waist to cup his balls. "Here. I'll help."

"That's helping?" Randall's words caught as Ellis gently squeezed. "Oh, fuck."

"It's certainly helping me." Ellis grinned again. He felt Randall's body squirm and squirrel around as the other man tried to find a position in which he could use the lube effectively, and did absolutely nothing to assist him. When Randall's slick fingers reached back and found Ellis' length, though, the grin wiped itself from his face. The fingers were strong and firm, and they worked to coat him and tease him at once.

"Fuck me," Randall snarled.

Christ, the werewolf was a horny little bastard when the mood took him.

Ellis used his entire body to shove Randall toward the bed and over it. He didn't wait for the other man to make himself comfortable; he followed with his weight on Randall's back and used his free hand to guide his head to Randall's entrance. His other hand he lifted from Randall's nuts so that he could use his arm to lock them together.

Randall writhed under him. His knees sprawled awkwardly as Ellis' pushed them apart. His back sloped so far forward that his head was probably against the sheets. His moans became muffled.

Ellis pushed himself in past Randall's tight, grasping ring of muscle. Randall howled into the bedding and pushed back, as though daring Ellis to enter him faster.

Fuck. Randall's insides were hotter than his skin, and they enveloped Ellis like molten silk. He drove on, pushing past each little quiver, every single squeeze of Randall's sphincter around his shaft, until he couldn't go any further.

Ellis clung to Randall to force the other man to take a moment. He knew Randall didn't want to, knew he'd insist he'd heal whatever Ellis did to him, but Ellis wasn't going to let it go that way. He pulled his left hand away from Randall's hips and slid it beneath him to feel tenderly up along his chest. His right drifted down to wrap around Randall's shaft, and he felt a trickle of pre-cum against his fingers.

"You gonna come for me, petal?" he whispered.

"Oh, shit," Randall mumbled.

Ellis brushed his lips over Randall's muscular shoulder and withdrew himself slowly, re-entering with long, slow strokes while he fisted Randall's shaft.

"Ellis," Randall pleaded.

He didn't answer. His strokes grew faster as he drove harder and deeper into Randall's tight, hungry arse and his arms clutched hard to keep them together. Randall's words became gibberish, the helpless cries of a man too close to the edge to use language.

"That's right," Ellis hissed. "Go on. Let it out."

Randall's short, powerful body bucked beneath him and his arse squeezed Ellis' cock so hard that Ellis could all but feel the cum as it rippled through his length. Randall shot forcefully against the bed and he heard every wad of it hit the cotton, even over the stocky man's roar.

They sagged as one. Randall's muscles gave out on him and he had just enough control to fall to the side rather than land in his own spunk. Ellis held him close and didn't try to unravel the mess of limbs.

"Oh," Randall whispered. "God."

Ellis laughed faintly, but couldn't come up with a response.

FIFTEEN

RANDALL BREATHED SOFTLY. For the first time in days he felt clear-headed. And *calm!* How did Ellis do this?

They had showered together, and Randall found himself mesmerised by Ellis' laconic smile, his gentle touch, and his piercing, unseeing gaze. Randall had been struck with the sickening thought that he hadn't done anything to deserve him and Ellis had shushed his concerns away and soothed him with soft kisses.

He watched the vampire now as they rested on the couch together. His head was in Ellis' lap and his feet hung over the arm rest. Ellis' eyes were closed, but his fingers idled across Randall's chest, and that smile still lingered on his lips.

"What're you grinning about?"

Ellis' lips parted into a wider smile. "I was just wondering if you only get turned on when you're running high on adrenaline," he teased.

Randall bit his lip. "It's got to be starting to look like it, eh? I'm sorry. It's not like that."

"Good. Not sure I could take the strain." Ellis' eyes cracked open, and he tipped forward to lean over Randall.

Randall could see the concentration on the vampire's features as he tried to see. He reached up and cupped Ellis' cheek, and the soft bristles of the taller man's stubble rubbed against his fingers. "Thank you."

"Any time." Ellis' grin became sly with innuendo.

"Pervert," Randall added.

"Definitely, aye." Ellis leaned back again. His face relaxed. "Now, tell me what's got you all of a bother."

He sighed a little and dropped his hands to rest together over his stomach. "Okay. I told you about this other pack nicking the cub, right?"

Ellis' head bobbed. His long hair fell forward, still damp from the shower, and a little drip of water flicked onto Randall's cheek. "Aye." He gently felt along the side of Randall's face, then wiped the drop away with his thumb.

Randall blinked. He knew Ellis could hear the tiniest of things, but a little drop of water? Randall had to be in his wolf body to hear so clearly. "Wow," he blurted. "Uh, yeah. So anyway. I got into a flaming row with Briar about it and he lamped me one."

Ellis blinked, and his face took on an expression Randall was relieved wasn't directed at him: cold fury etched his angular features, and his eerie blue eyes turned hard as diamonds. "He hit you?"

Randall swallowed. "Yeah. He's supposed to be calm, but he lost his shit and smacked me right in the jaw. Preeti thinks it's because there's a Blood Moon due and it'll be a supermoon at the same time."

Ellis rocked his jaw before he answered. "You mean a Harvest Moon?"

"Same difference. We tend to call it a Blood Moon 'cause

it's harder to resist than even a full moon, but Briar's usually okay with it."

"But not with a supermoon. Which is... what?"

Randall ran his fingers along Ellis' forearm. "Okay, so the moon's orbit around the Earth isn't at a fixed distance. It travels on an ellipsis. The distance actually varies by something like thirty thousand miles. Usually when it's really close to us it's not at the same time as a Full Moon, so it goes pretty unnoticed by most people. When it's close it looks way bigger in the sky, and when it's really close *and* a Full Moon, that's your supermoon."

"I get you." Ellis still frowned, but his angry look faded somewhat. "So we've basically got a massive red moon and it's making Briar punch people."

Randall winced. "Worse than that. He picked a fight with this other pack."

Ellis' eyebrows shot up. "When?"

"Earlier today. We went out and found them, and he totally laid into them."

The vampire pursed his lips, then said "Ahhh. And that's how you got blood on you?"

"How the hell did you know about that?" Randall blinked.

"I can detect the faintest trace residue of blood on pretty much any surface if I'm bothering to breathe at the time." Ellis grimaced. "Which is mostly pointless, since blood which isn't contained in something living and breathing is inedible, so usually it makes me hungry for no good reason."

"I had a shower before I came over..." Randall groaned. "Then I lost my shit and put my fist through the shower enclosure. That was probably my blood. Sorry."

"Don't be. I happen to find your blood-" Ellis broke off with a frozen smile on his lips. "Ah, I mean... That's not, like, the most romantic thing I could ever say to you, is it?"

Randall laughed. "Yeah, no. But thanks. I think."

"You're welcome. Any time you want me to tell you how delicious you are, you let me know." Ellis' smile relaxed, but the slightest touch of worry still creased the corners of his eyes.

"I'll try to remember that." He sat up enough to kiss Ellis gently. "Once this is all sorted out I'll tell Briar to stick it. More than I already have, I mean. Like, properly shove it up his arse."

"Is that wise?"

Randall shrugged as he laid down again. "It's a raging Blood Moon tonight and I've never felt happier. You do something to me. You give me my self-control back. I don't need to put up with the abuse if I've got you."

Ellis sat quietly. Randall tried to read his features, but it seemed Ellis was lost in thought.

"Ellis?" he ventured.

Ellis drew a faint breath, and said "Sorry. So, what do we do about this mess?"

"We?" Randall bit his lip. "Well, I don't know. What languages do you speak?"

The anger flashed back into Ellis' features, and his body became taut under Randall's shoulders. "Jesus Christ, Randall, how many times have I-"

"Ellis. It's all right." His fingers came to rest over Ellis' hand. "Listen to me, please."

It was difficult to face the betrayed, hurt cast of Ellis' features. The faint creases around his eyes became strained rather than worried, and his lips pressed together so tightly that they became little more than a hard, straight line.

"I know it's a secret, all right? I know it is." He used the sort of voice he'd put on to murmur assurances to a terrified dog; it came out of him entirely instinctively, and he hoped it didn't sound patronising. "But I think if you just happened to have learned Polish at some point it wouldn't be so bad, would it? You said they could kill you for speaking Polish." Randall sat up with care, trying not to spook the vampire with fast movements. "This is something you're not supposed to be able to do, isn't it?" He eased his feet to the carpet and turned so that he could face Ellis properly, then settled his hand on Ellis' bare thigh. "Talk to me. Please."

Ellis launched to his feet and strode away toward the kitchen, then paced back again. If he hadn't looked so pained Randall could have been distracted by his complete nudity, but at the moment it simply made the vampire look fragile, as though stripped of his armour. "If there's a vampire within a couple of hundred yards," he hissed, "they might hear."

"This is your patch though, right? They aren't allowed to stride on in?"

"There's no guarantee-"

"No," Randall cut in firmly, "there aren't any guarantees in life. But we need to talk about this, and we can't keep our mouths shut for the rest of our lives on the off-chance there *might* be a vampire nearby. Ellis. Tell me." He remained calm, and spoke quietly, but his tone didn't brook any argument. Ellis may not be a dog, but people tended to respond well to the same methods if they were on the brink.

Ellis stalked away again, then paused at the kitchen doorway to touch the frame. Maybe he was orienting himself after all the back and forth. "I think I stole Jonas' power," he whispered, still facing away.

Randall leaned forward. His head tilted as he tried to hear better. "Eh? How does that work?"

The vampire's slender shoulders hunched, and his head bowed. "I've no idea. I can't control it. I had no idea Barnes was talking Polish until he told me. He was the one who worked it out, and from there he figured out how I'd..." He shook his head. "I think he was right. I don't think he really *knew*, but I think he got it right."

Randall rested his elbows on his knees and pressed his palms together. The movement gave him a moment's pause, so that when he answered he remained softly-spoken. "It's all right. Can you tell me what he worked out?"

"I broke the law," Ellis whispered.

Randall had to fight the urge to ask how, or which law, or even whose law. Instead he waited.

"Jonas went to the gallery to kill me. He threatened Tiberius. I'm not a fighter, Randall. I've never hit anyone in my bloody life. It's not the kind of thing people do to each other, you know? I couldn't see him, I couldn't defend myself against him. He reeked of blood already. He was going to kill us." Ellis rubbed his forearm, then stepped back from the door frame and turned to face Randall. His arms wrapped around himself. "I knew that when we bite people it makes them unable to fight back. I *didn't* know if it would affect a vampire the same way - if I bit him whether it'd stop him from killing me. I figured I had nowt to lose, so I did it."

"You bit Jonas?" Randall murmured.

"Aye. I did it, and he just... stopped. Didn't say a word, didn't lift a finger, an' I realised we couldn't stand there like lemons 'til the end of time. Sooner or later I had to let go. But if I did that he'd come at me again, and I'd lose my only chance to stop him. So I-" Ellis' words cut out and he hurried to the sofa. He dropped back into his seat and curled in on himself like a condemned man.

"You fed off him?"

Ellis' head bobbed faintly. "Aye. And I didn't stop. I didn't stop until he was ash, and when they came to ask questions I told them I smashed his head in and they believed me. There are laws about how we can treat each other and our territories. Top of the forbidden list is cannibalism. Punishable by death. If the Council finds out-"

"You're dead," Randall concluded. "And because you seem to have picked up Jonas' power, questions would get asked if you started using it."

"It's not even only because it's Jonas' power. Whatever we get, we get it because it's a unique product of our bodies, our minds, and our blood. No matter what ability we gain, that's it. That's what we are, what we have. We can't shop around, it's not like we can go to Vampire University and learn silly powers off each other. We can't. They can't be taught. It's like trying to teach a tree to knit."

Randall inhaled sharply. "And now you've got more than one of these things, it'd raise questions," he realised.

"Aye."

Randall rubbed his jaw. He'd known Ellis had killed Jonas; he worked that out after Barnes' attack. Did the means make it any worse somehow? Ellis called it cannibalism, but his whole existence required that he drink blood, and Randall had to admit he was okay with that. Draining a guy dry in self-defence wasn't any worse, not when it was that or death.

Was this what they both were, then? Killers? And if they were, did it change anything?

His phone peeped from the floor, and his train of thought derailed itself. "Sorry," he mumbled as he went looking for it in folds of discarded clothing. "That's mine."

"It's fine." Ellis pushed his hair back from his forehead and began to gather up his own clothes.

Randall could feel the lump of his phone, right next to the lump of his wallet, but digging it out proved some Herculean task. "When'd you last eat, anyway?"

"The last time you let me," Ellis said simply.

He managed to fish his phone out, and the sudden bright light from the screen made his eyes water. "That was a month ago!"

"Haven't needed to since then."

"I didn't realise I was *that* delicious!" He thumbed the screen and his grin died.

Briar: They're on our turf again. Where the fuck are you?!

"Petal?" Ellis prompted, his voice soft.

"It's, uh. It's Briar." He cleared his throat. "Looks like he's spoiling for another fight."

Ellis snorted and offered a hand. "Ignore it."

Randall groaned as he reached for Ellis' hand. It was a tempting suggestion. He couldn't turn his back like that, though, could he?

Ellis tugged on his hand. "Come to bed. Get some rest. Let me hold you."

He stood and let his gaze take in Ellis' pale, lithe body in the light from the screen. It outlined him with an almost ethereal glow, and cast everything else into darkness.

"How 'bout," Randall rumbled, "I remind you how tasty I am?"

Ellis' lips curved upward in his sly half-smile. "Only if I get to remind you how sexy you are too."

Randall turned his phone off and tossed it onto the sofa. "Deal."

SIXTEEN

Ellis felt alive again. Randall had stayed all night and they'd slept in until mid-morning, when Randall's grumbling stomach had woken them both. The werewolf excused himself to get food and Ellis nodded off after.

Now he was up, and he'd decided to go straight to work rather than sit at home until the sun went down. It was earlier than his experiment with Jay, but he'd taken some of Randall's blood last night after they went to bed. Maybe it was that blood which made it possible for him to walk Tiberius in the mid-afternoon light, but it didn't really matter. The fact was that he could spend a little more time with Tiberius on their way to the gallery and let him run around one of the parks within Mayfair itself since they were all closed after dark. His skin itched like crazy by the time he let himself into the gallery, but the moment he was out of the sun's warmth the rawness faded. His body was using Randall's blood to heal the damage, and by the time he'd ascended the stairs to his office his face felt normal, without any of the sunburned tightness to it.

There were two people in the office. He heard Jay's voice, and tasted the lingering presence of a budget perfume in the air. Ryan, perhaps? The scent was familiar.

"Now, if these two figures don't match up, you've got a problem," Jay was saying, "and you have to work out where that problem is. Are we being over or undercharged? Has the agent or artist forgotten to include something in the consignment? Have they accidentally included VAT?"

Ellis pushed the door open and urged Tiberius forward. "Hey. Didn't mean to interrupt."

Jay picked up on the unspoken question. "You didn't. Ellis, this is Christy Ryan."

"Oh, of course!" Ellis smiled and nodded. He had no desire to feel the poor girl's clammy hand again. Hopefully in a couple of weeks once she'd settled in and wasn't as nervous her hands wouldn't feel like dead fish anymore. "Glad you could get started nice and quick. Poor Jay's needed another pair of hands around here for ages now."

"It's no problem, Mr. O'Neill," she said.

"Ellis, please," he replied as he urged Tiberius on toward his desk. "If you get stuck with anything, just ask. The sooner we can help you the quicker you'll learn, aye?"

"Aye. Um. Yes."

"Oh don't worry about him," Jay laughed. "He's the world's second-best boss."

"It's true," Ellis agreed. "But I'm afraid Jay's husband isn't hiring right now, so I'm the chopped liver."

"We'll survive, somehow," Jay chuckled. "Now, like I was saying. Reconciling our invoices with our consignment log book might take a bit of detective work now and then, but it's essential it's done right..."

Ellis smiled to himself, settled Tiberius down, and then sat at his desk to check his emails as he tuned out the chatter. It was nice though for that chatter to come from real, living people and not his television.

JAY PACKED Christy off home at five, and Ellis waited until she'd left the building before commenting "You're a good teacher."

"Ah, I've missed my calling, eh?" Jay's joints popped when he stretched.

Ellis winced at the sound. "Nope. Your calling is right here, I swear. How'd she do?"

"Not bad. I mean, it's probably all in one ear and right out the other at the moment. We'll see how she goes when she has to start doing some of this on her own." One of Jay's drawers slid open, then there was a light thud of plastic. "Oh, Edison called again. He tried pre-noon this time."

Ellis groaned.

"I know. It's almost like he's not going to give up when his inheritance is on the line." Jay laughed and headed over to fill the kettle. "You're looking hale and hearty. Been nibbling Randall all night long?"

"Every time I think I might forget about how filthy you are, you come right out and remind me."

"It's a burden I must bear." Jay gave a dramatic sigh. "Anyway, he seemed to have a proper mood on. Everything okay?"

The grin snuck across Ellis' face despite his best efforts. "Oh aye."

"You naawty!" Jay stirred his tea and carried it back to his desk. "Oh, shit. Now you're here, you're gonna find out my secret."

"You hate art?"

"Well, there's that. But around five's the best time to eat, too." The plastic popped, much like a lid opening. "Do you mind?"

Ellis tipped his head to the side. "Do I mind if you eat? No, of course not." He paused, then added, "Any road, I'm here early. You could go home and have dinner with Han?"

"Ooh." Jay tapped something against the plastic container. "Are you sure?"

"Aye. If you two aren't seeing much of each other lately, I insist." Ellis smiled softly. "It might even become a regular happening. I dunno if it's Randall's blood or just another thing Jonas cocked up, but I got here mid-afternoon just fine."

Jay popped the lid back onto his dinner. "That'd be amazing," he said cautiously.

Ellis moved his braille display aside, then leaned across his desk, his arms spreading idly over it. "The lady who came here the other night," he began.

"The vampire one?"

"Mm-hmm. Sorry about all the cloak and dagger. I had no idea who she was or why she was here."

"You don't have to explain all that to me, sweetie. I caught on."

Ellis chuckled. "Aye. You're far too smart to be a personal assistant, you know."

"Uh, I hate to disillusion you," Jay said, "but PAs have got to be pretty smart to keep all the balls in the air. The figurative ones. Not literal balls. That would be some kind of circus act, not a PA." He sipped his tea in small, faint slurps. "What about her?"

Ellis tapped his fingertips against the surface of his desk while he tried to corral his thoughts into some sort of order. "Her name's Barb. She lives in Soho apparently. And, ah." He lifted a hand and scratched at his scalp, then dropped it again.

"She wants me to join some kind of revolution. Overthrow the Council kind of thing, I think."

Jay coughed, and put his tea down with a thump. "Oh right. She doesn't want a lot, then."

"Yeah." Ellis gave a grim nod. "The way I see it I'm buggered either way now. If I refuse she probably has to kill me in case I run to the Council and blab. If I agree, what the hell do I bring to the party?" He took his glasses off, closed his eyes, and rested his forehead against the cool desk. "Urgh," he grunted.

"Sounds like just talking to her has dropped the average life expectancy in this room," Jay mused.

"That's pretty much my way of thinking, too," Ellis mumbled.

"Then I'd say you need more information." Jay lifted his cup for a gulp. "If nothing else it's a delaying tactic while you work out what to do. Maybe sell up and move out to the country. You might even have enough left over to pay your dad back and never hear from any of them again."

Jay's cheery lilt sounded forced. Nonetheless, Ellis appreciated his attempt to make light of the situation.

He pushed himself up off the desk and sat back in his chair, and when he cracked his eyes open the dim light wandered in, bringing a white haze with it. He didn't go for colour in the decor. It risked distracting the customers too much, so his office was anaemic and not worth looking at even if he couldn't see it properly. He grabbed his glasses and slid them back on. "That's not too bad of an idea," he admitted. "Apart from the countryside bit. That sounds way too rural."

"Well, I *am* a genius," Jay declared airily.

"So I've heard. Usually from you." Ellis allowed a ghost of a smile to return.

"Best person to hear it from. And while you're talking you

can ask her about this sunlight thing. Slip it in among a whole bunch of other stuff and hope her powers aren't lie detection. In fact, see if you can get out of her what they actually are. I mean, the Council knows everyone's, right? They keep tabs on that shit? It has to be something she's already had to tell, so hopefully she won't think it's a major secret."

"Bloody hell." Ellis pushed his shoulders back and lifted his chin. "You *are* a genius."

"Such pressure," Jay cooed.

"Don't let it get to you." Ellis pulled his portable display out of his pocket and flipped the case open. He turned it on and felt his phone buzz as the two devices connected.

"Wouldn't dream of it." Jay drank the rest of his tea quickly.

Barb had given Ellis her number. At first she'd tried to be all cool and pass him her card, but once he pointed out he couldn't read it she'd relented and read it out to him while he typed it into his phone. He searched for it now, and then pressed the keys to send her a text.

Are you free this evening?

"So if she's from Soho, is she a prozzie?" Jay deadpanned.

Ellis nearly typed complete gibberish. "Jay!"

The PA laughed and carried his cup over to the sink. The water ran and splashed while he washed it out.

Sure thing. Shall I come over?

Ellis' fingers darted across the display at Barb's reply. Her coming to him would be for the best. It put her at his mercy according to the Council's Laws and they both knew it. But Ellis was also grateful that it meant he didn't have to leave Mayfair. His mental map of CCTV cameras and glossy windows only covered his own stomping grounds. *If you don't mind? 10PM?*

Perfect, she answered. *I'll be there.*

"Well," he said. "That's that. She's coming over at ten."

He heard the rustle of paper towels, then the squeak of the swing-top bin. "I'd offer to stay," Jay said, "but what with the whole secret conspiracy thing it might be best if I were long gone."

"I agree, I'm afraid." Ellis stood and moved around his desk, then offered Jay his hand. "Give Han my love, areet?"

Jay took it, then enveloped him in a tight hug. "You do it yourself. You're going to be okay. You *better* be okay, or I will kick your arse."

Ellis squeezed him in return. "Oh, well if my choices are death with an arse-kicking or life with an intact bum, I'll take the latter."

"You better."

Jay let go and collected his things, then said to Tiberius "And you, don't encourage him so much."

Then he was off and away, and Ellis had to admit to himself that he really didn't fancy getting up to his eyeballs in whatever Barb's plans were.

SEVENTEEN

THE TROUBLE with allowing Jay to go home early was that it left Ellis as the only one available to speak with non-customers who wandered in off the street all evening. He had no idea that people still did this sort of thing, but it made sense: commuters used to do it back when he was alive and sighted, so why would they stop now? They'd dawdle home slowly to avoid the crush of the Tube, and some of them liked to dream about things they'd fill their fantasy house with when they won the Lotto or discovered a dead, wealthy relative they'd never known about. The occasional straggler would be someone trying to get out of the rain and wait for it to die down, so they used to pretend to be suddenly fascinated in art while they kept one eye on the windows.

This evening's intruders had been the commuter sort, so Ellis hadn't had to spend too much time with them. In the traditional British dance of politeness all it took was for him to offer to help: they would decline, then after a distance of time which seemed well-mannered to both parties - usually around two minutes - they would sidle out again with a mumbled thanks.

By the time Barb arrived the gallery had been still and silent for over an hour, and Ellis had entertained himself with an old audio game he had loitering on his hard drive which was made frustratingly difficult because he'd decided to leave his headphones off to keep an ear out for her arrival. Thankfully the gallery door swung open before he died a fifth time, and he shut his machine down.

"O'Neill?" she called.

"I'm here," he said. There was no need to shout. "Come on up."

The door clicked shut behind her and her boots clanged up the stairs. "Hey," she said when she barged into his office. "How's it hanging?"

Eighties, he had to remind himself. It was either that or she had a genuine interest in his penis. "Fine. You're well?"

"Yeah. Haven't yet been hunted down by a Constable for inciting rebellion, so we're all good." The chair facing his desk squeaked as she landed in it. "Unless this is a cunningly laid trap, which would be a bit of a let-down to be honest."

"If it's a trap, I've forgotten to do the important part of actually laying a trap." Ellis grinned. "Thanks for coming, though."

"Eh, I can't drop a bombshell like that then think you aren't gonna want to talk again at some point." Her clothing - leather, perhaps? - squeaked with some movement she made. "What can I do you for?"

Ellis leaned back and rested his hands in his lap, hoping he seemed non-threatening. "I wondered if you might be willing to tell me more."

Her nails drummed against his desk a while. "More like what?"

"Anything, really." He shrugged. "Whatever you'd feel comfortable telling me. I can't make a decision based on vague knowledge of the existence of some sort of revolution. What're your goals? How do you intend to achieve them? I don't mean, like, any information that could be used against you if that's what you're thinking. I mean... I don't know. Your ideological perspective, maybe, to start with?"

She drew a breath to sigh with, then another to speak. "I think the situation as-is exists to keep us apart and prevent us collaborating, forming opposition, discussing politics, that kind of thing. I think they also serve to stop us even getting to know each other. Travel is restricted unless you're on Council business, and if you ain't, anyone you meet has the right to kill you for the trespass. It increases the odds that we're likely to view another vampire as our enemy and skip any attempt at diplomacy or even trying to get to know each other. But these restrictions don't affect the Council themselves, do they?"

"No," Ellis agreed. He knew that much.

"No. And each Council Member gets to appoint their own Vassal, who can truck around in his master's name and do what he wants. Then there's the Constables, who can also travel around so long as they're doing it to police us - which, of course, they always are. There's no democracy at any level of this structure. Nobody voted for the Council, nobody gets to vote for the Vassals, nobody but the Council votes on the Constabulary. Every year we all have to travel to the Council to present ourselves like it's some fucking feudal fiefdom, and if we don't show up they send a Constable to find out why." She huffed. "If anyone's got a problem for the Council to discuss, they'd better be mates with a Vassal or the Council won't listen."

Ellis bobbed his head faintly as he listened. "For the most part, though, we're left to our own devices, right? I mean, like you've said, I haven't been around all that long. I don't really know."

"Oh, yeah," she agreed. "Left to our own devices to figure out where our borders are and patrol them like we're little more than dogs trapped in cages. You ever see animals in zoos, pacing backwards and forwards 'cause they're bored as shit? Can you imagine what the living would do if their government told them they were all restricted to a single patch of land and could be justifiably killed by their neighbours if they stepped outside of it?"

He rubbed his stubble as the memory of the riots a few years back flooded his thoughts. He'd been terrified that looters might burst in through the doors and destroy his entire livelihood, but thankfully it hadn't spread into his neck of the woods. "Aye," he muttered. "It wouldn't go down well."

"Nope. And London's got all these little areas. If you want art galleries, you come to Mayfair. If you want ad agencies and sex shops, Soho. If you're after museums you go to Bloomsbury or South Ken. But what if your territory isn't one of these little pockets of culture? What if you're out in fucking Brentford or something just as office-tastic and residential? You'd be bored to tears. There's literally nothing to do after dark in places like that. I mean, yeah, nobody's going to want your territory, but holy shit if you ever want to go find someone to eat you're going to have to keep hitting up the same two or three pubs and the landlord is going to notice you sooner rather than later. We're supposed to keep our existence a secret, but how can people do that if they have to keep on feeding off the same limited pool of humans week after week? Meanwhile some of us sit on territories which are full of bars, pubs, and clubs which see thousands of tourists pass through each month; we never have to feed from the same person twice."

"You're one of the latter, though," Ellis reasoned. "Soho's filled with bars and clubs."

"Yeah. And I think if someone is discreet and doesn't reveal what they are or start shit on my ground, why shouldn't they be allowed to come in and feed now and then?" Her clothing squeaked again. It sounded like she was a shrugger. "We should be helping each other. That way everyone benefits."

"But how do you intend to make sure vampires don't waltz in and mess up other territories?"

"There's nothing wrong with laws, but laws should be there to protect what's right, not whoever's the most powerful. I mean, the Council just so happens to be all the Elders in the city, doesn't it? Apart from the guy to your south, but that was a bit before my time."

Ellis shook his head. "I don't know who you mean." He uplifted the end in the hope that she'd answer the implied question.

"Charles Devitt?" She snorted. "Real piece of work. They say he's the oldest vampire in London now, 'cause of the Blitz. The rest either moved to the countryside or died in the bombing. He's like a hundred and fifty or something like that. He should be on the Council, but he's not; he got removed in the Eighties, I think."

Ellis' eyebrows crept up. "Why?"

"Dunno. Rumour is he was implicated in an unsanctioned turning. Not enough evidence to destroy him for it, but enough to screw his reputation, so they punted him off and replaced him." She hissed under her breath. "Nobody I know has anything to do with him. He claims most of Westminster and he's welcome to it."

A faint sickness sank into Ellis' stomach. He'd crossed Westminster without permission last month when he and

Randall had tried to work out who had been threatening to kill him. It was bad enough when he thought he could be trespassing on another vampire's territory, but that it belonged to the oldest and potentially most powerful vampire in the city made him uneasy. "Great," he said faintly.

"That's not the half of it. The guy's got some fucking insane mind control power. Apparently it's rare as shit and only comes along like once every few centuries, but this bastard's got it. That's why everyone avoids Westminster like the plague. All he has to do is say a few words and that's it, you're doing whatever he tells you to." Her chair creaked. "It's not right. All he'd have to do is ask and we'd spill the beans about this whole thing, but he stays in Westminster as far as we know. You're nearest to him, so don't go down there. Okay?"

"Should be fine. I've got no reason to go there," Ellis lied. "But everyone's got their own power, right? I mean, just the one? It's not like he'd have anything more than that because he's older?" *Do as Jay says*, he urged himself. *Hide your important questions.*

"Just the one," she agreed. "But that one's nasty as hell. Plus the word is we get better at whatever our thing is the older we get, so if he's had like a century or so to practice that shit..." She grunted. "I don't even wanna think about it."

"How about you?" Ellis shifted to a slight and hopefully disarming smile. "What's yours?"

She let out her cynical laugh. "Careful now, it's amazing. I wouldn't want you to get all jealous."

"I'd only get jealous if you had the power to magic a million pounds out of thin air," he said.

"Yeah. Fuck yeah, that'd be awesome. But no. I can walk up walls and across ceilings and shit."

Ellis pursed his lips.

"Don't laugh."

"I'm not laughing."

"You are. On the inside. I can tell."

"How do you even figure out something like that?" he wheezed through his teeth, desperate not to smile.

"Trial and error. When nothing mysteriously manifests itself you start trying to do all kinds of weird stuff. Fun fact: I cannot turn into fog or a wolf or a flock of bats, and I know this after many nights of straining like I'd shat meself."

The laugh escaped Ellis despite all his best efforts. "Oh god, I'm sorry."

"Yeah, yeah. Shut up. One day the power to run up a wall will save my arse and you'll all be in awe."

He clapped a hand over his mouth, then rubbed his face as though he could wipe the smile off it. "Sorry. Sorry. Uh." *Change the subject!* "I didn't get taught much of this before the guy who turned me went bonkers and tried to kill me. Obviously by now I've figured out we need to drink blood. The stuff about reflections and cameras and phones seems pretty true, too. How about…" He paused as though he was trying to think up a question. "Sunlight?"

"Oh god no. Don't do sunlight. Not unless you're tired of living."

"Right. Running water?"

"If you want to go insane, by all means try walking across the Thames. If you're lucky you'll never reach the other side."

"Sounds lovely." He pushed hair back from his forehead. "I can't keep food down. Is that normal?"

"Oh yeah." She laughed. "Gross, isn't it? Better bring it back up yourself or it'll all come out at sunrise and there's nothing you can do to stop it."

He crinkled his nose. "Aye. Yeah. Not a nice way to find out."

"Eh, we've all been there. Most of us just don't admit it." She chuckled. "Anyway. I should get back. Let me give you my address. That way if you ever want to visit you know where to find me."

"That's kind of you, but I don't like to go places I don't know."

"Oh? Why not?"

Ellis propped his elbows on the arms of his chair. "I don't know the routes, I don't know what traffic hazards there might be, I've no idea where the CCTV is or where all the glass is. It's better to stay where I am."

She was quiet a while, then said "Okay. Well. I'll give it to you anyway, just in case. Yeah?"

"Areet." There wasn't any point fighting it. He typed it out as she rattled it off, then stood to shake her hand. "I'll have a think," he said. "Thanks for your time."

"It's fine, but if you rat us out, I'll be mega pissed off."

"I won't," he assured her. "It's a lot to think about, you know?"

"Yeah. I know. See you later, okay?" She left, and her boots clumped down the stairs until the front door opened and closed with her passing.

Ellis remained in his chair while he mulled over her information and tried to work out which part of it had been the most troubling.

EIGHTEEN

RANDALL HID out in his flat all day mainlining DVDs and waiting for the sun to go down. After mopping up the mess in his bathroom he'd gone through an entire season of Battlestar Galactica, called for pizza, and hadn't even bothered to shave since he'd got home from Ellis'.

Things never seemed to go to plan of late, though. Preeti arrived just as he was about to head on over to the gallery, and now she sat cross-legged on his sofa stuffing a cold, leftover slice of pizza into her mouth.

He watched her eat and tried to work out how he could get shot of her fast.

She swallowed the last of her crust, then slurped her fingers clean. "Cor, I needed that. Cheers."

"It's fine." He smiled a little. "How's Briar?"

Preeti's tiny shoulders hunched into a half-arsed shrug. "Blood Moon last night, and it was huge. I don't think he's gonna hold it together, not with this other pack stirring it up." She used the side of her hand to rub her forehead. "And if he can't hold himself together, he can't help the rest of us."

Randall still felt blissfully calm. "Maybe it'd be a good idea to get out of the city for a few days. Wait until the environment's not working against us all."

"Not all of us are freelancers who set our own schedules," she grunted. "Sure, me and Briar can be slack for a few days over at the garage, but everyone else has got their jobs to worry about."

"Then they can pull sickies, can't they?" he reasoned.

She shook her head. "Even if they do, then what? Suppose we go out there and there's a pack and it's us who are the trespassers all of a sudden? It'd be every bit as bad. At least here we know where everything is and where to leg it to when the shit hits the fan."

"I suppose." Randall leaned back, since it looked like she was here to stay. "Why aren't you out with the others?"

"'Cause I'm here with you." She flashed a grin.

"I'm not coming."

"Thought you might say that." She leaned over and grabbed another slice out of the open box which sat splayed on the coffee table. "Not to worry. How's this boyfriend of yours anyway?"

Randall rocked his hand in a so-so gesture. "Oh, you know. Fine."

She grinned impishly, her dark eyes bright with mischief. "So the sex is awesome, right?"

"Preeti!"

"You can tell me!" she crowed. "All the juicy deets, c'mon!"

"Yeah, the sex is awesome," he coughed. His cheeks felt like they were on fire.

"Did he turn out to be a mole shifter? Oh my god, you've been to his burrow, haven't you?" Her words were muffled as she spoke with a mouthful of pizza.

"No. Not a mole, not a spider, nothing like that." Randall pointed to her. "You've got sauce on your chin."

She wiped it off with her palm, then licked it. "So what is he, then?"

"Er-"

"It's been a month already. You've been all up in his butthole. Or he's been all up in yours. Or maybe you swap, I dunno. Do you swap?"

"Preeti!" There went his cheeks again, radiating heat into the air.

She chewed in satisfaction. "Either way you can't tell me you haven't had your nose all over him by now, you dirty git. And you won't have got this far with him without finding it out. So come on, spill the beans!"

Randall rubbed his hair and scratched his scalp through it.

"He's not human. We already know that. Humans smell, this guy doesn't. He's not a Shifter or you'd have pegged it right away. So what *is* he?"

Randall scowled at her. "I don't know."

"Bullpats. You're a shitty liar." She waggled the leftovers of her second crust at him. "I'll tickle it out of you if I have to, don't think I won't."

He had no doubt. She was a ferocious tickler, and completely merciless.

Could he tell her? He owed her his family's lives, but how deep did that debt go? There had to be things it didn't cover, otherwise he'd give her everything until either he ran out of anything to give or one of them died. Surely other people's secrets weren't covered, especially when those secrets didn't threaten the pack in any way and weren't going to harm anyone.

Preeti's grin faded slowly. She wiped her fingers off on her jeans. "You know there's only one real reason you wouldn't tell me, right? I mean, this is one of those times where a failure to deny kinda confirms instead. It's because you're a good bloke. An honest man. You ain't even thought to come up with a lie for when you get asked, have you? You were just hopin' it'd go away. That's sweet and all, but he's gonna ask, sooner or later."

"For fuck's sake," Randall said, resigned. "Preeti, you can't tell him."

"Oh my god!" Her eyes widened again. "You're shitting me! He *is* a vampire?"

Too late, he realised he'd been played. "Fuck! Preeti! No-"

"What the hell! You *know* what Briar said! How long have you known?"

He sagged against the sofa and looked away from her, studiously examining the wall while he pushed down the sudden fury that struggled to erupt from him. He should've been with Ellis by now. Yet again his pack had come between them, and this time it might have signed Ellis' death warrant. Stupid pack. Stupid fucking Blood Moon.

"How long?" she snapped.

"A month!" He rounded on her and gripped the cushion to keep himself in his seat. "Okay? One lousy bloody month! Yes, he's a vampire. No, he doesn't kill people. Yes, he has to drink blood to survive. Yes, he's drunk my blood. Just leave him alone!"

"You know Briar ordered you to kill him, right?" She bared her teeth, then shook her head. Her long gold earrings glinted in the low light. "Shit, Rand. What'm I supposed to do?"

He blinked rapidly, and his anger cooled. "Eh?"

"I love you to pieces. And you're a good judge of character. You're protecting this guy for a reason, and either that's 'cause you've been brainwashed by super evil vampire powers, or-" she shrugged "-it's 'cause he's a nice guy. Briar swears up and down whoever you're with is bad for you 'cause it's making you distant from us, but I ain't ever seen you happier than when you're off in outer space somewhere, daydreaming about him. And check you out right now: you've calmed yourself down and Briar in't even here." She puffed her cheeks out and laid back against the sofa. "I dunno what to do."

"Let the moon pass, all right? We can work it out after, but if he's not keeping it together he'll demand Ellis be destroyed and there'll be no reasoning with him." Randall gazed at her as though he could implore her to do as he asked with the power of puppy eyes alone.

"I can't *not* tell him," she muttered.

"I'm not asking that. But hold off for, like, three nights. Until the worst of the moon's passed, yeah? Give him a fair chance at taking the news without exploding in our faces."

Preeti's lips scrunched together and her eyes narrowed. She didn't use her thinking face often when she wasn't working in the bowels of an engine, so Randall said nothing. He didn't want to interrupt whatever process was taking place between her ears.

"What if Briar's right?" she said slowly. "What if he's doing something to you to make you fall in love with him and it's messing with your head?"

Randall shrugged. "I don't think he is."

"Well yeah. You wouldn't if you'd been brainwashed, right?" She tapped her chin. "You been out all night, yeah?"

"Er."

She sniffed. "Your bathroom smells like you didn't clean up last night. That water's through your lino and into your flooring by now. It'll take ages to dry out properly, especially this time of year. Too cold to make it evaporate. We should take your lino up to give it all a chance to breathe."

"Um." Randall wasn't sure where she was going with any of this. "So?"

"So that means you were with him, since you weren't with us." She gestured to his feet. "And you got your boots on. You were off out again tonight, weren't you? I got 'ere around sunset. You were going to spend the night at his again, weren't you?"

"Uh…" Randall dipped his head a little. "Yes?" he said slowly. "So?"

"So he's expecting you." She burst into a wide grin, her eyes alight, and sprang to her feet. "C'mon. Let's go."

Randall stood, wary. "Wait, what? Go where?"

"You're gonna take me to go meet your fella," she declared.

The blood rushed from Randall's face, and he felt dizzy. He sat heavily and the cushion *floomphed* at his sudden weight. "What? No!"

"Uh huh." She planted her little fists on her similarly little hips. "It's perfect. Listen to me." One hand came up and she began to wave it through the air while she spoke. "We can delay Briar a few nights, yeah, but when we do tell him he'll be livid we kept it from him. So what we do is I go meet yer man and I'm investigating to see whether he's a danger or not. That way when we tell Briar we have evidence and observation and if your guy's as innocent as you seem to think he is there's *two* of us telling Briar this. Right? But if we go to him and say "Oh Rand's known for a month but he did shit all, and I knew a few days ago but didn't tell you" he'll flip his lid, moon or no moon. You know he will."

Randall stared at her. He wanted to tell her she was wrong, but he had the cold, hard feeling in the pit of his stomach that she wasn't. Briar's order had been clear, and Randall had disobeyed it.

"I can't take you over there," he protested weakly.

Preeti shrugged. "It's that or I go tell Briar now."

"He'll kill Ellis if you tell him now!" Randall shot to his feet again.

"Then it's sorted, innit?" She bounced on her toes. "Take me to your sexy vampire lover!"

Randall rocked his jaw and glared at her, but her mind was made up. There was no getting around her once she'd reached a decision.

"Fine," he growled. "But this better work out."

"Hey. If he's worthy of you, Rand, it will."

He wasn't so certain, but choice wasn't on the table anymore, so he snatched his jacket and stormed out of the flat.

NINETEEN

Ellis had barely locked the gallery's door when his pocket buzzed.

"Sit," he murmured to Tiberius. He felt the dog do as ordered, and dragged the mini reader from his pocket to check it.

The message was from Randall: *Are you free?*

He smirked to himself. *For you? Always.*

I've got someone who wants to meet you.

Ellis lifted an eyebrow. *Threesome? You pervert!*

Randall's reply came quickly: *Can't text about it. It's urgent.*

Ellis sighed. That didn't sound like it'd be fun at all, so he texted back *All right. Come to the gallery.*

Then he let himself back in, and returned to his office to wait.

It took another twenty minutes for Randall to arrive. Ellis

heard two people enter the gallery, but one was much lighter than the other.

"Woah. This is well posh, innit?" It was a woman's voice, with a strong East End accent to it. He didn't recognise her, but that was to be expected.

"Yeah." Ellis straightened in his seat when he recognised Randall's voice.

"Is 'e minted, then?"

"Nah. Costs as much to run as it makes, I reckon."

Ellis shook his head and wished Randall wasn't quite so correct about that.

"Where're we going?"

"Upstairs," Randall said.

"After you."

Randall snorted slightly and came clomping up the stairs. His companion did, too, and her boots thumped with surprising weight for someone who had sounded lighter at ground level.

Ellis had already cleared his desk. His display was tucked away in its drawer, and nothing remained on the surface in case Randall's friend was here to tear things apart. "Come in," he called.

"Ellis," Randall said once they were in the office. He was hesitant. "This is Preeti."

"Wotcher!" She said. Her cheer was forced, and she didn't approach his desk.

Ellis kept his voice neutral as he murmured "How can I help you both?"

He heard sniffing. "It's well weird," Preeti said, as though continuing an earlier conversation - and as if Ellis weren't even in the room. "I can see 'im, but all I can smell is some cheap perfume."

Ellis gritted his teeth. He couldn't tell whether she was treating him like a non-entity because he was blind or because he was a vampire; either was unwelcome, but not exactly unfamiliar.

"Is it all vampires, or just this one?" she added.

Randall had told her. God damn it, Randall had *told her!* Ellis' nails dug into his chair's arm-rests as he fought to keep himself from screaming in anger. How many times did Randall intend to betray him? How far would this go? Was Preeti here to destroy him?

"Randall," he hissed.

"I had to," Randall whined. He rushed toward the desk, but Ellis flashed his teeth to prevent the werewolf from coming closer and he stumbled to a halt and fell into the chair instead. It squeaked in protest. "She was going to tell Briar."

"After *you* told *her*," he supplied with short, clipped words.

"She guessed." Randall sounded utterly miserable.

"Hey. Guys. I'm right fucking here," Preeti grunted.

"Well now you know how it feels when people are talking about you and not to you, don't you dear?" Ellis faced her heartbeat.

She snarled, and Ellis pushed his chair back from his desk to stand. Buggered if he was going to wait around for this nonsense. He had better things to do with his time. He didn't yet know what all of those things might be, but one of them was certainly to take Tiberius for his late-night poo, and standing around waiting for his dog to take a dump sounded far more appealing than taking any more of this crap in his own office.

"Ellis," Randall blurted. "Please. She guessed because of what I talked to her about after I met you. Since then I haven't said a word, I swear, and she put two and two together 'cause if I'd found out what you were I would've said, *unless* you were a vampire. And I-" he sucked in air. "I'm a lousy liar."

Ellis placed a hand on his desk and leaned across it a little. "You are at that," he conceded.

"Yeah. Well she confronted me about it and I couldn't lie. So she guessed that the only reason I'd cover up what you were is if you *were* a vampire." Randall's discomfort made his heart race and his voice shake. "And she told me either I brought her to meet you or she'd go tell Briar right away, and it's a Blood Moon and he'd probably storm right over here and murder you himself. We're trying to buy time."

Preeti stepped so lightly that human ears might not have heard her. She was circling the room. Whether to sneak up on him or just be nosey he couldn't tell. He inhaled now that she was closer and caught the distinctively woodsy edge to her scent. It was a little different to Randall's, but the underlying theme was the same.

"If you're buying time," Ellis said flatly, "why is she trying to creep up on me?"

"I'm *still* here!" she huffed.

"Preeti, stop mucking around," Randall pleaded. "Just pull up a chair, eh?" He sighed. "Can we all just pop a chill pill? Blood Moon and all that? I really don't want anyone to lose their shit and spread my boyfriend all over the walls."

Ellis heard her grousing under her breath, but Randall had a point: regardless of how angry Ellis was, he'd have to work his arse off here to keep either of the werewolves from foaming themselves up into some kind of rabid state. He felt backward with his leg until he reached the chair he'd shoved away, and then carefully lowered himself into it, taking the time to compose himself.

Preeti clomped across the carpet and dragged the chair from Jay's desk over with her, then dropped into it. "Fine," she huffed.

"All right," Ellis said softly once he'd reined himself in. "I apologise. I was taken by surprise. I'm afraid I'm also used to people talking like I'm not in the room, so that rubbed me up the wrong way. How about we start over, eh?"

"I'm sorry," Preeti grumped. "That was rude of me."

Ellis lifted his chin, then presented a small but genuine smile. "Water under the bridge," he assured her. "Now, I think I probably have a vested interest in helping this delaying tactic you've both concocted. What do you need from me?"

"I wanna know if you've brainwashed Rand."

He heard Randall draw a sharp breath.

"No," Ellis cut in smoothly, "I haven't. I have fucked him a couple of times, if that counts?" He gave his best dirty grin and was rewarded with the sound of Randall's breath rushing out of him again. Good. With Randall defused, he'd be able to focus more of his attention on Preeti. "He asks so nicely, though, I can't say no."

Preeti snorted. "Why've you got sunglasses on? If you're blind it don't matter, right?"

"Preeti!" Randall sounded mortified.

"It's fine. I wish more people would ask this kind of thing." Ellis wished nothing of the sort, but keeping Preeti calm was suddenly at the top of his to-do list. He dipped his head and raised his hand, then eased the glasses free and set them on the desk. "But I'll take them off if it makes you more comfortable."

It made him *less* comfortable. The office lightened and formed into a mockery of sight just in the centre of his old field of vision. It was like looking through binoculars whose lenses had been smeared with mud and Vaseline, still dark around the twin points of dreary light which revealed a couple of blobs in front of him. Those blobs were Randall and Preeti, but at this distance even if he tried to focus on either of them it'd be wasted effort. Instead they tormented him with their unattainability.

"Woah," Preeti gasped. "Those are the bluest fucking eyes I ever seen. Is that a blind thing?"

Ellis shook his head. "No. It seems to be a vampire thing. They were cobalt before I was turned." They were the first thing Jay had commented on back then; he'd described them as aquamarine, almost too bright to be natural. Ellis thought Jay was joking, since he'd lost the ability to check for himself in a mirror, but when Han asked if he was wearing coloured contacts it sank in. "I wear glasses because I don't like the light."

"Because you're a vampire," Preeti concluded.

"Nope." Ellis moved his chair forward so that he could lean against his desk. "I have - had, I suppose - a form of retinitis pigmentosa. It's a degenerative disease which kills off various cells in your retinas. There's several different kinds, and there are no cures for any of them. I can't speak to the experiences of others but mine began with a gradually-reducing peripheral vision which I pretty much ignored because for ages I didn't really notice it. I got a bit clumsy, bumped into a few things, but for the most part I just carried on. When it got to proper tunnel vision I was already well into the progression. By then other stuff started happening: my eyesight got worse at night until I was totally night blind; I lost most ability to tell colours apart unless they were right at the centre of my field of view; and what little sight I had left I became really short-sighted with. Eventually it pretty much all went away within the space of a couple of years. I went from running my own business to functionally blind even in bright light." He nudged the glasses with his fingers. "I went out and got totally hammered, got picked up by a bloke in a bar, and he turned me."

"So the glasses are for what?" Preeti prompted, though she

sounded uncertain now. *Good*. Derailing her from murdering vampires into the disability talk had taken the wind out of her sails too.

"The senses of vampires are all enhanced. Sight, hearing, touch, taste, smell… All the traditional ones, and all the ones people never used to think about: temperature, balance, vibrations, acceleration, all that. It wasn't enough to restore my sight. I'm still night blind, but in light now I can just about make out the kind of rubbish I had to deal with a few weeks before I lost it all." He grimaced. "I'd accepted that I was blind. I didn't accept it *well*, but there it was and there was nowt I could do about it." He grimaced and leaned back against his chair, trying to keep his expression neutral. "Then it transpires if I'd been turned a year previous it would've likely been enough to restore my sight to what it was when I were just starting out with this disease. One year." His teeth ground together and he closed his eyes a moment to rub at them with his fingers. "The glasses cut out the light."

Preeti gasped faintly. "You wear 'em to make yourself blind as you were before you were turned," she realised.

"Aye."

"Surely any sight's better than none," she argued.

"Nope. No, it isn't. It's like getting trolled by your own body." Ellis reached for his glasses, but forced himself to open his eyes. He hated it, but Preeti needed him to be in a vulnerable position. She wasn't like Randall. She wasn't calmed by having her power taken from her: her calm came from her empathy, so he fed it.

"You can put 'em back on. If you wanna," she mumbled.

"Thank you." He slid them on slowly rather than startle her out of her current state. "Any more questions?"

"Yeah. Have you ever killed anyone?"

Randall groaned.

"Yes. Both tried to kill me, and I killed each of them in self-defence." Ellis tilted his head aside. "Have you?"

"Hey, I'm not the blood-sucking vampire here!"

Ellis grinned. "Are you a vegetarian?"

Preeti's huff answered that one for him.

"Your mum'd probably be disappointed, eh?" he guessed.

"Too right she would," Preeti grumbled. "Okay, look. Briar's ordered you dead. Rand was supposed to have done it by now, but he's been protecting you instead."

Ellis tutted and faced Randall. "Randall, were you sent here to kill me?"

"That's not fair," Randall whined. God, he was so sexy when he was trying to wriggle out of something. "I didn't know. He told me I had to kill you if it turned out you were a vampire, but by the time I found out I couldn't do it."

"Why not?" Ellis heard Randall's heart clamouring like a runaway train.

"Because I love you," Randall blurted.

Ellis blinked. Randall's pulse still raced, and his breathing had a rough edge to it like he'd been backed into a corner and forced to speak truth. But he'd *said* it.

Holy shit, Randall had *said* it.

"I think we'd be able to persuade Briar if you had something you could bring to the table which benefited him," Preeti said, oblivious to the sudden silence from the two men in the room.

"What?" Randall and Ellis both spoke at once.

"Randall?" Ellis said, uncertainty gripping his chest. Had Randall told her? Christ, he'd told her everything else; had he given her the one thing Ellis had asked him to swear secrecy on?

His jubilation crashed like a lead balloon.

TWENTY

RANDALL'S JAW WORKED, but he couldn't speak.

It was out there now. It sat between them like a living thing. He'd told Ellis how he felt, and for a moment they'd shared some kind of absurd, wonderful connection across the expanse of desk which separated them.

Then it was gone, whisked away by Preeti's question; replaced by that wounded look that Randall hated seeing on Ellis' face but which kept on coming back.

"Randall?" Ellis repeated, his voice growing urgent.

Randall shook his head numbly. "I didn't," he whispered.

Preeti looked between them. "Didn't what?"

Jesus, why did Briar have to be such an arsehole about the whole thing? Why couldn't he have decided to maybe find out more about this creature if it had been a vampire? Learn about it, maybe, find out if there were others and whether or not they could coexist. But no. Briar had to decide that he found the very idea of vampires offensive, and like that he'd called for Ellis' destruction without bothering to stop and think what it might mean to the people around him or to Ellis himself. It was a selfish decision, taken without thought, reason, or data, and Randall found it harder each day to respect the man who had been his Alpha for over ten years.

"You didn't *what*, Rand?" Preeti nagged.

"Break my confidence," Ellis murmured. The hurt faded from his features, but his body remained tense. "Preeti. I might have something to bring to the table, as you put it."

Preeti looked between them, then leaned in slightly. "What is it?"

"I'm not willing to discuss it. Not here."

"Okay." Preeti hopped up from her chair. "Then we go to Briar."

Ellis laughed faintly. "Are you bonkers? You've both spent the better part of the last half hour telling me he wants me dead and that this is the absolute worst time of the month to try and negotiate with him."

Preeti shrugged. "I know. But he won't leave our territory for the next few nights. I shouldn't have either, but whatever."

"He's not coming over here anyway," Ellis stated. "I'm not having some moon-frothing nutter near my dog."

Preeti leaned over the desk and eyeballed Tiberius, then straightened. "Then what're we gonna do?"

Ellis reached into his jacket and pulled out a small bundle of keys and an electronic key card, which he offered to Randall. "You take him home," he murmured. "You know how to let him go to the loo on the way, so take him home and we'll wait here for you."

"Why don't we all go?" Preeti blinked.

"Well, because I don't want Briar to know where I live, and I've got no right to ask you to keep secrets from your own husband. This way you simply don't know," Ellis pointed out to her. "I'm sure you could sniff Randall's trail out if you wanted, but I have every hope that you don't want to."

Randall took the keys and card and frowned between them. "You two gonna be all right while I'm gone?"

"Oh aye." Ellis grinned. "I've already eaten."

There went Randall's cheeks again, flaming hot with his embarrassment.

Preeti gasped. "Oh my god!"

"Shut up," Randall mumbled.

He coaxed Tiberius out from behind the desk until he could take the German Shepherd's harness in hand, then hurried out of the office before Preeti could pester him for details.

RANDALL WANTED to run all the way to Ellis' flat and back again, but Tiberius was on the harness, so he wouldn't run. Randall couldn't let him off, either, because that signified the end of the working day. He went for the best middle-ground that they could achieve and strode at a brisk pace.

He hated leaving Ellis with Preeti. Ellis seemed to have the situation in hand, but the moon was fat and red in the sky, low on the horizon and peeking out over the houses and shops, and Randall was filled with dread at what he might find when he returned to the gallery. What if Ellis said the wrong thing? What if she turned on him and decided everything would be simpler if Briar's wishes were seen to?

"Come on," he hissed to Tiberius. "Please. Hurry up."

Tiberius trotted along peacefully, but his glances back at Randall told him that the guide dog wasn't sure Randall knew what he was doing.

Randall knew exactly what he was doing. The problem was that Tiberius and Ellis were paired, placed together because they understood one another. Randall could read the dog's signals every bit as well as he could any other dog's, but Tiberius didn't know that, and wasn't sure the man currently in his driving seat was capable of giving the right instructions either. It led to some disconnect between them which Randall had to hope wouldn't impact the dog's training by the time Ellis got back.

He was so busy running over horror scenarios of what the gallery might look like on his return that he almost forgot to let Tiberius do his business.

He fumbled with the key card and hurried across the antique black and white marble tile floor. Tiberius' claws clicked neatly and echoed in the lobby, and Randall hurried them both upstairs as quickly as he could. He unlocked the flat, let the dog out of the harness, and checked his water. Was there anything else? Randall tried to remember Ellis' routine, but came up empty.

"Shit. That'll have to do, Tiberius. Good boy. We'll be back later, I promise."

He locked the door after himself and fled.

HE RAN ALL the way back to the gallery while his mind spooled through one god-awful scenario after another. Every single one involved Ellis being nothing more than a pile of dust by the time Randall arrived.

He heard noise up ahead. The Mews was dark, lit only by the Victorian streetlamp up the far end, but two figures stood close together outside the gallery. Ellis' tall, slender body and Preeti's far tinier one, both doubled up in laughter.

Randall skidded to a halt a couple of feet from the odd sight. His chest heaved, and he all but swallowed air as sweat ran down his face and tickled between his shoulders.

Preeti straightened and howled at the sight of him. "Oh god, did you run?"

"Wha-" Randall gasped.

Ellis raised himself up and dusted himself off, though there wasn't anything *to* dust off, and tried to smother his smirk. "Randall. Great! You were quick!"

Randall stared at them both.

Ellis had done it *again*! Randall had left him for twenty minutes, tops, with a werewolf who'd been ready to punch his lights out when they first met, and now Preeti was relaxed and laughing while the baleful light of the moon washed over the streets under its ruddy gaze.

"Yeah," he wheezed.

Ellis reached out until his hand brushed against Randall's bicep, then he felt his way down and slid his fingers under and around Randall's elbow. The vampire stepped up alongside him and laid his other hand atop Randall's forearm. "Remember to watch out for low-hanging flower arrangements and the like, eh?"

"Right. Gotcha." Randall leaned into him in relief, and smiled when Ellis responded by kissing his cheek. "I'm sorry about all this," he mumbled.

"We'll worry about that after," Ellis said gently. "Let's just go see this fella and see if we can't get the whole thing resolved quick as you like. Where are we going?"

Preeti's smile slid away. "Er. Maybe better not to-"

"Whitechapel," Randall said.

Preeti scowled at him, but Randall shrugged. "What? You know where to find Ellis. It's only fair he at least knows where we're taking him."

"Whitechapel," Ellis said carefully. "That's, er, t'other end of London."

"Yeah." Randall nodded and gave Ellis' hand a squeeze. "That gonna be okay?"

Ellis' hands tightened around his arm in response.

Randall knew it was a big ask. Ellis wasn't comfortable leaving Mayfair. The vampire knew his own territory like the back of his hand, but the problem with leaving it meant they were potentially crossing into areas controlled by other vampires. He'd been nervous as hell when they strayed into Westminster on the trail of Ellis' would-be murderer, so the idea of going all the way through Central London and out the other end must be terrifying. Preeti was right though; Briar wouldn't leave the East End while this other pack was roaming around it.

Ellis didn't seem to want to tell Preeti that there *were* other vampires. Back in the gallery he'd simply mentioned two people had tried to kill him, but not that one of them had been undead. That made sense to Randall - after all, if Briar did decide to kill Ellis, he at least wouldn't then have any reason to go on some kind of citywide pogrom to clean up the rest. Yet again Ellis was putting everyone else ahead of himself.

Randall felt sick with shame. How could he deserve this kind, selfless man when all Randall had to offer in return was betrayal and fear?

"Randall," Ellis said softly.

"Uh?" Randall looked up. Had Ellis been speaking to him? He couldn't tell.

"It will be fine." Ellis dipped down to kiss him.

Randall leaned into him, desperate for his assurances. Ellis' lips were warm, soft and gentle, and the kiss lingered well beyond Preeti's mocking huff.

"There." Ellis lifted his head again. "Just stay calm, petal. We'll be okay."

Randall swallowed. "But-"

"It'd be better if we took a taxi, aye." Ellis' lips twitched into his beautiful little ghost of a smile. "Back before sunrise and all that. And I'll need to tuck up into a corner so the driver doesn't notice that he can't see me in the rearview. You'll have to work that part out, okay?"

Randall dipped his head. "Okay."

"Good boy." Ellis gave Randall's arm another little squeeze. "Best get cracking. I reckon if you want to find a black cab this time of night Piccadilly's our way forward."

"Right." Randall set off, slowly at first. "This way, then."

Preeti scurried after them. "For what it's worth, you seem like a nice bloke. I really hope Briar doesn't kill you."

Ellis laughed at that. "I think it's safe to say you're not the only one."

Randall said nothing. If Briar so much as sneezed at Ellis, Randall wasn't going to give him the benefit of a warning. A small part of him fervently hoped that Briar would try something: it'd give him the excuse he needed to repay Briar for his broken jaw, and at this point Randall couldn't care less whether or not that was the moon talking.

TWENTY-ONE

Ellis stayed silent in the taxi so as not to draw the driver's attention to his little corner of the back seat. Randall and Preeti chatted on occasion, mostly about the shops they drove past, but Ellis kept his head down and stayed out of it.

If his heart were still beating he'd have to take a good, hard look at whether or not it would be able to cope with all the strain he'd been under lately. Now here he was, willingly paying for a cab fare to meet a fella who wanted him dead and would most likely not listen to reason when he came face to face with the man he'd condemned. At least he'd managed to get Tiberius to safety. If Ellis disappeared, Jay would go looking, and he'd find a way into Ellis' flat. From there it'd just be a call to Guide Dogs for the Blind and they'd come rescue the daft ball of fluff and take good care of him. If Randall survived the night, he too had Ellis' keys and could go rescue Tiberius himself.

All Ellis could do to influence the outcome of this meeting was to remain calm. He couldn't afford to let himself rise to any baiting or get angry over Briar's treatment of Randall.

There'd be time for that later if they made it to sunrise without incident. For now he had to tread carefully and keep his mouth shut for the most part.

The taxi halted, and from the way Randall moved at his side Ellis presumed it wasn't for another traffic light. He fished some cash out of his wallet and passed it to Randall, then hurried out of the car while Randall distracted the driver with the cash.

Ellis found the kerb with his heel and eased out of the cab, then took a few short steps away from it. There he stopped, unable to go any further without guidance.

He took a breath while he waited and analysed the information it gave him. There was an undercurrent of rotted fruit and vegetables, the mixture of sweet and rancid carried on a cold breeze. The air had the fresh, slightly salt tang of the Thames. The street was fairly quiet, although there were at least two crowded pubs nearby, both filled with loud music and even louder conversation. The door to one opened for a moment and spilled the noise right out onto the street before it was muffled again.

Layered over the street level he could hear the distinctive sound of hundreds of humans sleeping: sluggish heartbeats, slow breaths, faint snores. They all mingled together to form a background level of noise which, once he grew accustomed to it, became easier to ignore. Wherever the taxi had let him out seemed to be mostly residential, and probably hosted a street market during daylight hours - that or the bins hadn't been collected in two weeks.

Randall and Preeti left the taxi at last. Randall brushed his hand against Ellis', and Ellis smiled.

"Thanks."

"Any time. Ready?"

"As I'll ever be." He patted Randall's arm and then hooked his fingers around it. "Lay on, MacDuff."

Randall moved forward. "I thought it was 'Lead on'?"

Ellis chuckled. "Lay on, MacDuff. And damn'd be him that first cries, 'Hold, enough!'"

Preeti sucked air between her teeth. "I reckon you've got nuts of steel coming 'ere, Ellis. You're all right by me. Just try not to wind him up, okay?"

"I'll try my damndest, I promise you," he murmured.

Preeti darted ahead and he heard the rasp of a large key in an old lock. The chambers squealed so faintly that he doubted the werewolves could hear them, and then the bolts thunked back into the heavy-sounding door. Hinges creaked, and Preeti stepped aside. "After you."

"Right," Randall said as he led Ellis forward. "There's a shitload of stairs. Is that going to be okay?"

"No," Ellis deadpanned. "I need you to carry me."

"Oh. Well, okay-"

"Joking," Ellis chuckled. "Is there a hand rail?"

Randall clicked his tongue. "Just to your left."

Ellis reached for it until he hit cold, hard metal with the back of his hand. He grabbed at the rail, then nodded. "Areet. Let's go."

They descended slowly. Ellis clung to both Randall and the rail for stability. The steps were uneven, each one out a fraction of an inch from where he might expect it to be based on the previous one, and he stumbled several times. The handrail was encrusted with sharp edges of rust which crumbled under his touch. The air grew colder still down here, and smelled of damp and mould.

"Are we underground?" he asked. Logically they had to be, as they were descending from the street, but for all Ellis knew they could be going down an embankment toward the river.

"Yeah. It's an old tube station," Randall murmured. "We meet up in it 'cause it's been disused for something like seventy-odd years. It got flattened in the Blitz and wasn't ever rebuilt."

The door clanged shut behind them, and Preeti's boots thudded down the metal stairs. "Rand," she hissed.

Randall's shrug radiated all the way up to Ellis' own shoulder.

Ellis didn't like it. Bad enough to have taken a taxi all the way over here, but now he was being dragged deep underground too, where he could be horribly murdered and nobody would ever know.

The stairs ended and the ground had the dull *whump* of concrete underfoot. There was very little echo down here, as though the place were built to subdue sound. That made it an even more ideal location for slaughtering vampires.

Don't panic. Stay calm!

Ellis lifted his head and waited as Preeti opened another door for them.

He heard claws and animal sounds. Not the gentle noises of dogs, but more primal vocalisations that he only half-understood.

Who's this?

Why is he here?

No scent!

What have you done?

Well, if nothing else, that confirmed Ellis' suspicions about how Jonas' gift interacted with the intelligent chatter of werewolves in their wolf bodies. Why he only half-grasped it, though, he didn't know, and now wasn't the time to try and work it out.

The wolves began to change. It was a sickening sound when Randall did it, but to hear four of them change all at the same time made him freeze on the spot. The sound of wet flesh tearing itself apart while bones ground against cartilage and dragged themselves into new configurations became violent and grotesque.

One werewolf was enough to snap Ellis like a twig, and here he was deep underground with six of them. Worse, one sounded absolutely massive, if the height of his heart and breath were anything to go by.

He could at least try to amuse himself with the knowledge that these people were butt naked.

Bare feet slapped against the floor as the giant came nearer. There was a rumble deep within his chest that burst up and out of his mouth as a snarl.

Preeti darted between them. Her boots hit the ground like a miniature thunderstorm. "Back the fuck off and listen," she barked.

Ellis bit the inside of his cheek. That wasn't *exactly* how he would have handled it. Randall was tense at his side, so maybe Ellis wasn't alone in his way of thinking.

"Preeti," the big man answered. His tone was laden with displeasure.

"No. They all go outside and wait, right now. We need to talk, and we don't need a peanut gallery."

God, she was a pugnacious little sod. Ellis began to see why Randall valued her friendship so highly.

Voices broke out in dissent. Two men and a woman.

"Hey, if Briar can hear it-"

"Who the fuck is this-"

"He's got no scent!"

"Silence!" The big man roared, and his booming voice drowned out the others. "Go wait."

They filed out of the room and the door slammed after them. Ellis could already hear them shifting back into their wolf forms, most likely to eavesdrop more successfully. This meant the big man had to be Briar, which was nice. He couldn't have been a little fella, could he? Oh no. No, he had to be the biggest bastard Ellis had ever shared a ceiling with.

Stay calm. It became his mantra.

"Stand aside," Briar rumbled.

"No." Preeti had to be half this bloke's height, but there wasn't an ounce of fear in her. "Briar, this is Ellis. Randall's boyfriend."

"And you bring him here because... what? You felt like giving our secrets away? What the hell were you thinking?"

"Oh will you shut your mouth for two bloody minutes?" Preeti slapped some part of his body, and Ellis didn't want to know which one. "We've got to sort this out."

"Sort *what* out?" Briar growled. "It's a damn Blood Moon, Preeti. We need to stay together, and we need to keep our heads. What part of bringing a stranger down here struck you as a great idea?"

This would go around in circles for hours. He could see it now. Preeti would argue that Briar had to listen, and Briar would counter that she'd betrayed them. Tempers would rise, and Ellis would become collateral damage. He didn't have time for all that, and he really didn't fancy decorating a deserted underground bunker with his body parts, so he drew a breath and cleared his throat.

The shifters stopped arguing immediately.

Before they could start on him instead of each other, he piped up, "I'm here to help with your translation problem."

TWENTY-TWO

RANDALL STARED AT ELLIS. The vampire looked calm as anything, his head held high and his shoulders back. He was facing Briar with reasonable accuracy despite being unable to see him.

Ellis had been so angry whenever Randall asked him about this language thing, yet here he was now about to just lay it all out on the table. It stung, that was for sure, but then Preeti had suggested Ellis bring something to the table. This was the ace up the vampire's sleeve, and the only one which might stay Briar's hand. That understanding helped mitigate the sting, if only a little.

Briar's lip curled, but Preeti still stood in his way, and he didn't seem about to shove her aside. "And what translation problem would that be?"

Ellis didn't smile. He didn't so much as twitch. "You have a language barrier which is causing problems," he said, speaking evenly. "It's already led to violence. I'm offering my services to you as a translator."

Randall looked between them as they faced off above Preeti's head.

"How can you translate," Briar grated as though speaking to a child, "when we don't even know what language we need?"

"That's fine," Ellis replied. "I speak them all."

Randall felt Ellis' fingers tighten their grip on his arm. He was readying himself in case Randall had to pull him aside, he realised.

Briar's anger all but rippled off him. His face contorted into a mask of rage. "You're wasting my time," he snarled. "All of you."

"Well there's one way to find out, ain't there?" Preeti snapped. She glanced over her shoulder to Randall, then spoke to Ellis in Hindi. Her voice was musical, rising and falling in intonation as the words spilled from her.

Ellis answered smoothly, his own intonation matching hers. He didn't pause, but he didn't smile either. Unless Preeti had told him she'd switched languages on him, he probably didn't even realise what he was doing.

Randall swallowed. It was exactly like watching him speak with Barnes. Everything was automatic; Ellis didn't seem to have any control over this ability whatsoever, and it became horribly clear how easily it could betray him if he did it in front of anyone who'd ever seen Jonas in action. No wonder Ellis had been so insistent that Randall not say anything about it, yet Randall hadn't listened, and hadn't kept quiet about it. Now here they were, because of Randall's damn mouth, with Ellis forced to use an ability he shouldn't possess to save his own skin.

Why couldn't Randall have kept quiet? He would have worked out what Ellis was sooner or later. He hadn't needed to ask Preeti.

Ellis' fingers gave Randall's arm a gentle rub, and Randall glanced up to him. His expression was placid, and he still faced Briar, but his hand patted Randall's sleeve.

Randall took the hint and exhaled slowly to try and calm himself.

"'S pretty fuckin' impressive," Preeti admitted in English. "I mean, I'm assuming you never actually learned Hindi, right?"

Ellis' jaw flexed slightly.

He didn't know! Randall felt ill.

"No," Ellis answered, voice flat. "Basic French at school, even more basic German. No Hindi."

Briar's stance shifted. He straightened up a notch, and his expression slid from anger into suspicion. "It's a trick. How is that possible?"

"Because he's a vampire," Preeti barked.

"Preeti!" Randall tugged Ellis back a step, just in case, but within seconds the whole situation had exploded in his face.

Nazim flung the door open so hard that it slammed against the wall and propelled a spray of old plaster into the air. Lara and Jim were at his heels, still mid-change back to their human shapes, and Randall realised with a sinking sense of dread that the whole pack had eavesdropped.

Briar flung himself at Ellis, massive hands reaching for the vampire's neck, but Preeti stepped neatly in way and jabbed him in the throat. He coughed, wheezed, and staggered to a halt.

"You fucking arsehole," Nazim screamed, coming straight for Randall. "You utter cunt!"

"Woah, wait," Jim yelled. He grabbed at Nazim's elbow, which forced the stockier shifter to slow his approach.

"You fucking *liar*," Briar coughed. He pointed at Randall over Preeti's shoulder. "You total shitweasel!"

Randall snarled. "You think killing an innocent man's going to achieve anything?"

"Innocent?" Briar stepped forward, but didn't seem to have the ability to push Preeti aside. "He's a *vampire*. A leech. A flea. And you, you've told him what we are, where we are, even what problems we're having!"

"Yeah well maybe if you hadn't encouraged this entire pack to treat me like shit all these years-"

"Randall," Ellis said softly.

"Briar's right," Lara yelled, raising her voice to be heard. "He gave you an order, Rand, and instead what've you done? We're your family, for crying out loud!"

"You are *not* my family!" Randall stepped forward, only barely aware that this meant dragging Ellis into the fray with him. "Only Preeti's ever been my family out of you lot. The rest of you can rot in hell!"

"Yeah well maybe it's time we cut you out, if we aren't your family," Briar snarled. "All this time I've wasted trying to make you feel at home-"

"Are you *insane*?" Randall felt his skin ripple.

"Randall," Ellis said again.

"What?" He rounded on Ellis, teeth bared.

Ellis leaned in to kiss him.

The rage around them faded. Randall's skin retracted the fur that it had begun to sprout, and the itch passed. Nothing mattered but this: Ellis' lips on his, possessive and warm, demanding that Randall's respond. It was gravity to him, an event horizon that he couldn't pull away from, and he gave himself to it completely. The fire in his blood sputtered and died, replaced with the cool, soothing calm which had suffused him last night.

Ellis broke off reluctantly and squeezed his arm. "Better?" he whispered.

"Oh god," Randall replied. "How do you-" He stopped himself. It didn't matter right now. The pack around him was in danger of breaking out into all-out war with itself.

He moved back slowly, drawing Ellis with him. It wasn't safety, but it could give them a few seconds if necessary. He turned to press Ellis against the wall, then whispered "Thanks."

Ellis smiled slightly. "Any time."

Randall wanted to kiss him again. He wanted to ignore the idiocy at his back and lose himself to Ellis' lips, his arms, his body... But while it was a great fantasy, it'd be a fatal tactical decision, so he released Ellis and turned back to the shifters.

"Briar's right," Preeti snarled. "Randall *did* lie. But can you say you've never lied? We lie about what we are, for god's sake!"

"That's different," Lara countered.

"How's that?" said Nazim.

Randall saw the anger in their postures, the wild moon-ridden look in their eyes. How the hell was he going to stop this?

Ellis cleared his throat and stepped around Randall, hand to the shifter's back. "Bickering like children," he called across the room, "won't solve your problems. This other pack you're fussing about will win if you tear yourselves to pieces over rubbish that doesn't matter."

Something cold and hard gripped Randall's heart. Was Ellis *trying* to get them killed?

"You shut your filthy fucking-" Briar yelled.

"He's right!" Preeti cut in.

The pack seemed to hold its collective breath as the Alpha pair disagreed so openly.

"Well then we sort him out quick-" Briar gestured to Ellis "-then get on with the bigger problem."

"Oh, yes," Ellis said. There was a faint hint of sarcasm to his voice, but his words were smooth enough to gloss over it. "Great idea. When the negotiator offers you his help, why not murder him first and *then* go to the negotiating table?"

Briar sneered, but there was an uncertain look in his eyes. "Just because you've got some fucking language magic doesn't make you a negotiator."

"No," Ellis agreed. "But I do convince people to buy paintings which cost more than the average Londoner's annual salary. Or do you think they sell themselves?"

"Some people have money to burn," Lara grunted.

"And so many things to burn it on." Ellis' lips quirked softly. "For the cost of a painting they could have a guided tour of some of the world's most guarded archaeological digs, or a small piece of jewellery personally designed and hand-crafted for them by London's premier goldsmiths. They could have a bespoke suit from Savile Row's finest tailors, or a Georgian chimneypiece for their fourth house. There are as many people vying for their money as there are for yours, and there is an art to selling art - to convincing someone that oil on canvas holds the same intrinsic value as a Chaumet watch."

Briar huffed, but looked toward Ellis with something other than outright loathing at last.

"You are the Alpha here, correct?" Ellis murmured.

"Yes."

"Then behave as such. There is a Blood Moon, and you must control yourself for the good of your pack. You cannot lose your temper like some playground bully, because it will cost lives. And you sound like a big fella to me, so I think none of the lives lost will be yours, eh?" Ellis grimaced. "Just those of people you love, instead."

It was a low blow, whether or not Ellis knew it. It seemed

like the entire room had paused, waiting to see how Briar would respond.

"They've got a cub with them," Randall said quietly. "Saving cubs used to be your priority."

Time stretched to breaking point. Sweat inched down Randall's back.

Briar curled his lip, then padded away toward his discarded clothes. "Fine," he snarled. "But if you bugger this up, leech, I will fucking end you."

"Bargain," Ellis said.

Randall wasn't so sure, but conditional death later had to be preferable to certain death right now, so he at least understood the sentiment.

TWENTY-THREE

ELLIS HEARD the sound of shapeshifting as he was led back up the metal stairs. It was only one of them this time, and it wasn't until the remainder began to grumble among themselves that he worked out it was Preeti who now walked on four paws.

"Is this wise?" he whispered to Randall as they stepped back out onto the street.

"Preeti's kinda more like a coyote than what people would recognise as a wolf," Randall murmured. "Her and Lara are the only ones who can really wander around like this. Everyone else is more, you know." He hesitated. "Obvious."

Briar stomped off ahead with Preeti at his side. The pace of her claws matched his boots, and Ellis supposed that it helped with the charade when the 'dog' walked alongside a fella so huge nobody would quibble with him.

"How's that work?" Ellis kept his voice soft to avoid drawing the ire of the pack around him. "Aren't wolves, you know, wolfy?"

"There's a lot of different breeds of wolf," Randall

answered as he steered Ellis down the pavement. "We assume there's different breeds of wolf shifter too, but most of us are pretty much what you'd expect in this part of the world: your regular Eurasian Wolf." Randall sighed faintly. "Or, you know, what you'd expect if people hadn't wiped them out in this country. Preeti looks more like an Indian wolf, and a small one at that."

Preeti huffed up ahead.

"Sorry," Randall whispered. "But you *are* tiny."

Whatever her response, it wasn't audible to Ellis, but Randall chuckled briefly.

"What was that?" Ellis leaned into Randall as his foot caught on a crack in the pavement, and he clung to the shifter for stability. "Shit," he added.

"I got you." Randall's muscles grew pleasingly hard for a moment as he stabilised them both. "A lot of the way animals - and us when we're in that shape - communicate isn't sound, it's body language. That was her ears twitching."

Body language. No wonder Ellis only half-understood the wolves' chatter: the rest of it went unspoken. His revelation was short-lived, interrupted by his left foot butting against another crooked paving slab. He ground his teeth in frustration. "Are there *any* decent pavements around here?"

"Er. I dunno, to be honest."

"Do me a favour, petal. Can we try to stick to the flat bits?"

"Oh." Randall's guilt made his answer sound small. "I'm sorry. I didn't think-"

"It's absolutely fine. Leading takes practice." Ellis ran his palm down Randall's forearm to try and reassure him. "And I haven't taught you how to do this. You'll get the hang of it." *If we're given long enough.*

He heard Nazim muttering to Jim about Randall's openness and couldn't decide whether the shifters didn't realise that he could hear them, or didn't care. Either way, it didn't really matter to Ellis. All he had to do was make it through the next three nights without getting killed. How hard could it be?

Yeah, okay. Best not to think of all the ways in which it looked utterly impossible. He focused instead on guiding Randall, on explaining to him the hazards to look out for and how to communicate them to him, all while silently cursing the fact that he'd forgotten to ask Randall to pick up his cane when he dropped Tiberius off home. That would've made life far easier, but he was so used to going about his business without it that it hadn't crossed his mind.

Randall's main problem was that he kept slowing down when Ellis began to let him lead. This wasn't ever an issue when they were dawdling along together, but at the pace Briar had set it made it difficult to read the position of Randall's arm. Ellis corrected him a few times, but the urge to walk side-by-side seemed to be strong in the werewolf. Could it be a pack instinct? Randall was at the very back, and he might well think that by walking a step ahead of Ellis he wasn't in the right position. Whatever else Ellis corrected, Randall took up quickly, but he seemed incapable of letting Ellis lag behind him.

He'd take more work than this, it seemed, to get it right.

"Where are we going?" Ellis asked after what felt like hours. He didn't tire the way that he had before he'd been turned, but he was growing bored of the seemingly endless hike across the East End.

"We're not really going anywhere specific," Randall said softly.

Ellis groaned. "Are you telling me we're just wandering around in't middle of t' night wi' no actual goal in mind?"

He felt Randall's shrug. "We're following Preeti's nose.

Patrolling's not easy if whoever you want to find isn't scent marking."

"Great." Ellis drew his left hand back up Randall's arm and wrapped it around so that he could slip his right free of its grip for the moment and instead slide his fingers beneath his shirt sleeve to feel the ball bearings of his watch. "Christ," he groused. "It's nearly two." He re-took Randall's elbow and dropped his watch arm to his side again. "Do they plan to be at this all night?"

Randall grunted, then stopped so fast that Ellis overtook him a step.

Briar's boots ground against the pavement, and soon the giant was stalking toward them both.

"It will take," Briar snarled into Ellis' face, "as long as it fucking takes."

Ellis wrinkled his nose. At least the Alpha brushed his teeth, but having some stranger's breath in his face was still not his favourite experience. Heat poured from Briar and touched his skin, and he had to fight to hold his ground against such lousy manners. "You should be aware," he said lightly, "that there is a daylight concern."

Not that there was. Damned if he was going to let Briar know that, though. He hadn't even worked it out himself yet, and it could prove useful if Briar decided that leaving him out for the sun was a convenient way to get shot of him.

"I don't give a shit. Stop whining."

Ellis raised his left hand, fingers spread wide in surrender. "Not another word," he swore.

Briar remained in his face for another handful of seconds, then turned on his heel and strode off to the front of the pack, where Preeti waited.

There wasn't any way Ellis intended to remain quiet for

long. "Where are we?" he whispered, leaning toward Randall's ear.

"Tower Hamlets," Randall breathed back to him.

Ellis hadn't come this far east while he'd had sight, so had no real idea of what it might look like here. It sounded even more residential than Whitechapel, with several storeys of sleeping people on either side of a deserted street. He heard the creak of metal and the distant snuffling of some animal or other, although their current mission had him half-thinking it could be a wolf instead of a hedgehog.

Preeti made a soft rumble in her chest. *Got it.*

"She's found their scent?" Ellis whispered.

"Yeah." Randall's muscles tensed under Ellis' touch.

The pack slowed. He could hear Preeti's intense sniffing. The others stopped complaining about the vampire in their midst and were quiet at last.

There was another creak of metal - like a time-worn gate swinging in the breeze - which paused.

"In here," Briar grunted.

Randall led him through the open gate. Ellis' hand automatically went to find it, and found wrought iron near-freezing to the touch and bumpy with several layers of terrible paint jobs. It swung closed with a clang behind him before it went back to squeaking.

"Stealthy," he muttered.

The pavement gave way to gravel, which was far less subtle with seven of them crunching across it. Even drunkards would be able to hear them coming a mile off, never mind the delicate ears of wolves. Maybe that suited Briar just fine, since the fella seemed to be hankering for some confrontation, but it wasn't Ellis' idea of a sensible approach. He didn't like to draw attention out in public at the best of times, but when on the trail of a pack of unknown werewolves it seemed unnecessarily antagonistic.

They weren't on the gravel for more than five minutes, thank god. One by one they stepped off it and onto dry grass, but only a minute later the grass turned into a long and unruly mass. It wrapped around his shoes and ankles to transform the walk a hard slog. Every step was sluggish, and the ground was treacherous underneath all the grasping blades.

"Where?" he snapped.

"Cemetery Park," Randall whispered.

"Never heard of it. Tell me it's not actually a Cemetery."

"Uh…"

"You have got to be joking!" Ellis hissed.

"It's more of a nature reserve kind of thing," Randall mumbled.

"It's a fucking *cemetery!*"

"Abandoned, though."

"Oh that's *so* much better," Ellis snipped.

Preeti's growl brought them all to a halt.

Ellis clamped his mouth shut and leaned forward. He could hear those animal sounds again. Snuffling and sniffing, along with heartbeats. Not the tiny, rapid flutters of a bird's heart, and not the cute little snuffling of a hedgehog. No, that'd be too pleasant, wouldn't it? These were big, strong hearts; primal snarls and yips. The more he listened, the more he was able to separate out the different pulses, the distinct voices.

The park was riddled with wolves. He tried to count, but they were too distant and too many. More than ten, he was absolutely certain. Maybe more than twenty.

How the hell did that many wolves get here when Randall's pack were so careful not to be seen? Had they come here and then shed their human skins, or were they so brazen as to walk through the streets without a care?

Either way, Ellis had the distinct feeling that he was buggered. They were outnumbered, and if the other Alpha felt the same way about vampires as Briar did, making it through three nights might suddenly become the least of his worries: surviving the next ten minutes would be his new pressing concern.

If it turned out that all he'd done was buy himself an extra three hours, he was going to be right pissed off.

TWENTY-FOUR

"THEY'RE HERE," Briar snarled.

Ellis pulled himself upright. *Head up. Shoulders back. Don't let them see that you're shitting yourself.* "I'll go," he said softly.

Briar snorted at him. "No you won't."

Ellis released Randall's elbow and straightened his coat. "Look, I can't do this with you breathing down my neck. I'll go over and talk to 'em, and then we can go from there."

"How do we know we can trust you?" Lara snapped.

"Yeah, that's pushing it a bit far," Nazim threw in. "We're supposed to just stand back and wait for you to go hand us over?"

Ellis raised his hands to try and placate them. "It's a Blood Moon, right? You lot stomping in there is going to get their backs up, and before we know it you'll be at each other's throats and my entire night will have been a total waste of time. So how about you all let me do the thing you dragged me along for, and we see how it goes?" He lowered his hands slowly. "You've got Preeti here with you. She can hear everything right where she is and tell you if it goes wrong."

"Except she won't understand a word that's being said," Briar snarled.

Ellis cursed silently. Briar was brighter than he seemed.

"What does that matter," Ellis countered, "so long as nobody gets hurt? And I guarantee you that if she can hear them right now, they can hear us. It's not like we've got a couple of hours to argue about this before you make your mind up."

Briar gave a long, deep sigh. "Fine," he rumbled. "But-"

"Yes," Ellis cut in. He was growing tired of hearing Briar's threats. "If I screw it up you'll roast me over an open fire. I get it." He re-took Randall's elbow. "Areet," he added. "On we go."

Randall only got to take one step before he stopped abruptly.

"Not him," Briar said. "He stays."

Ellis closed his eyes a moment and fought the urge to call Briar an imbecile. "Without him," he whispered, "I can't *get* there."

"Just walk."

"Not sure whether you've noticed-" *you great wazzock* "-but I am blind, and there are obstacles." Tripping and falling over some poor sod's abandoned grave didn't seem like it'd be all that dignified, especially on his way into a dangerous negotiation. "I need a guide, and Randall's the only one of you who knows how to do it."

"Actually," Nazim said, "I know how."

Ellis' eyebrows crept up.

"I work on the Underground," Nazim explained.

"There's a choice, then," Ellis said evenly to Briar. "Who're you going to let me go in with?"

Briar ground his teeth, then snapped "Fine. Take Randall."

Ellis nodded, and didn't wait for him to change his mind.

RANDALL LED him across the snagging, treacherous ground. Their route zig-zagged and Randall occasionally murmured "grave" or "tree" to explain why.

Ellis could hear the wolves more clearly the closer they got. There were eighteen of them. Easily enough to murder Briar's entire pack, he reckoned, if things got out of hand.

The wolves stopped their vocalisations now. They had to be aware of Ellis and Randall's approach, that was certain, and they were choosing to lie in wait rather than come forward. Was that confidence? Was it a trap? Or was this simply how packs met each other?

It didn't feel friendly, not in the happy way that dogs might come up and greet a stranger. They were spread out and still, and it seemed like he was walking straight into the jaws of predators.

What if they didn't have their Alpha with them?

Ellis grimaced. God, why hadn't he thought of that sooner? What if they were out with a ruddy moon so close overhead without their Alpha to rein them in? Or what if, like Briar, their Alpha wasn't in full control of himself tonight?

"Randall," he breathed.

"Yeah?"

"If this goes south, promise me you'll frame thissen like yer britches are on fire."

Randall hesitated. "I think I got about half of that. Sorry."

"Leg it," Ellis hissed. "If this doesn't work out, get yourself to safety. Promise."

Randall laughed abruptly. "You don't get it, do you? I ain't leaving you, here or anywhere."

Ellis frowned slowly.

"I won't ever leave you behind, Ellis. Never."

He drew breath, then held it. How could he answer that? There weren't the words, especially not with Briar's pack behind them and this other pack ahead. "I love you," he exhaled.

"Me too," Randall whispered. "Er. I mean-"

"I know." Ellis' features pulled into a lop-sided grin. "Let's get this done, aye?"

He started forward, and Randall moved with him.

THEY SLOGGED toward the waiting wolves. Ellis spoke as they approached, not knowing whether he used English or not; not knowing whether they could understand him.

"I'm here to talk," he said. "To see if I can help."

A couple of the wolves moved closer, from the outer edges of the pack. A pincer movement.

Ellis raised his chin. "Only to talk. The rest won't come closer until we ask them to-" he hoped. "You and me for now. Is that okay?"

Muscle ripped itself apart. Bones and cartilage tore and rubbed and popped. He couldn't determine how many of them were changing shape out there until they were done.

Three. Three human shapes now, their hearts higher, their breathing slower than that of the wolves around them. Was there no CCTV in this park, or did the trees Randall had mentioned block the view of where they were right now? If the cemetery was abandoned, was it even supposed to be accessible, or had the gate been forced at some point?

Werewolves seemed to have a knack for hanging out in places where it'd be right easy to kill a man without getting caught in the act.

They waited, which forced Ellis and Randall to move closer.

Another wolf broke free and came toward them. It sniffed. He felt its nose brush against his trousers, then it circled them both and returned to its previous position.

"What would you like to talk about?" The middle of the three spoke. Male, he sounded just a little shorter than Ellis, and his rich tenor seemed measured and polite.

Ellis released Randall's arm and gently removed his glasses. It made no difference at all, so they were well away from any artificial lighting, but the shifters might respond better if they could make eye contact with him. He tucked them away into his coat pocket. "Well, there seems to be some dispute going on which has led to a fight already. I've come to see whether we can open up a dialogue before things go too far."

"And you are..?"

"Ellis O'Neill." He dipped his head. "This is Randall Carter, but he's here as my eyes, not as a representative of his pack."

Grass rustled and a twig snapped as the shifter approached him. "Yes," he murmured, only a foot away now. "I know of this one. But I don't know you."

Ellis felt the Alpha's warmth come closer a moment, and the man sniffed him.

"Randall's pack is led by a man named Briar," Ellis said, trying not to let himself be put off by the shifter's behaviour. "The moon is, I believe, red at the moment, and very large. It's affecting them badly."

"It isn't affecting this one," the Alpha said. Ellis had no way of knowing whether the man had indicated Randall in some way or was simply being rude. He wore no clothes to give away his movements.

Ellis pursed his lips. The old adage of imagining one's audience to be naked was not what he wanted running through his thoughts right now. "No," he agreed. "He's okay for now."

"Interesting." The man chuckled, and it wasn't an unpleasant or unfriendly sound. "I am Zev Uddin. Is it wrong of me to presume that you are blind?"

"No. Not wrong at all."

"That is also interesting," Zev decided. "Although neither of these things are as interesting as the fact that you have no scent. Why is that, Mr. O'Neill?"

Ellis gave a frozen smile. This was it. This was the crunch, where the next words out of his mouth would make or break his chances of getting home in one piece. Hopefully the shifters weren't bonkers enough to carry silver weapons around with them: you'd have to be mental to do that, surely? Mental *and* rich, and he didn't think people who wandered naked around Tower Hamlets in the wee small hours were especially laden with money.

No, even those who had taken human form had no clothes, so no way of carrying weapons. Not that the teeth and jaws of fifteen wolves wouldn't make short work of him anyway, but at least he wouldn't get stabbed.

There really was no good way to spin this situation, no matter how hard he tried.

"I don't know," Ellis answered. "Briar believes that it's because I'm a vampire."

Zev laughed again, but this time it wasn't with good humour. "And are you a vampire?"

Ellis licked his lips, then nodded. "Yes."

The wolves bristled and began to growl and mutter to each other. He could only catch the vocal parts of their chatter.

Is?

Eater?

Of blood?

Can it?

"This isn't right," a woman hissed.

"I say it's a lie," said a man. "If there is such a thing, why haven't we ever found one before?"

Randall took Ellis' arm, but Ellis shook his head and slid free. Later on he'd have to explain to Randall about who held onto whom for guidance, but for now he had to quell this ruckus before tempers were lost.

"I'm telling the truth," Ellis stated, raising his voice to be heard above the growls. "I have no reason to lie about this."

"It would be a curious thing to lie about," Zev agreed. "Perhaps, then, you might tell me why we should not kill you?"

Ah, Ellis thought. *Here we go again.*

TWENTY-FIVE

RANDALL WAS LOST. He stood in the dark of an abandoned cemetery surrounded by wolves, and the man by his side - the man he loved - was talking to them in a language he didn't understand.

He half-recognised the three who had come forward and taken human form. The tallest was their Alpha, a couple of inches shorter than Ellis and far more wiry. He was flanked by a man and a woman, both around Randall's height. The light of the moon wasn't much to see by: the red hue made it far less useful than it would normally be. With the trees and ivy all around, the dim light hardly made it through all the leaves, so the naked bodies standing before him were only barely outlined in the weak starlight.

One of the wolves had come forward to sniff them both, and now the Alpha himself was sniffing Ellis.

Randall swallowed. He hadn't thought this through. The vampire's lack of scent flagged him as unnatural to every shifter present.

Ellis' features were mostly calm. As the only white person

here, his pallor was oddly ghostly among the group. It also made his expression the easiest to read, especially once he had pocketed his sunglasses.

The Alpha had looked intrigued by Ellis' eyes, but it wasn't long before the tone of the conversation turned. Words were sharper, people waved hands with swift and angry motions as they argued.

Randall tried to take Ellis' arm, ready to drag him to safety, but Ellis slipped free of him with a shake of his head.

Had he gone mad?

A few wolves slid forward, easing around tree trunks and crooked, broken gravestones.

The hair on the back of Randall's neck lifted. His skin prickled. He wanted to run, to toss Ellis over his shoulder and get the hell away from here.

Ellis kept his head, and he was still talking. His hands moved slowly, palms toward the trio of naked shifters, and the heat seeped out of their replies.

The wolves stopped where they were.

Ellis bowed his head to them and murmured something, then his fingers found Randall's elbow and tucked into the crease of it. He turned to face Randall, pale eyes colourless in the dark, and said something.

"I think you're still speaking... whatever it is," Randall whispered.

Ellis clicked his tongue and his eyes narrowed in concentration. "How about now?"

Randall gave a half smile. "Got it."

"Good. Let's go."

Randall looked to the Alpha, whose expression was unreadable, and carefully stepped back. "Okay. Let me get us turned around first, yeah?"

"Take your time."

Randall slowly picked his way back toward his pack. The undergrowth was like tentacles that grabbed at their feet. There were broken chunks of headstone hidden among the wild flora which were covered in moss or lichen to make it even harder to see in the already difficult terrain. Many gravestones still stood, jagged fingers pointing toward - but rarely straight at - the stars, and he couldn't help but imagine the families who once thought their loved ones would have memorials which stood for centuries. If any remained alive today they'd have to be bitterly disappointed at this mess. The place looked like a bomb had hit it, and with the pounding the East End had taken in the Second World War that probably wasn't far off the truth.

He glanced back over his shoulder, but couldn't see any of the pack. They'd disappeared back into the trees.

Briar stood like a mountain, arms crossed. Preeti sat at his heels with her tail wrapped around her paws. Jim and Lara paced behind them, with Nazim at the back keeping an eye toward the way they'd entered the park.

"We need to leave," Ellis said softly. "Now."

Briar snarled. "You fucking traitorous flea! You lied to us!"

Ellis sighed faintly. "We have got to go. I'll explain once we're back at your batcave or whatever it is."

"No. You explain *now*."

"We've been given ten minutes to clear out or they'll chase us out. We probably used nine of those walking back here." Ellis tugged on Randall's arm gently. "With or without you, Briar, we are leaving. There's eighteen of them. You're welcome to get your arses handed to you, but Randall and I are off."

Randall avoided Briar's glare, and went with Ellis' hint instead. He steered the vampire around Briar's towering bulk and led him back to the broken, creaking gate as quickly as they could move.

"What are the odds of us finding a taxi 'round here this time of night?" Ellis muttered to him as he slid his glasses back on.

Randall shrugged. "Nil, I reckon."

"Great."

TRUE TO FORM, there weren't any cabs to be found. They had to walk all the way back to Whitechapel, although at least they could take the more direct route now that they weren't searching street by street for any trace of a scent. What had taken around two hours in one direction was only twenty minutes back again.

Ellis looked exhausted by the time Randall got him down the stairs into the disused ticket hall of St. Mary's. He leaned against Randall's side, his lips pressed tight together, and Randall slid an arm around his waist to support him.

"You look knackered," Randall whispered.

"I've been up for like-" Ellis felt his watch "-fifteen hours straight, and as nice as it's been holding your arm for the last few of 'em, it's been pretty stressful otherwise."

Randall blinked. Ellis *was* tired.

Why did that surprise him? He knew Ellis slept. Of course he did; they'd done it together only last night. He'd kind of assumed vampires slept the day away and were up all night to avoid the sun, though, instead of just... needing to sleep.

"Sorry," he murmured.

"It's been a long day." Ellis tried to muster a smile, but it was flat.

Preeti re-took her human form and grabbed her clothes.

She dressed efficiently, without any care for whether or not she was watched. Each of them had seen the others naked so often over the years that they'd become inured to it.

Briar swept around them and grabbed Ellis by the lapels. "Now," he snapped in the art dealer's face, "tell me."

"Briar!" Randall glowered up at him. "Let him go!"

Ellis released Randall's arm. "It's all right," he said softly. "Although I do remember events more accurately when people aren't shouting in my face."

Briar exposed his teeth, but Ellis couldn't see them to respond, so the Alpha pushed him away and growled "Talk."

Randall caught Ellis around the waist to keep him from falling.

Ellis straightened his clothes out. "They speak Bangla," he explained once he was satisfied.

Nazim and Preeti exchanged a look, and Nazim shrugged. "Urdu, not Bangla," he said to her.

"Close enough, innit?" she grumbled as she tucked her t-shirt into her jeans.

"Fuck off is it," he snapped. "Closer to Hindi than Bangla!"

"Enough!" Briar yelled. Then to Ellis he added "Go on."

Ellis straightened and lifted his weight from Randall's arm. "Their Alpha's name is Zev. He was pretty reasonable, all things considered, what with having you lot grumbling around in the background like a bunch of yobbos."

Preeti smirked quickly.

"Zev believes your pack is dangerous, reckless, and aggressive. He isn't interested in fighting you but he says he will if he has to. He gave me the impression he considered you lot a bunch of nutters." Ellis slid his hands into the pockets of his trousers. "His own pack's safety is his number one concern."

"What about the cub?" Briar crossed his arms again.

"She's in hospital, which could lead to problems if she changes while she's still there." Ellis shook his head. "They're going to try to get her out tomorrow, if she can move well enough. They say once she's out the change should heal her."

Briar glanced toward Preeti, and Randall caught a sliver of guilt in his gaze. "Those arseholes started it," Briar rumbled.

"I don't care who started what," Ellis said smoothly. "You've got the opportunity to end this peacefully."

"How?"

"Zev's willing to meet with you tomorrow night. He's also willing to let me return as your interpreter."

Randall blinked. "That's awesome!"

Briar didn't seem to think so. "And what're we supposed to talk about?"

Ellis' lips curved into a wolfish smile. "Boundaries."

The shifters erupted into swearing. Even Lara let rip with a few choice words Randall rarely heard pass her lips.

"The bastards!"

"They're on *our* turf!"

"How *dare* they!"

"QUIET!" Briar roared.

His voice echoed dully for a second, filling the emptiness of the pack's sudden silence.

"I'll think it over," Briar said to Ellis. "But in the meantime, you stay right here. I'm not letting you out of our sight."

Ellis snorted. "No. I'm going home."

"Like hell!"

"I have a dog to feed and a business to run." Ellis seemed unflappable, which he might not have been if he could see Briar's face. "I don't have time to lay about in your grimy underground lair all bloody day. And what am I supposed to do after that? Turn up in dirty clothes smelling of rat piss and rotten veg? No. I am going home, and I'll be back here tomorrow night. Take it or leave it."

"We don't need you!" Jim snapped. "Who the hell do you think you are?"

"Well," Preeti interjected, "we kinda do need him actually. Unless any of you lot suddenly learned Bangla on our way back here? Anyone? No? No takers? No miracles? No, didn't think so. Shut the fuck up." She tossed hair over her shoulder with a flick of one delicate hand. "If Ellis wants to go home, Rand can go with him, then lead him back here after sunset."

She glanced to him, and Randall nodded quickly. "I'll go with him," he agreed.

"Oh yeah. But you're a traitorous ratbag yourself," Briar snarled.

Preeti kicked him in the shin. "How fucking *dare* you talk to Randall like that!"

Briar blinked, taken aback.

"Don't give me those eyes. I've had enough of it. He's right. You treat him like shit and he's done nothing to deserve it!" Preeti poked Briar in the ribs. "Take yer man home, Rand. Go get some sleep. We'll be 'ere when you get back."

Ellis took Randall by the arm. "Thank you, Preeti. We'll be back here by eleven. You have my word."

"You better be, or-"

"Yes, yes. Crucified at dawn with sporks in me eyes." Ellis waved a dismissive hand. "Let's go, Randall."

Randall led him up the stairs and didn't dare look back.

TWENTY-SIX

THERE WAS a warm body at his side when Ellis woke. For the second night in a row Randall had stayed, and Ellis began to imagine that he could get used to this.

He listened to the slow and gentle sounds coming from the shifter: the slumbering breaths and subdued heartbeat were almost musical. When faint rumbles from Randall's stomach underlined them, though, Ellis laughed softly and slid an arm around the other man's chest.

"Mmnh?" Randall began to stretch, and his sounds quickened.

"Good morning," Ellis murmured into his shoulder. "Or afternoon. I've no idea." He drew his palm slowly down muscle and let his fingers stray over each little valley and ridge on his way to Randall's groin.

Randall gasped and shuffled to roll over and face him. Ellis didn't mind. It left his hand cupping Randall's tight arse instead, so he squeezed slowly.

"Bet you've got no food in yet, have you?" Randall's hand went to Ellis' chest and his soft palm began to explore.

Ellis chuckled at him and slid a leg around one of Randall's. "I don't think you really want to steal off Tiberius, do you?"

"Er, no. Not really. I mean, generous though the offer is…"

"I know." Ellis released an exaggerated sigh. "You're just a picky eater." He leaned in to gnaw playfully at Randall's shoulder. "So am I."

"Oh my god!" Randall laughed and pushed him back. "Ellis!"

Ellis grinned and slipped his hand from Randall's backside to his cock instead. "*Very* picky," he insisted. "But I reckon this here tastes good." He squeezed as he spoke.

Randall released a jagged moan as his words failed him, but his length began to harden in Ellis' hand.

"Thought you might agree," he murmured. He slowly wriggled his way down Randall's body until he was able to run his tongue along the stiffened flesh. Randall's scent was strongest here, and Ellis inhaled deeply as he trailed the tip of his tongue along Randall's damp slit, then he took Randall past his lips, and slid down him until the shifter's thick cock couldn't go any further. Randall rolled onto his back and his fingers threaded through Ellis' hair, but Ellis focused on giving the best damn blowjob he could. He swallowed around Randall's engorged flesh, then began to bob his head slowly, his tongue pressuring the underside of Randall's cock and ensuring the head slicked along the roof of his mouth.

Randall's hips jerked. "Oh… Oh god… Ellis-" He groaned, and his body tensed. He lost his grip on Ellis' hair and his hands thudded against the sheets.

Ellis didn't need to breathe and he had no desire to pause to answer Randall. He slipped a hand down beneath himself and grasped his own cock, stroking idly as he focused most of his attention on Randall's.

The shifter's moans grew louder, and his words devolved into nonsense.

Ellis lifted his head free and Randall's noises became pleading, urgent whines.

God, he loved Randall beneath him. The shifter's powerful frame was desperate for release, and all because of Ellis' touch.

He slid up Randall's body and used his skin to rub over Randall's trapped, slick member until his own dragged up the inside of Randall's thigh and nestled between his cheeks.

Randall bucked like a fish out of water. His legs parted, the insides of his thighs sliding over Ellis' hips, and he offered himself up with a moan.

Ellis guided himself to Randall's entrance and circled it, teasing at it, slicking it with his wetness.

"Ellis," Randall cried. "Oh shit! Fuck me! God, please, I need you!"

Ellis didn't argue, but he hadn't taken Randall dry before, and he sure as hell wasn't about to rush it no matter how enticing Randall's begging became. He nestled his face against Randall's shoulder to best be able to listen to his body, then he slowly, *slowly* pressed against his tight muscle.

Randall lifted his knees, but his body stilled. His breathing deepened, catching at the back of his throat in tiny little whimpers while he struggled to relax.

Ellis withdrew, then pressed again.

And again.

Randall's whimpers turned needy. Eager. Then his muscle quivered and took Ellis' tip inside, smothering it in tight, wet heat.

Ellis shuddered and stopped. His teeth gripped Randall's skin, his fingers clenched into the sheets.

Randall panted like he'd run a marathon, and they lay there

together. Ellis fought to hold still as the sweating, trembling body under him tried to lure him on.

"More," Randall croaked.

Ellis didn't dare listen to Randall's words. Every ounce of him was tuned into the other man's body instead, waiting for its cues, for the signals that would allow him to continue. He could feel every little squeeze and relaxation of Randall's arse around his shaft, every tiny flutter of his muscles and pulse.

"Ellis." Randall's voice cracked with lust.

There. The shifter's body began to relax, to let him in, his sphincters less of a death grip and more a tight embrace now.

Ellis inched deeper inside. Every little motion felt like torture, and the need to bury himself grew stronger. But he couldn't. He *wouldn't*.

Randall lifted his hips and eagerly drew Ellis into his passage, and Ellis was finally able to come to rest in him.

"You are so sexy," Ellis whispered against his skin. "Take your time."

Randall swallowed, then slid his arms around Ellis' shoulders. He gripped tightly and turned to kiss Ellis on the lips, his tongue darting between them to draw Ellis' out.

Ellis returned the kiss as he slid a hand between them and took Randall's cock in his grasp. He stroked firmly over the wet shaft and nudged his thumb to Randall's slit, gathering up moisture and trailing it over his head.

"Jesus," Randall growled. He curled his legs around Ellis' waist. "Fuck me!"

Ellis did. He moved carefully until it became easier, and then he drove deep inside Randall's hot body. Each thrust was divine, and made him push harder, faster, with the next.

When Randall came, it was with enough force to hit Ellis' collarbone. The sounds Randall made - his delirious and wanton cries had to be loud enough to wake the neighbours - wove themselves around the trembling of his body and were enough to drag Ellis over the edge with him.

Spent, satisfied, they lay together, and Randall's chest heaved enough for the both of them.

THEY SHOWERED, then Randall popped out to get some food in for the next few days. Ellis thought that was optimistic, but he didn't argue.

As Randall ate a breakfast that was so late it could only really be called lunch, Ellis lounged on the sofa and listened to the sounds of life in his own flat. His fridge was switched on for once, and gave off a low hum that blended into all the hums from the other flats quickly enough.

"What did Zev really say last night?" Randall asked between mouthfuls of tea.

Ellis couldn't help but laugh. "What *are* you suggesting, petal? That I left information out when talking to Briar? You wound me!"

Randall snorted. "I know you," he said. "You're not daft enough to give away your hand to a guy who wants to kill you."

"Too bloody right." Ellis pushed hair back from his forehead and lay with his arm over his head. "I'm keeping too many plates spinning right now. I need time, and I don't think Briar's going to let me have any."

"We've got this afternoon." Randall was calm again.

It was as if being away from his pack was enough to overcome the moon's effect, which if what Zev had said was true could well be the case.

"What's going on?" Randall prompted.

Ellis sat up, slowly swinging his feet to the carpet and resting his elbows on his knees. "I think your blood's letting me go out in the sun."

Randall coughed as he inhaled his tea. "Shit! Really?"

"I don't know. It could be. All I seem to get is a touch of sunburn, then it heals right up once I'm inside."

"What-" Randall put his cup down. "No, wait. How the hell did you find this out? If sunlight's dangerous, what made you think going out in it was such a great idea? You could've-"

"It wasn't my idea, Randall." Ellis sat back and gripped his knees with his hands. "The Mobility Instructor had to come visit and check up on Tiberius, and she opened the curtains while she was here. By the time I realised what she was up to it were too late to stop her."

"Shit."

"Pretty shit, aye. Then I get visited by this vampire from Soho."

"The blonde woman?"

"Probably?" Ellis shrugged.

"Sorry. I meant-"

"The one who was leaving when you arrived the other night, aye." Ellis waved fingers slightly. "It's fine. Anyway, she came to talk politics at me. Reckons herself a proper Che Guevara she does. She's looking to overthrow the way the Elders run the city and install some sort of Communist collective instead. And if there's one thing I know all too well it's that art never flourishes under Communism."

"Bloody hell." Randall's footsteps padded lightly across the carpet, then his weight settled at Ellis' side.

"And my dad wants his money back, which I don't actually have available. It's all tied up in the gallery. Rent, bills, marketing, wages..." Ellis sighed. "I think Han might be ill, too. Jay says he's sleeping a lot, but I haven't had the time to press him on it now that we've taken on a new employee and Jay's time's all focused on training her. I can't just go over and visit to check up on him, either. I could already get into enough shit with Briar dragging me through god knows how many territories just to do his talking for him. If someone sees me and takes it up with the Council I'll get censured. If they see me and take it up with me directly they have the right to kill me for trespassing. All of which is irrelevant if Briar pulls my head off tonight."

Randall took his hand and gripped tight. He didn't speak, and Ellis couldn't blame him.

"Sorry. That was all a bit stream-of-consciousness." He closed his fingers around Randall's.

"I'm sorry. I've been so distant lately, and I dunno-" Randall drew a breath. "I dunno what's up with me. I've got no excuse."

Ellis smiled a little. "It's fine. You got a touch of cold feet, that's all. I know I come on a bit strong. Reckon that's the artist in me. I get carried away sometimes-" He chuckled. "Especially when there's a gorgeous man in my life."

The truth was that Ellis couldn't help but suspect that there was a deeper issue than mere early relationship jitters. Randall had mentioned once that his dad had walked out on the family when he was still a child, but it wasn't something he'd lingered on. That kind of thing was bound to leave a man with commitment issues, and when faced with someone who loved as easily as Ellis did it had probably terrified the poor fella. Letting him dwell on it now would probably run the risk of dredging that fear right back up to the surface again, and Ellis didn't dare risk it. He had to steer Randall elsewhere.

"All that'll have to wait. Zev said a few things last night that you need to hear."

"But-"

"They think Briar's pack is dangerous." Ellis faced Randall, and could make out the faint difference in tone between the werewolf and the rest of his flat. "They think he's reckless and treats you like shit. They patrol his territory to rescue cubs before Briar finds them because they don't want anyone else to end up the way you did."

Randall's heart thudded, and Ellis heard him dry-swallow. "I... They... They *what?*"

Ellis pressed his lips together tightly. He couldn't begin to imagine how Randall felt right now. To find out that his name was used as a cautionary tale to frighten the kids with had to be awful. *Don't go near Briar's pack or you'll end up like Randall.*

He wished there was a gentler way to say it. Dancing around it would have made it worse than laying it out. He wondered whether this was what police officers felt like when they had to deliver what they delicately referred to as sympathy messages. Still, he supposed they got some kind of training for it. Ellis had to work it out for himself, and whatever option he chose felt like it would be the wrong one.

"What am I, the poster child for abused werewolves?"

"Yes," Ellis said simply.

"Why didn't they ever come to me? Try to help me out? If they're so dead-set on saving everyone from Briar, why didn't they pull *me* out?"

Ellis leaned in and pressed soft kisses to Randall's neck. He trailed his lips up to the shifter's jaw, then down to the soft crook of his neck. "I think," he finally whispered, "that werewolves are very loyal creatures."

"So?" The hurt in Randall's answer was palpable. Ellis wanted nothing more than to make it go away.

"Even if Zev spoke English," he murmured, "even if he

came to you and offered to take you from Briar's pack, I don't think you would have gone with him, would you?"

Randall's silence was answer enough.

"No," Ellis agreed. "You wouldn't. Because you weren't ready."

He didn't think Randall was ready to hear what else Zev had said, either, and so he didn't mention it.

TWENTY-SEVEN

IF RANDALL never saw Briar again it'd be far too soon. Bad enough to hate his own Alpha, but now to find out that Zev's entire pack not only knew who Randall was but also used him as their impetus to rescue every stray cub they could find?

How was he supposed to feel about that? Fuck, he'd been standing right there next to Ellis while Zev had told him all this. They must've thought he was pathetic.

The longer the day dragged on, the less Randall felt like he could follow through on the promise to return tonight. He made himself useful around Ellis' flat, vacuuming and dusting while Ellis worked from home. Then they walked to the gallery together, stopping off at a small park to let Tiberius do his business and have some play time.

Ellis' skin burned like that of a white bloke in Marbella on his summer holidays. He was pink within quarter of an hour, and well on his way to a lovely shade of cooked lobster by the time they reached the gallery, but just like he'd said, the burn faded away by the time they made it upstairs to his office.

Randall met Christy Ryan, who seemed nice and friendly,

but spent most of her afternoon downstairs with customers. Jay hovered near her like a helicopter parent, always poised to swoop in and rescue her if she faltered.

And still the day dragged on. Ellis had work to do, which left Randall at a loose end, and he couldn't occupy himself with cleaning like he had at the flat. The gallery was spotless already.

He kept chewing over what Ellis had told him until his sour mood had deteriorated into a vile one.

The day limped on. Christy left work at five.

Jay came in and sank into his chair, then cast Randall a grin and a wave. It seemed strained. "Hey, Randall. What's up?"

Randall shrugged. "Not much. You?"

"Same."

Randall had the nagging suspicion that Jay's claim was as much of a lie as his own.

"Mind if I nick off early again tonight, Ellis?" Jay said, looking over to his boss' desk.

"I think it'd be a good idea," Ellis answered.

The tension in here was thick as treacle, and Randall wasn't sure he understood the source of it.

"Cheers. See you tomorrow. Take care, eh?" Jay added to Randall, and Randall thought it sounded like a threat.

"What was *that* about?" he grunted once Jay had gone.

"He knows you told Preeti what I am," Ellis replied.

"What?" Randall sprung out of his chair.

"He doesn't know what you and Preeti are." Ellis pushed his braille display aside and faced Randall. "But he did offer to scratch your eyes out."

"But-"

Ellis shook his head. "I haven't so much as *hinted* at what you are to him, petal. That's not my secret to give."

"So now he thinks I'm just some guy who's found out what

you are and blabbed it to his friend!" Randall shook his head. "How's that any better?"

"It isn't."

Randall prowled around the desk. Was Ellis manipulating *him* now?

"I was angry and upset," Ellis murmured. He nudged his chair back from his desk, and his head unerringly faced Randall as he moved. "Jay asked why, so I told him. But I glossed over it, nothing more."

"And now he hates me," Randall grumped.

Ellis reached out and ran his hands up Randall's thighs to his hips, then drew him forward, and Randall had to step in against Ellis' chair to keep from losing his balance. "It'll pass," Ellis murmured. He pressed a kiss to Randall's stomach, lips resting against his t-shirt.

Randall grimaced and perched on the edge of Ellis' desk. Ellis had to bring his chair forward to remain in contact with him.

"What if it doesn't pass?"

Ellis ran his hands tenderly over Randall's thighs. "We'll worry about that once this is all dealt with, all right? Let's get the situation with Briar squared away, and then we can talk to Jay."

Randall scowled down at him.

Ellis tugged his glasses off and set them to Randall's side, then leaned in and slid the t-shirt up so that his kiss could land against bare flesh this time.

"This is serious," Randall grumbled. He ran his fingers through Ellis' thick hair, so at odds with his own, and marvelled at how soft it felt.

"I agree." Ellis didn't sound all that serious. "Especially this-" he ran his fingers over Randall's jeans, rubbing along his length "-here."

Randall leaned back a little and planted his free hand on the desk surface. "I don't think that'll solve anything."

"Ah, on that I *dis*agree." Ellis' deft fingers worked Randall's fly, and his lips darted in before Randall could object.

"Jesus," Randall hissed. He gripped Ellis' hair while the rest of him turned to putty. All he could do was stare as those pale lips closed around his shaft and slid down it before it had even had the chance to fully harden.

Ellis' mouth worked its magic. His hands grasped Randall's thighs and pinned him to the desk while his head rose and fell. His hair cascaded back and forth, long enough to brush against Randall's stomach and the tops of his thighs every time his lips drew tight around the base of Randall's cock, and his throat...

Randall groaned, and his hips bucked. Ellis had a way of swallowing him which pushed him toward the precipice so fast he barely had time to recognise that was where he was headed.

"Fuck," he wheezed. "I'm... Ellis, I'm gonna-"

Ellis lapped at his slit, then took him all the way in again. His throat closed and flexed around Randall's head and didn't break free, and Randall was undone in seconds. He howled as he spent himself, then his muscles gave up on him and he collapsed back, sprawled across the desk like so much discarded clothing.

He stared up at the clean white ceiling while he struggled to give a damn about anything that had seemed really important before Ellis had sucked him dry, but it wasn't going to happen, and he grinned feebly. "You're a dirty bastard," he breathed.

"Oh, you noticed?" Ellis chuckled and idled his fingers over Randall's stomach.

"Ha." Randall let his eyes close a moment. "God, I love you."

Ellis' fingers halted.

Randall's fog lifted and he became acutely aware of the words that had just left him. "Er."

Ellis chuckled. "I love you, too. And I'm proud of you. You're amazing."

Proud of him? "For what?" Randall struggled up onto his elbows to try and read Ellis' features, but the vampire had already slid his glasses back into place.

Ellis just smiled and offered his hands to help Randall sit up, and Randall took them. Ellis wasn't exactly overburdened with muscles, but he did all right for his build, and Randall slid to his feet to tuck himself back into his jeans. Then he frowned.

"Hang on."

Ellis' brows lifted. "What is it?"

"We went out for dinner, right? I mean-" he blushed "-we bailed on it halfway through, but we did eat."

"Mmhmm…" Ellis leaned back.

"And you, er. You just, er. Well, you didn't, you know. Just then." Randall's cheeks were definitely burning now.

Ellis laughed. "A dirty bastard never spits."

"But you're a vampire." Randall leaned against the desk once he was straightened out. "Do you have to eat *and* drink blood?"

"Oh!" Ellis' expression was priceless. He shot through understanding and straight out the other side into embarrassment. "You don't want to know."

"Well, I obviously do." Randall watched Ellis, fascinated at the sudden squirming. "Otherwise I wouldn't ask."

Ellis felt his watch.

"Don't pull 'oh, is that the time?' with me!" Randall smirked. "Come on. Tell me."

"You'll regret this…"

"Tell meeee," Randall whined.

"Okay. Areet. Fine." Ellis put his hands up in surrender. "I can ingest whatever I choose to, but unless it's blood I have to, er, evacuate it, so to speak. Well, I don't *have* to, but if I don't it'll come up of its own accord at sunrise."

Randall stared at him. "Ew."

"I said you'd regret it!"

"*Eww*! Shit! You're going to-"

"Yes."

"Couldn't you just-"

"I told you you didn't want to know!"

Randall grimaced. "Well, I was about to ask you to dinner."

"You're welcome to, but don't be offended if I choose not to join you." Ellis grinned. "Waste of money, if you ask me."

"You know, weird as it might sound, I'm not all that hungry now." Randall hopped up onto the desk and swung his feet idly.

Ellis' smile faded, and he rubbed Randall's thighs. "I won't be offended if you don't come tonight. I can take a taxi to wherever it was in Whitechapel and go with them to the park."

"What?" Randall stopped his feet and stared at Ellis. "Have you lost it? I'm not letting Briar anywhere near you without me there."

Ellis tipped his head aside. "He does sound like he's around the same size as Snowdon," he admitted.

"Yeah, pretty much." Randall sighed and reached out to brush Ellis' hair back from his face. "He could probably turn us both into mincemeat without breaking a sweat. Still not letting you go in on your own, though."

The thought of Ellis never coming back was horrible, but time after time the vampire put his life on the line to protect Randall. What kind of bloke hung back and let a blind man defend him from a creature like Briar?

Ellis had killed twice, both times in self-defence, but tackling a vampire whose power was a gift for languages and a crazy human who was an artist, not a soldier, didn't mean he was at all prepared for what Briar could do. He didn't have a wolf shifter's strength or speed. He didn't have any kind of power to get himself out of harm's way. Sure he could heal his injuries if he'd fed, but sooner or later Briar would just do so much damage that it wouldn't matter anymore.

And what if Ellis came to realise Randall was almost as much of a horror as Briar?

God, what would Ellis think of him if he knew what Randall had done to his own bathroom in a momentary tantrum? What would his reaction be to the gigantic monster Randall was capable of becoming at a moment's notice? And Randall's halfway shape was *nothing* compared to Briar's. Where Randall was five feet eight inches in his socks, he barely topped out at around ten feet on the handful of occasions he took on his worst shape. Briar was six foot five and half as wide, and when he changed Randall reckoned he hit maybe fourteen feet tall. He was *terrifying*.

Ellis turned to kiss Randall's palm. "Penny?" he offered.

Randall sighed and shook his head. "Nothing. Shall we get going?"

"All right."

Ellis shut everything down and gathered Tiberius, and they walked back to his flat in no particular hurry, talking about meaningless things like weather and the price of different brands of dog food. Randall stopped off to grab a sandwich on the way just in case he felt hungry later, and flirted with the idea of calling the whole night off.

Then the moon rose.

TWENTY-EIGHT

ELLIS DID his best to distract Randall as the night drew in, but there were only so many times in a twenty-four-hour period that a man could put his mouth on another man's cock before things got strange. The shifter seemed tense, but thankfully not as upset as he was before Ellis took matters into his own hands at the office.

Once the sun set, they made their way straight to Cemetery Park. Ellis suggested that they stop off at Whitechapel, but Randall's response to that had been "Fuck 'em. I'll text."

The park's gate squeaked nearby. Randall had found them a bus stop to sit in while they waited for Briar's people to turn up, except the "seats" were more like a slanted shelf to lean the arse against rather than sit on with any degree of comfort. Ellis couldn't work out what the point of them was at all; his bum kept sliding across the near-frictionless metal and he had to stand with his feet apart to maintain any kind of stability. They probably looked like a pair of criminals hanging around near a dodgy cemetery, Ellis in his tailored-fit smart casuals, and Randall in his off-the-rail t-shirt and jeans.

He coughed into his hand to stifle a laugh.

"You okay?" Randall asked.

"Aye. I'm fine. Just letting my mind wander." He tilted his head at the throaty chug of a black cab, so unlike any other vehicle in the city. With the scarcity of taxis out in Tower Hamlets, he added "Is this them now?"

Randall's clothes rasped and the row of bum-rests moved as his weight left them. "How the hell did you know that?"

Ellis shrugged and stood upright. "Black cab," he answered. "Diesel engine, four cylinders, intercooler, muffled tyre noise implies low-slung body. Basically," he added with a grin, "most varieties of black cab pretty much sound like no other car on the road."

"All right, show-off." Randall sniffed. "Didn't know you were a secret petrol-head."

"Not me. I just have Top Gear on in the background and pick up a lot of nonsense words." Ellis grinned and felt for Randall's arm. He slipped his fingers into the crook of the shifter's elbow and leaned in to kiss his cheek. "No matter what happens," he whispered quickly, "I love you. Got it?"

"I got it." Randall sounded bemused.

"Good."

The cab stopped and disgorged Briar's entire pack. Either it had been a tight fit in there, or they'd called for one of the bigger cabs that held up to eight people - or four normal people and Briar. Ellis said nothing while Jim paid, and once the cab pulled away he remained quiet, waiting for it to leave the street.

"You were supposed to meet us at St. Mary's," was Briar's snarl of a greeting.

"Didn't fancy it." Ellis smiled. "I wanted to spend some

time with Randall. But we're all here now, as promised, and on time."

"And I'm to believe you just sat here waiting this entire time and haven't already gone in and made arrangements?"

Ellis laughed. "What sort of arrangements? I'm here to translate, not arrange. I might advise one or the other side to take a few minutes to calm themselves, but tonight is up to you, Briar. If you want peace, this is your opportunity to make it happen, for everyone's sake."

Briar snorted, but Ellis faced Randall and murmured "Ready when you are, petal."

"Okay." Randall led towards the creaking gate, and the pack trailed at their heels.

They passed into the park with a surprising lack of muttering or complaining from Briar's people. Could it be that, in spite of Briar's gruffness, he had mellowed out tonight? That would sure as heck make things much easier if it were true.

It would have been nice if someone had happened to charge through this place with a flamethrower and destroy all the bloody undergrowth during the day, but Ellis' luck was against him and he had to slog through the grasping plants with the random-seeming deviations around whatever lay in their path. Thank god Randall was sturdy or they'd both have fallen flat on their faces several times.

He could hear the wolves up ahead, lingering in the same places as they had the night before. Soon Briar's pack would hear them too, and the night would likely all come down to luck more than judgement.

Ellis hated relying on luck. He did it enough at work without it consuming his free time and risking his life too.

The grotesque noises of shifters changing shape filled his world, and then the bickering began, both ahead of and behind him. He really hoped werewolves weren't like this every month and that there was some truth to all their Blood Moon talk, because otherwise this could get irritating.

"Briar, Zev," Ellis said firmly. "As Alphas, bring your packs to order, please."

He said nothing as the Alphas subdued their own people; Briar with grumbled words and Zev with softly-spoken ones.

"I'm here to negotiate," Ellis said once the hubbub settled. "But I need you to know that I can't control this ability I have with languages very well. I might need you to speak to me first before I switch to your language, so if I'm talking and it's nonsense to you, please say so and I'll try again. All right?"

"Understood," said Briar.

"Sorry?" Zev said. "What was that?"

Ellis tried to concentrate on Zev's words. The gentle way that the vowels fluctuated and the tones rose and fell throughout his speech. Was that simply Zev's way of speaking, or was it a factor of the language he used? Either way, Ellis repeated himself as he tried to emulate that fluctuation.

"I understand." Zev sounded wary, and Ellis really wished he could keep an eye on what all these highly volatile werewolves were up to.

"What are you saying?" Jim snapped.

"I'm just repeating what I've already said to you." Ellis struggled to keep his frustration out of his tone.

"How do we know that?"

This would be a long night if both sides questioned every single thing he said.

TALKS STUMBLED along like a dog with a broken leg. Zev and his pack would comment on Briar's temperament and untrustworthiness - which Ellis couldn't possibly translate - and Briar and his pack would repeat their demands that Zev's pack leave Tower Hamlets and never come back. Ellis' attempts to find some neutral middle ground had floundered and were at risk of drowning in despair.

"The fact remains that they come into our territory without any regard for our markings!"

"Why should we respect the territory of a pack who do not respect themselves?"

"What did he say?"

"Your Alpha is a fathead."

Ellis bit his tongue before that one came out of his mouth, and he rubbed his jaw. "Maybe a break is in order," he suggested.

"Maybe we should break some fucking heads," Jim rumbled.

"Don't be ridiculous," Ellis sighed. "They outnumber you three to one."

The wolves were griping among themselves as they prowled back and forth among the dry-sounding grass.

Waste of time.

Don't like this.

Should retreat.

Should attack.

Moon. Danger.

Weapon.

Ellis hesitated, then leaned in to Randall and kept his voice low. "Randall?"

"Yeah?"

"Is anyone here armed?" God, why hadn't it occurred to him to insist that nobody brought any weapons? Because he was a bloody art dealer, that was why. Because nobody in their right mind took weapons to peaceful negotiations.

He might have made a horrible mistake.

"I dunno," Randall whispered after some movement. Ellis presumed Randall had been looking around. "Jim brought a knife the other day, though. He's the one who stabbed the cub."

"*What?!*" Ellis hissed. Zev had said that the girl was in hospital after this fight they'd all had, but he hadn't mentioned a knife, or who had been the one to hurt her. And now either someone had spotted a weapon, or they were concerned that Jim might have brought one; either way it was a disaster waiting to happen.

"Tell me about it," Randall grumbled, his anger all well and good but not useful right now.

He turned toward Briar. "I need Jim to leave the park," he said quietly.

"Fuck off!" Jim snapped.

"Why?" Briar said.

"Because he stabbed the girl," Ellis explained. "They think he's armed now. It's making them nervous."

"You carrying, Jimbo?" Briar growled.

"What if I am?"

"You fucking idiot. Get out and wait outside!"

"Ellis?" Zev prompted.

"I'm just asking Jim to leave," he said, attention returning to the calmer of the two Alphas. "His presence seems to be upsetting some of-"

Several wolves snarled at once.

"What are you saying?" Briar growled. The more often he asked it, the more Ellis thought he sounded like a drunk tourist on the Costa del Sol. "Is he starting?"

"No, I'm-"

"What's set them off?"

"Fuck this," Jim hissed.

There was a sound very much like cloth whispering over metal.

Weapon!

Traitor!

Liar!

Feet trampled grass. Bodies thundered toward each other. Breathing became laboured as hearts sped into action. Bones ground and meat tore and Ellis couldn't be sure whether it was due to people changing shapes or because they'd impacted against each other hard enough to do serious damage. He heard snarls and yips, screams and yells.

It was chaos, and it was too much. He couldn't keep track of over twenty people in a full-on brawl, especially when the number of people and wolves kept changing. He had no idea who anyone was any more.

Tonight had gone to ratshit incredibly quickly.

"Fucking leech!" Briar screamed. "What did you do?"

What? How the hell was any of this *his* fault?

Zev barked orders to his people, urging them to calm and keep their heads, but his shouts were abruptly stopped.

Something whipped past Ellis' face.

"Fuck," Randall snarled. "Hang on."

"Wh-*oof!*"

The air was crushed out of him as he slammed against a hard surface and bent almost double. He scrabbled to grab at something - anything - as his feet left the ground and his head dangled upside-down, and he found only clothes and taut muscle beneath him. Arms closed around his thighs and kept them pinned to a living, breathing body, and he clutched at the clothes he'd found as he began to bounce so violently that his glasses shook loose and fell off.

The snarling and yelling faded into the distance. Now the only thing he heard with any real accuracy was Randall's heart, his breath, his feet slamming against grass, gravel, then finally pavement.

It slowly sank in that he'd been tossed over Randall's shoulder like a rag doll and Randall was running away from the fight as fast as he could.

He drew breath, but the bouncing crushed it right out of him again, and all he could do was hang on for dear life as Randall sprinted away from the park.

TWENTY-NINE

RANDALL RAN. All it had taken was the murderous gleam in Briar's eyes and he'd made his decision. Sod the lot of them. He had to protect Ellis.

He didn't know which direction he ran in and he didn't care. All that mattered was getting away from that damn park. With Ellis slung over his shoulder in an undignified fireman's carry he sprinted through housing estates and across a main road. He leaped the short fence surrounding another, less grave-filled park and shot across it like his arse was on fire. Out the other side, over the fence again, and he hared over a bridge which crossed a canal.

Ellis grabbed at his waist in terror. A whimper slipped out of him.

Fuck. Running water.

No time to worry about that. Too late. He'd crossed it now. He kept going, through into another housing estate, this time with lower buildings interspersed with two-storey terraced houses. It was late, dark, but there were still people here and there and Randall darted down side streets and through alleys to avoid them.

He skittered past Limehouse station and under the railway bridge. A group of locals poured out of a fast food place across the road, so he sped away down the first turning he could take.

Another few minutes and more twists and turns than he could keep track of, he had to stop. They were on a little path that ran alongside the Thames, and the only thing separating them from the river was a low iron rail and a three foot drop.

"Randall!" Ellis gasped in panic. "For god's sake, put me down!"

Randall looked back the way he'd came, but they were alone, so he crouched forward and set Ellis down on his feet.

The vampire's hair was a mess, and he'd lost his glasses somewhere. He turned toward the water with real fear in his eyes. "Where are we?"

"Limehouse," Randall gasped. "By the river. No way to cross it, though."

"Thank Christ for that. Did we go over water earlier?"

"Just a small canal."

"Randall!"

"Briar was going to pull your bloody head off!" Randall wiped his forehead with his arm, but it just smeared the sweat around, so he tugged up the hem of his t-shirt to use as a mop instead. "Anyway, if you're okay with sunlight, you might be okay with running water, too."

"P'raps. But I'll 'appen as we don't wanna be findin' out reet now, eh?"

Randall winced. Ellis had gone all Yorkshire again, which meant he was likely pretty upset. "Sorry."

Ellis' ice-blue eyes flitted blindly toward the sounds of the river, then he reached for Randall's arm and gripped it. "Not your fault," he said. "What happened?"

Randall bit his lip. "You asked Jim to leave and he got pissed off about it. Then when Zev started talking I think things got a bit frayed and our lot thought they were going to attack Jim 'cause he was the one who stabbed the cub and that's why you'd suggested he leave, so he pulled his knife out, and-" Randall gasped for breath. "They saw the knife and it set 'em off."

Ellis clenched his jaw and stepped closer. "Are you areet?"

"Me?" All Randall could think of was the chunk of gravestone that had narrowly missed Ellis' head. "Yeah, I'm fine. Briar seemed to want to blame you for everything so I figured it'd be better if we just legged it."

Ellis' grip relaxed at last. "Thank you."

"Any time." He looked to the water to work out which way it was flowing, then began to lead Ellis along the path. "Train station's shut," he said. "We passed it on the way here. I reckon if we just follow the river west we can turn at Westminster and cut through St. James' Park to Mayfair."

Ellis shook his head, and his hair began to point downward at last. "Can't go through Westminster. We need to cut north."

"I can't go north from here. That'll take us straight through Briar's territory, and if they've left the park they could be trying to track us down." It was tempting, though. If he headed north from here he could cut straight across Whitechapel and out into Spitalfields. He and Ellis could hole up with Randall's mum until public transport opened up again.

'Course, that meant introducing Ellis to his mum in the middle of the night, then legging it before dawn. She'd give him a flea in his ear for treating her flat like a doss-house, and with the glowering red eye of the moon above there was no guarantee that Briar would stay away from his mum or his brother.

It was too risky. Ellis' place was safer, but it was further away, and Randall had no way to know where one vampire's turf ended and another began. He doubted they ran around pissing on the street corners to mark their ground.

"What's wrong with Westminster?" he asked.

"Barb says the fella who owns it is a reet nasty piece of work," Ellis murmured. "I can't run the risk of bumping into him. But if we can cut up through Soho she'll let us through, I'll 'appen."

"Okay. If we head up through Holborn that'll get us to Soho. Anyone in Holborn we need to avoid?"

"No idea." Ellis shook his head.

"Okay, well." Randall checked over his shoulder, but they were still alone. "Anyone else's areas we have to go around?"

Ellis looked pained. "I don't know. All I know is what Barb's told me."

"It's okay." Randall nodded to himself. "We'll just get there as fast as we can, and make sure we're not caught."

He wished this could have been a romantic stroll along the river's edge. It was a beautiful thing at night, the Thames; gentle ripples caused the reflected lights from both sides of the water to dance and bounce like playful will-o'-the-wisps. The buildings which overlooked the water here were mostly blocks of flats four or five storeys high. As Randall led Ellis along the path the river curved, and the view opened out to a long stretch of the waters which looped again in the near distance.

It was gorgeous, and Ellis couldn't see it.

Randall's heart sank. He looked to Ellis, who had fallen a half-step behind him, although matched him for speed. The taller man seemed content to walk quietly, lost in thought.

"Why do you walk behind?" he asked, curious.

Ellis' head tilted toward him. "It's easier to read and respond to your movements. If I'm alongside you I can't keep my own arm straight, and I have to twist slightly." His lips quirked, and he added "It's not because I don't want to walk beside you, believe me."

Randall smiled a little. "Am I doing better at it tonight?"

"You're doing grand, petal." Ellis patted his arm. "Just don't swing your arms around like you're a windmill and you're fine. And, er. Please don't take my arm like you did last night, eh?"

Randall's smile left him. He remembered how Ellis had pulled free at the time, but he'd put it down to wanting to look independent in front of Zev's pack. "I'm sorry."

"Shh." Ellis' lips twitched. "You weren't to know. And while it's reet endearing that you keep apologising for things you have no control over, it seems a lot of effort." His fingers squeezed gently. "When you lose your sight, you lose a lot of agency. You become reliant on others for things you always used to be able to do for yourself." His gaze drifted toward the ground. "If I hold you, I get to retain some illusion of that agency, you see? If I hear something or I want to stop I can let go. But if you are holding me I have no choice and no control. I don't get a say in my direction and I don't get to stop if I want to. I have to tell you what I want and wait for you to action it." He smiled wryly. "I suppose that sounds daft, eh?"

Randall shook his head. "No. God, no. It makes total sense." He puffed his cheeks out, then sighed. "I know what it's like to lose the control you think you have over your life, you know? Everything was fine when I was a kid. Then when dad walked out had to grow up a bit, I s'pose. Kieran had it harder. I think he felt like he had to be the man of the house, you know? Take care of mum, look out for me, all that. He was always getting into fights at school when I got picked on for not having a dad, like I was the only kid around that didn't."

Ellis' eyes flitted toward him, and Randall saw the tell-tale squint, the furrowing of his brow that suggested the vampire was attempting to focus on him.

"It's too dark," he murmured, trying to save Ellis the trouble.

"Aye," Ellis said quietly. "Go on."

"Eh." Randall almost shrugged, then remembered what Ellis had said about moving his arms around. "Anyway, after that I was all set to go into a proper job, you know? I had it all planned out. I'd get through my A-Levels then I was going to do accounting at Uni-"

"Accounting?" Ellis blinked.

"Hey, I was fourteen when I made this plan. All I was thinking about was earning money and supporting mum. I didn't know how boring it could be." Randall chuckled. "Then of course that all went out the window when Preeti found me and I changed. I had to stick to London, couldn't go to the Uni I'd planned. 'Cause of what I am, I lost the ability to make that decision, about where to study, where to go to map out my entire future. I had to stay in the city to be near Briar every full moon. Preeti and I talked it over and the more we talked, the more I realised I wanted to do animal behaviour. I didn't know what I wanted to *do* with it at the time, but it really interested me, so I went to the Royal Veterinary College at King's Cross. Just kinda fell into training dogs after that, 'cause I got a job as a vet's nurse and-"

Randall broke off. That job had been a nightmare. There were customers who couldn't afford the treatment so opted to have their pets put to sleep; others who could afford the treatment but couldn't be bothered with the time or effort it would take to rehabilitate their pet. There were customers who mistreated their animals, then threatened the staff when they called the RSPCA in.

Of course there were the great customers, too. The ones who gave a damn, the ones who genuinely understood - as Ellis did - that that they were utterly responsible for the wellbeing of the animals in their care. There were *lots* of those customers. But all it took was one of the less awesome kind and it pushed Randall's day downward. Combine one of those customers with a full moon and he'd wound up launching himself over the reception desk to try and strangle the bastard.

"Didn't go well?"

"Nah. I needed something where I could be my own boss, set my own schedule."

"That would make sense," Ellis agreed.

"Yeah. So I set up my own business and trained dogs. Been doing it ever since. It's amazing." He smiled again. "Really rewarding, you know? To be able to make a difference to the lives of the dogs and the people who come to me, it's a real honour."

"That drew me to you, you know."

Randall blinked and looked back to him. "What?"

"Your passion. Your love of working to make things *better* for your client's animals." Ellis flashed a grin. "That and Jay said you were gorgeous."

"He did?"

"Oh aye." Ellis slowed to a halt and pulled Randall toward him. "And he was right."

Ellis dipped his head toward Randall, and Randall lifted to meet the kiss. Ellis' fingers drew a line across his chest, and Randall felt for Ellis' hip as they each tilted their heads in unison.

"How 'bout we go home, and I'll show you how gorgeous I think you are?"

Randall gazed into Ellis' eyes. He knew the vampire couldn't see him, but his eyes were so captivating that Randall couldn't resist looking. They lost most of their colour in the dark, yet had a faint gleam to them that made them almost unnatural; breathtakingly beautiful, much like the man himself.

"Yeah," Randall mumbled when he realised he hadn't answered. "Okay."

He let Ellis take his arm again and led along the embankment. They passed the Tower of London soon enough, and the Millennium Bridge. The peaceful walk gave Randall's mind too much time to think, and he began to worry about Preeti.

God, he hoped she'd be okay. Every time he relayed some important part of his past to Ellis, Preeti was part of the telling; she had been there from the beginning, and now he'd left her fighting for her life in a park full of angry shifters. The guilt gnawed at him the more he worried at it, so he drew out his phone and tapped out a text to her, hoping she'd answer sooner rather than later.

Ellis occasionally asked where they were, and Randall answered with the nearest landmark or street sign. Once they reached Temple station Randall veered away from the river and up past the clean white buildings of Aldwych. Holborn was, if he remembered correctly, just north of here, but Mayfair was west, and he could shave some time while still avoiding Westminster if he cut through Covent Garden.

He led along Drury Lane. This end of it was relatively light on theatres. Instead there were more theatrical and artist supplies shops, all of which were closed at this time of night. The street was narrow and deserted, so they could get to Covent Garden quickly and quietly.

Ellis slowed down, his head tilting. "Where are we?"

"Drury Lane. Heading up on Covent Garden."

Ellis pressed a finger briefly to his lips, then gestured toward a small side-alley dotted with slim trees and old Victorian streetlamps. He dropped his hand back to his side before they drifted far forward enough for Randall to look down the narrow street. There was a restaurant on the corner, lights off inside and no sounds coming from it, and further down the path it looked lined with private properties.

Randall frowned as his gaze searched the street and he tried to work out what Ellis had warned him about.

Then he saw the dark figure detach from a doorway and saunter toward them, and in the brief gleam of a streetlamp the man's eyes flashed bright and pale.

THIRTY

THERE WERE FOOTSTEPS, but no heartbeat.

Ellis quickly indicated the direction of what was most likely a vampire and had to simply hope that the signal was simultaneously understood by Randall and unnoticed by the newcomer. The way the stranger's steps echoed implied that they were around a corner, but Ellis had no real way of knowing for certain.

Randall's pulse gained pace, and the other person's footsteps came directly toward them now.

Ellis ran the tip of his tongue along his teeth. Tonight was going straight down the toilet.

It was definitely a vampire, and the closer it came the clearer the footsteps grew. For all the stranger knew Randall was a human being, and Ellis had to keep it that way without damning himself in the process.

"Nice night," the stranger started. Male, his voice was surprisingly cultured, like some middle class Sloane Ranger who'd drifted too far east. He sounded a little shorter than Ellis, and had the smoothness of youth to his vocal chords.

He'd likely been in his early twenties when he was turned, but that knowledge told Ellis nothing about the other vampire's actual age.

"Not bad," Ellis agreed. *Not bad; it's shit.*

"Are you lost?"

Randall's body twisted briefly. "What's it to you?"

Ellis smiled inwardly, but kept himself composed. Randall had to have picked up on the signal; that or the vampire was close enough for him to notice the lack of scent. Either way, playing the oblivious card would help maintain the charade.

"Always willing to help point people in the right direction." There was a faint, almost inaudible touch of frustration to the vampire's answer.

Good. He's going to play by the rules. Ellis desperately rifled through the information Barb had shared with him. Had she mentioned Covent Garden? Did she tell him whether it was a safe patch to pass through?

No. She hadn't mentioned it all. Ellis had been so keen to steer her toward his question about sunlight that the only other vampire she'd mentioned was Devitt. They were well away from his patch, but that meant Ellis was blind in more ways than the obvious one now. He had no information, and had been caught trespassing.

"We're heading to Soho," Ellis said. It wasn't strictly untrue: they had to pass through Soho to reach Mayfair from here if they wanted to keep on in a straight line.

"Now why would you go there?" The stranger's voice became a purr, almost threatening.

Did he know about Barb's plans? Was he trying to protect her, or did he view her as a threat? Had Ellis just associated himself with a known troublemaker to someone closely allied with the Council?

God, he *hated* leaving Mayfair.

"It's on the way," Ellis said, pretending that it was nothing more than the next hop of a longer route.

"We just keep heading this way, right?" Randall butted in, body moving with some gesture. "Cut left at the pub, head toward the tube station?"

"And where are you going after that?"

Ellis squinted, but there wasn't nearly enough light to see by. Fine. Well if he was as gossiped about as Barb had said, perhaps he could use that to his advantage. "Mayfair," he said casually. "I live there."

"And this is your..?"

"Friend. I can't get around without a guide, alas." *Yes, that's right. The blind one from Mayfair. The one who kills his enemies.*

He heard the vampire click his tongue. "How kind of him."

"Hey. I'm right here," Randall muttered.

"It would be unfortunate if you failed to reach your destination."

Ellis smiled coldly. "Oh, I won't fail."

Was the vampire considering whether he could get away with killing Randall too? It shouldn't be too hard to justify. Once Ellis was dead he could claim that Randall had known what he and Ellis were and so regrettably the human had to be disposed of too. The man had no way of knowing that to attack Randall - tonight of all nights - was at best a terrible move and at worst a suicidal one.

Then there was the unknown factor of the vampire's power and status. If he had some ability that gave him the edge over Randall in a fight it might not be as clear-cut as Ellis had first thought. If he was on the Council, or Vassal to one of the Council Members, his word might well count for far more than Ellis' if they both survived this encounter.

What a ridiculous thought. Ellis had been yanked out of

open warfare between two werewolf packs, yet here he stood at risk of destruction only a mile or so away from home.

"You seem so sure of that." The vampire didn't hide his sneer. The wazzock probably thought he was superior just because of his accent.

Ellis didn't dare mention Barb. It could be his ticket to a free pass, or it could condemn them all. The risk of exposure was too great. He'd just have to lie and hope it didn't bite him in the arse later.

"Had to go to the office in a hurry," he murmured, hoping this stranger would pick up on the inference. "Didn't have time to arrange something more convenient. You know how it goes." He reached into his pocket. "Tell you what, why don't I call the authorities in and we can waste their time as well?"

It was a gamble. Ellis would be screwing himself more than anyone else if he dragged Hughes all the way up here from Battersea, and he didn't know any other Constables. None of them would lie on his behalf, but they might be willing to escort him off this vampire's territory and back to his own; or they may walk away and leave him to his fate. Sometimes all it took to win a conflict of words was balls the size of a man's head, and Ellis prayed this was one of those times.

"Yes," the stranger hissed. "You turn left at the pub and go down Long Acre, past the tube station."

"Great," Randall chirped. "Thanks, mate."

Ellis could almost feel the other vampire's hatred burn a hole between his shoulders as Randall led him past.

"WHAT THE HELL was all that about anyway?" Randall said once they were past the pub.

Ellis grinned toward him, but said in a resigned tone "Who knows, eh? You Southerners are all bonkers."

"Oi. Walk yourself across town next time you get a late night phone call, eh?"

"Suit yerself." He ran his thumb across Randall's elbow in gratitude and nodded to him.

They had no way of knowing whether they were being followed. In theory the other vampire's hearing would be every bit as good as Ellis' own but there were no guarantees. What if the stranger could turn into a bat, or fog, or could move silently? No. Randall was right to maintain the ruse, and he was getting better at it too. The beat of his heart could easily be taken for fear of getting stabbed by a stranger in a dark street, which any Londoner worth their salt would feel in that situation. He'd been quick on the uptake, and that alone could well have saved them both.

They passed through Soho quickly. Occasionally a neon glare would be bright enough to bring some brief glow of colour into Ellis' life, and he could hear the mixture of late-night clubs alongside the less distinct noises of humans doing the kind of things they did when they found some private space surrounded by sex shops.

By the time they got home, Randall had calmed, and they got up to Ellis' flat before the werewolf said, "Safe?"

"Safe as we can get," Ellis admitted. He shrugged his coat off and hung it, then kissed Randall's cheek. "You were amazing."

Randall huffed. "No, I just did whatever popped into my head."

"Don't sell yourself short." Ellis wandered into the living room. "You've saved my life twice tonight." He flopped onto the couch and nudged his shoes off, then leaned back and closed his eyes.

He just wanted a moment's rest. His body didn't seem to produce adrenaline any more, but terror was still exhausting in its own right, and a little time to settle into safety would be greatly appreciated.

Randall *had* saved his life twice in one night. There was no doubt in Ellis' mind that either pack would have torn into him sooner or later had Randall not lugged him away. Briar seemed to take it on himself to accuse Ellis of causing the fight instead of ever taking a moment to examine his own pack's behaviour, and the threats from the vampire they'd met in Covent Garden were so thinly veiled as to be almost crass.

When had his existence become so fraught? He kept to himself, ran a quiet and inoffensive business, and while he might have been lonely at least he hadn't been threatened by gigantic werewolves or harangued by vampires.

No, that wasn't fair. Jonas had come to try and kill him long before he ever met Randall. His dad would still demand his money back, regardless of whether Ellis was happy. Barnes would still have attempted to stick a knife in him, except without Randall there he would have succeeded. Saving Ellis' life seemed to be Randall's favourite pastime.

"You okay?" Randall came over and sat beside him.

Ellis considered the question. He was alive, and he had the most wonderful man in London by his side. After everything Randall had been through here he was, worrying about Ellis. He smiled slowly. "Aye. Better than okay. I'm good. Thank you." He felt for Randall's thigh and set his hand on it. "How are *you*?"

"I'm fine."

"Don't give me that." Ellis raised his head from the comfort of the couch and opened his eyes. Randall hadn't turned the light on, which was a kindness Ellis appreciated.

"This must be painful for you. If there's anything I can do, tell me."

Randall sighed and slowly leaned into him. Ellis shifted his position and draped an arm around the shorter man's shoulders to draw him close.

"This is all I need," Randall whispered.

"Then I'm happy to provide it," Ellis replied. He pressed his lips to Randall's short, wiry hair.

They sat in silence. Randall sounded as though he had drifted off to sleep now and then, but Ellis remained awake to hold him and stroke his shoulders when he fidgeted.

He could live like this, he reckoned. Randall was worth it.

His stomach convulsed.

Oh god. How long had they been on the couch?

Ellis sprang to his feet. "Sorry," he called after himself. "Sorry. I need-" The spasm wracked his body and he couldn't talk anymore, so he concentrated on his sprint to the bathroom and ignored Randall's sounds of confusion.

He slammed the door after himself, and made it to the sink with seconds to spare.

THIRTY-ONE

RANDALL JERKED awake as Ellis leaped away from him. He groaned as he tried to work out what was going on. Were they under attack? Had they been followed here after all?

Then he heard retching from the bathroom, and everything fell into place.

Ew. *Ew.*

He sat up and rubbed his face. He could hear Ellis brushing his teeth through the recently-slammed bathroom door.

This had to be horrible for him, didn't it? As much as Randall's own reaction had been one of revulsion moments ago, what was Ellis going through? Bad enough that he had to do this in private to maintain the charade of living and breathing - Randall had seen him drink tea and eat food to maintain that illusion of normalcy - but to have an audience for it now? Even in the next room, poor Ellis probably felt lousy enough without Randall adding to the strain by making some insensitive comment when the vampire was ready to emerge.

What should he do? Go ask whether Ellis was okay? No, that'd just hammer home what had happened.

Randall felt his way through to the kitchen instead. He found a cup and poured himself some water, then drank it slowly. He refilled it and worked his way through the second cupful. He'd run a mile or so with Ellis over his shoulder, and then they'd walked all the way from Tower Hamlets to Mayfair, so he needed rehydration.

He placed the cup in the sink. That should have given Ellis plenty of time, he reckoned. He tugged clothes off over his head as he wandered back through to the living room, and laid them over the back of the couch, out of the way where nobody could trip on them. He unfastened his jeans and stepped out of them, added them to the pile, then placed his socks and briefs on top. His brain sluggishly ground itself into gear and his fears for Preeti resurfaced, so he searched his clothes for his phone, only to find a barrage of angry text messages from most of his pack about how they wished he'd never been born. Thankfully Preeti had also answered his question, and wanted to check whether he and Ellis were all right, so he replied to her and ignored the rest.

Thank god for that, at least. If Preeti hadn't responded he didn't know what he'd do. Go over there, he supposed. Try her garage, then her home. Run into Briar. He grimaced and put his phone away. None of that mattered. She was okay, and the rest of them could take a long walk off a short plank.

He walked toward the bedroom, pushed the sheets aside, and got in. Then he waited.

When Ellis came to bed, Randall moved over and drew the duvet up around them both.

"Sorry about that," Ellis whispered.

"It's okay." Randall drew him nearer and nuzzled against his chest. "What are we gonna do about Briar?"

"We could give it another go once everyone's cooled their heels," Ellis mused. He began to relax, and his legs slid against Randall's before entwining with them. "See if they're remotely willing to give diplomacy another try or whether they're dead-set on blood."

"How can you even suggest that the way they've been treating you?" Randall drew his lips across Ellis' soft skin.

Ellis laughed faintly. "If I gave up at every hurdle I ever encountered I wouldn't be here now with the man I love in my arms, would I?"

Randall couldn't object. He was tired and comfortable, and it wouldn't kill him to just once accept that he might actually be good enough for the love of a man like Ellis. "I s'pose not," he mumbled.

"No," Ellis agreed. "And you don't have to be so hard on yourself. I know how you feel."

Randall blinked and pulled back a little, but he couldn't see Ellis in the darkness no matter how hard he tried. "What do you mean?"

"Hm." Ellis rolled onto his back. One of his legs was pulled free by the motion but the other remained sprawled between Randall's as though he were too comfy to move it. "Depends on how willing you are to believe something Zev said to me."

Randall shifted onto his side and draped his arm across Ellis' stomach. "Considering the bloke's handled himself with way more decency than Briar has every time I've seen him, I'm willing to give him a try. Why, what'd he say?"

"He said he knew the difference between an Alpha and any other shifter. Said he knew what elevated anyone to Alpha."

Randall blinked. "Anyone?" he echoed. "Isn't it genetic?"

"Not according to Zev." Ellis rubbed Randall's forearm idly. "He says that the ability to control yourself during the moon's 'gaze' is a gift, and other werewolves can sense that gift. They pick up on it and defer to it. That's how an Alpha can calm his pack down during a full moon: they're drawn to his gift." He hesitated. "His gift is more powerful than his own temper, and so long as his pack respects him and he cares for them it is more powerful than their tempers too. That's why Briar's struggling to control his pack. Few of you stick with him because you care for each other. You stick with him because he's the Alpha, but the real problem is he isn't the Alpha."

"What?" Randall sat up, which prompted Ellis to untangle his right leg. "You've lost me."

"He said that the Alpha's gift is love," Ellis murmured. "You have it, and that's why you can control your temper. It isn't me, Randall, it's you. You feel love strongly enough to push the moon's influence down and regain your senses." His hand brushed across Randall's back. "I reckon Preeti is your pack's Alpha, but both she and Briar are stuck in these ideas of how wolf packs work so they assume he's the one. She's Indian, isn't she?"

"I- what? Yeah." Randall nodded numbly. "Why?"

"I reckon she's got a good, traditional mum somewhere. She speaks Hindi despite being with you lot for all her adult life so she must've learned it as a child. And she agreed her mum'd be disappointed to find she wasn't a vegetarian. She was just a kid when she and Briar found each other. Her dreams pointed her to him. That's such a powerful thing for a teenager, and if he's this big, strong, powerful lad and she's this tiny little thing they might both think that he has to be the one in charge. He's used this weird idea about wolf packs to bully you all these years when you know Omegas aren't a real thing, right?"

"Yeah," Randall breathed.

"Put two people together," Ellis explained. "Make one of them a young girl with a really traditional upbringing and the other one a ballsy young lad who thinks he knows everything because he watched a couple of documentaries. When they meet others like themselves it turns out they can help them stay calm during the full moon. Your pack *believes* Briar is their Alpha, but when he tells you all to calm down he's not alone, is he? No. Preeti's by his side." Ellis paused for breath. "I think you all do it for her," he concluded. "I think she's the Alpha. I think that's why Briar's out of control under this Blood Moon thing: because she's standing by and waiting for him to pull it together and he *can't*."

Randall shook his head. "But if he loves her, that'd make him Alpha anyway, right? Like a proper Alpha Pair?"

"Reckon so, aye," Ellis said. "I reckon that's how everyone's thought it was just him all these years. But what happens when there's a third Alpha in a wolf pack?"

"Well, a proper wolf pack's a family unit. Parents and their offspring. You get mum and dad in charge, and everyone pretty much does as the family needs. The Alpha Pair are usually the only ones who get to mate, and once offspring are adult and sexually mature they'll wander off to go find or form a new pack. It maintains genetic diversity. There's no fighting over it or anything."

"But you lot aren't actually wolves. Maybe there's something in that which explains things, eh?" Ellis sat up slowly and traced down Randall's arm to take his hand. "You're all sexually mature, and none of you are Preeti and Briar's children, but only one of you is in love. Suddenly there's too many Alphas. Briar's got this whole macho thing going on so he sees you as a threat. Your presence weakens his position."

Randall stared toward Ellis. He could almost make out the slight outline of his lover, but nothing more.

What if it was true? What if even only half of it was right?

If Briar was losing his ability because of Randall's presence, did that make it Randall's fault that the cub had been stabbed and sent to hospital?

He sucked in a breath. "Wait. You're saying that's how you know I-" He broke off. "How I feel about you," he finished. "Because I haven't torn your face off?"

Ellis chuckled. "That's if what Zev said is true. But why would he lie about it? Anyway. I think if Preeti took command of your pack they'd all be happier. She's compassionate, that one. Cares about people. Oh aye, she's rough around the edges, but she's honest. Honest people who give a shit are rare as hen's teeth."

Randall rubbed at his scalp, fingernails bumping over his hair. He drew his knees up to his chest and rested his elbows on them. "It can't be that easy, can it?"

The vampire at his side burst out laughing.

Randall huffed. "What's so funny?"

It took Ellis a few moments to calm himself enough to answer. "Since when's love been easy?"

Randall felt behind himself, grabbed a pillow, and smacked Ellis across the chest with it.

"Haha ow! Help! Help, I'm being murdered in my own bed!"

"I'll bloody murder you all right!" Randall smooshed the pillow against him again, trying not to laugh. "You and your bleedin' fortune-cookie words of wisdom. What's next? Nothing worth having was ever easy? Love is not for the weak of heart?"

"Oh, you don't want to get into a Chinese proverbs fight with me!" Ellis wriggled under the pillow and tried to grab it off him, but Randall held it tight. It ended up a playful tug of war, neither of them pulling too hard. "Dig the well before you are thirsty! Failing to plan is planning to fail! Han's mum is full of these, I could go on for hours!"

"I know someone right here who's full of something," Randall snorted.

"I know someone right here who'd *like* to be filled with something," Ellis retorted with a dirty laugh.

Randall's body tingled. His cheeks grew hot. "Ellis!"

"Oh, no. No, you know full well what I'm like, petal. You can't pretend you're shocked now." Ellis released the pillow and grabbed Randall's arm instead.

Randall found himself dragged back down to the bed, and curled against Ellis' body. They lay together, in one another's arms, and Randall allowed his eyes to slowly close.

"I do love you," he finally breathed.

"Aye," Ellis murmured. "I know." He kissed Randall's forehead. "Let's get some sleep, eh?"

"Yeah."

It took a long time to doze off. Randall's mind whirled with what Ellis had said - all Zev's claims - and tried to unpick it all, to find the flaw that meant it couldn't be right.

Because if it was true it meant that Randall was an Alpha, and that was total nonsense.

THIRTY-TWO

THEY WOKE late in the afternoon, and Randall realised he didn't have any clothes at Ellis'. Ellis had given him directions to some clothes shops up around Bond Street, since Randall wasn't going to stick to Mayfair and shell out two digits for a t-shirt or a pair of undies. He picked up a few toiletries, too, since Ellis didn't own a razor or any shaving foam.

He grabbed something to eat on the way back, and they'd showered and lazed about on the couch together, then taken Tiberius out for a walk. Ellis stayed under the shade of a tree and it seemed to mitigate some of the sun's damage while Randall threw a ball for the German Shepherd.

It was almost everything Randall had imagined a normal life could be. They'd laughed together, kissed beneath the bare branches of a tree in Berkeley Square Gardens, then gone back to Ellis' flat and idled around checking emails and schedules. That they'd both come close to dying the night before seemed a whole world away.

In the time since they'd been back at the flat, Randall had reached a decision.

"I'd like to tell Jay," he said.

Ellis paused at his desk and tilted his head toward him. "Tell him what?"

"What I am. If I'm going to be hanging around you all the time I'm going to bump into him and I don't want him thinking I shopped you to Preeti the way he does."

Ellis swivelled his chair back and forth, his lips pursed. "Aren't you kind of dropping Preeti in it by doing that?"

"Jay can keep a secret." Randall nodded. "He keeps yours, and you trust him, right?"

"Aye."

"Then I think I'd like him to know. I don't fancy getting the cold shoulder off him for the rest of my life."

Ellis smirked. "You're thinking long-term, eh?"

"Well, I, er... I mean, uh, I just-" Randall stammered.

The smirk became a teasing grin. "Uh huh. Just admit it. You want to stick around because you *loooove* me."

"God, you're such an arsehole!" Randall bit his lip. "Remind me what I see in you?"

"Great hair."

"Oh, yeah. That's it!" He stood up and went over to nudge Ellis' shoulder, but wound up leaning over to kiss him instead. "So what do you reckon?"

Ellis leaned back and faced Randall. "I reckon it's up to you, petal. Whatever you choose, I'm with you all the way."

Randall braced his bum against Ellis' desk and crossed his arms. "You still think we should give it one last go with Zev and Briar?"

Ellis sighed faintly. "I think we have to try. And if what Zev says is true, and my guess about Briar and Preeti is right, maybe we can help them come to understand the friction and deal with it too. Everyone gets to walk away happy. Even better, if Zev's information helps Briar's pack sort their issues out, hopefully in the longer term they can become... not necessarily friends, but allies at least."

Randall considered it. Ellis had good points, and Randall dearly wanted to pick Zev's brain at some point about his claims. Being able to have a line of communication with him in the future would be worth the aggravation now if it bore fruit the way Ellis suggested.

"I agree." He moved his knee to rest it against Ellis' thigh. "Let's wait for your new employee to knock off, then go bring Jay up to speed. At least then he'll know what it was all about if anything happens to us, eh?"

Ellis rubbed his stubble thoughtfully. "Good point."

"Right. Sounds like a plan."

The world felt a little less terrifying with a plan.

JAY STARED at him in stony silence.

Randall shifted his weight uncomfortably and glanced to Ellis, who had his lips pressed tight together.

Ellis had explained most of it, with Randall filling in the occasional detail, and Jay had gone through anger, disbelief, bitchiness, a moment's sulk, and now he seemed to have settled on irritation. For such a slight, lanky thing, the lad had a surprising force of personality when he applied it, and all of it felt like it was being applied to Randall's face through that stare.

"What I don't like," Jay said at last, "is that you two idiots have been putting yourself in harm's way without even telling me."

"It wasn't my-"

"Secret to tell, I know," Jay cut Ellis off. "I get that. But you-" he pointed at Randall "-have to be his-" the finger swung toward Ellis "-common sense, because he gets ideas into his head-"

"-Oh like you've never-" Ellis interjected.

"This isn't about me-"

"What about the time you-"

"Oi, oi! Not in front of Randall!"

Randall sighed. "Guys, can we just focus for a minute?"

Ellis and Jay stopped their bickering and turned their attention back on him. He felt like an ant under the magnifying glass of petulant schoolboys.

"The whole point of this is so we can move forward, innit?" He rolled his shoulders slowly. "And part of that is the fact that we're going to go try to get these people to talk to each other one last time, but if it goes wrong we wanted you to know what had happened."

Jay frowned and slouched in his chair. "And what if you don't come back, either of you?"

"You have my spare key," Ellis said quietly. "If you could pick up Tiberius and take care of him, I'd appreciate it."

Jay's frown turned into a scowl. "Will you stop talking like you're going to die?"

Ellis smiled tightly, but there wasn't any mirth to it. "It's a very real possibility."

"Then don't go!"

"Does he ever back down from things he's decided to do?" Randall asked.

Jay glowered at him, then hopped out of his chair and went to fill the kettle. "No," he grumbled. "Fine. Yes. You know I'll take care of Tiberius if anything happens. But you two better promise me you'll do your best, okay? I can't be dealing with losing you. I've got plans for the weekend and everything."

"Oh, areet, well. Wouldn't want to spoil your plans." Ellis' smile slowly softened.

"Good. And you, Randall, better make sure he doesn't. Because I am going to eat pizza and overdose on all the Star Wars films with my husband, and I won't have you two ruining it, okay?"

Randall dragged his index finger across his ribcage. "Cross my heart, Jay."

Jay huffed, then pulled down mugs from the cupboard. "Tea?"

Randall nodded and pulled his phone out. "Yeah, please."

While he waited, he typed and re-typed a text to Briar until he was happy with it enough to send it.

Ellis and I will be at THCP at 10PM. Willing to try negotiating one last time. Come unarmed or don't come at all.

RANDALL FOUND A TAXI WITH EASE. Mayfair was their natural habitat, it seemed, but then Ellis' gallery was right beside one of the city's most prestigious hotels - the staff entrance, sure, but it meant that there were plenty of cabs roaming the night hunting for fresh wallets to devour.

Ellis wedged himself in the corner once Randall worked out the driver's most likely field of view, and they sat quietly to avoid drawing his attention. Once they were at Tower Hamlets, Ellis slipped out again while Randall paid.

"What if they don't happen to hang around in this one rotten park all night, every night?" Ellis whispered as they approached the squeaky gate.

"That's fine," Randall said. "Contacting them should be fairly easy."

Ellis lifted his head, eyebrows quirked in curiosity.

"Well, you know." Randall cleared his throat. "Wolves."

It took Ellis a few moments, then his lips parted in understanding.

Randall held the gate open, and soon they walked across the gravel on their way to the thick, dark tree-line. He steered Ellis onto the grass as soon as he could to minimise their noise, but doing so slowed them down as always.

"What if people hear wolves howling in the middle of London?" Ellis finally asked.

"I think this time of night most people will assume it's a dog. We don't do it often, 'cause it'd get suspicious if people heard it like every other night, but once in a while is okay. It's just a communication thing anyway, and a pack that sticks together doesn't need it. One that splits up can use phones instead." Randall peered ahead into the dark, but couldn't discern any movement other than the idle sway of bare branches and dead ivy ahead of those few evergreens which provided more shelter further into the park.

Ellis head dipped briefly. "Well, you might have to do it tonight. I don't hear them."

"You just want to get me naked in a park." Randall grinned.

"Maybe I do." Ellis laughed lightly. "But if I were after that I'd likely as not come all the way out here for it, eh?"

Randall snorted and came to a halt where they'd been last night. The undergrowth was trampled and torn, but it was messy enough to begin with and hard to work out the extent of the damage or the fight. "Can you smell blood?" he asked Ellis.

Ellis inhaled through his nose, then said, "Aye. Not much, though, and it's well dried now. Probably nothing more than a few scrapes or bloodied noses."

"That's good." Randall sighed. "If they broke it up before it got serious then hopefully nobody's got a grudge to bear." He unzipped his jacket and laid it over a gravestone, then pulled the t-shirt off over his head. Shifting into his wolf body while dressed wasn't impossible, but it made changing back again a pain in the arse until he'd shrugged out of everything, so he stripped as quickly as he could while occasionally batting Ellis' hand away from his backside. "Stop it," he laughed.

Ellis grinned. "What'm I supposed to do while you're stripping off next to me, eh? Cruel and unusual punishment that is."

"My heart bleeds," Randall deadpanned.

He stood on the ground with bare feet and felt the brittle plants and dry mud underfoot. Then he began the change. Fur prickled through his skin and his hips realigned. His spine curved his body forward. The world around him became clearer, sharper, even as it lost some colour. Now he could see, as he fell onto all fours, that they were truly alone in the park. He detected the scents of the two packs and saw how they intermingled and separated, especially those who had been in their wolf bodies: the scent glands in their paws left a trail that was clear as daylight. The splatters of blood invisible to his human eyes stood out like flares of colour to his sensitive nose.

The fight hadn't lasted long. He prowled the area, looking back to Ellis now and then to check that he was all right, and worked out the sequence of events from first punch through to the places where shifters on both sides had quickly dragged the rest of their pack out of the fight. Preeti, he wasn't surprised to find, had managed to pull Briar from a brawl with three of the other pack while Zev pushed his own people to disengage.

The other pack had lingered longer, but only another hour or so. They had re-scented the park before they left.

"Y'areet?" Ellis murmured.

"Rr."

"Good." The vampire nodded.

Randall hopped up onto a moss-covered crypt that had partially sunk into the earth, and faced east. He filled his lungs with the crisp, faintly salted air, then howled at the sky for all he was worth.

It felt weirdly satisfying. Natural. *Right*. He called out to any who would listen. He sang his peaceful presence to the moon and it sang back to him, stirring the wolf that he so rarely listened to.

The wolf was pleased.

THIRTY-THREE

IT WAS a good half hour or so before anyone else arrived. Randall had changed back and got dressed, then he and Ellis had sat on the wonky crypt while they waited.

Ellis' head tipped toward the trees. "Someone's here."

"Is it them?" Randall hopped off the cold stone.

"Can't tell. There's-" He paused. "Ten? Eleven. None talking. Seems strange behaviour if it *isn't* them."

Randall touched Ellis' arm and waited for the vampire to take his elbow. "You okay getting down?"

"Aye." Ellis slid forward until his toes found the earth, then he stood and brushed dirt off his trousers. "Good luck, eh?"

Randall shook his head. "You're doing the hard work, not me."

Ellis didn't answer him, and now Randall could hear the approach himself: undergrowth crunching under boots and snagging in clothing; twigs creaking or snapping altogether under the weight.

Zev stepped forward warily, and Randall's heart sank. The Alpha had a short baton in his right hand, black and dull, hard to see until he was close enough. Randall looked between the others as they emerged from the dark of the trees, and they were almost all armed: batons, knives, even a heavy and vicious-looking chain. One who wasn't armed crouched to pick up a chunk of stone bigger than his own fist.

Randall swallowed his own words before they could break free. Anything he said could be taken the wrong way by people who didn't understand him.

Zev spoke to Ellis, and his voice was as unsure as his body language. Did he think this was a trap? If so, why had he brought fewer people with him than the night before? Surely if he suspected a trap it would be better to arrive with overwhelming numbers?

Ellis answered. His hands danced gently as he spoke. He looked calm and relaxed; confident, even.

Did he even know that they were armed?

Randall chewed his lip and kept watch as people paced back and forth, or weighed the weapons in their hands. But they were holding back. That was good. It *had* to be good, because there was nobody there to distract them if they kicked off. Ellis and Randall were their only available targets.

Zev tucked the baton into his belt and patted the air toward those behind him. The one with the stone tossed it back down to the ground, and half of the others sheathed knives or pocketed their own batons. Four, though, kept their weapons in hand.

"Yes," Zev finally said.

For a surreal moment Randall half-wondered whether he'd been around them long enough to learn Bangla by osmosis.

"But I didn't want Briar's lot to know this," Zev continued. He eyeballed Randall as he spoke.

"Wait, what?" Randall snapped his head up. "You speak English?"

Ellis pressed his lips together grimly. "Why not?" he asked of Zev.

"Because Briar's a dick. We didn't want anything to do with him or his crazy pack. No offence," he added to Randall. "I thought it was better to make like none of us spoke English and he'd just fuck off and leave us alone, but no. I underestimated the level of batshit there."

Randall's anger flared. "You-" Words failed him. Zev's accent was pure East End. There wasn't any hint that he was anything other than a Londoner, born and bred. "We dragged Ellis all the way over here, put him in danger, all because of your bullshit! Why didn't you just talk to us?"

"How the hell was I supposed to know that you had some gay vampire boyfriend tucked away who was like a bloody Babel fish, eh?" Zev planted his hands on his hips. "How does that even work, anyway? Is it a vampire thing?"

Ellis tugged his glasses off and rubbed the bridge of his nose. "Christ," he sighed. "No, it isn't. Well, it is, but only for me. Every vampire's power is different, and we keep it a closely-guarded secret."

Randall glanced to him at the half-truth, but Ellis slid his glasses back on to hide his expression.

"So I would really appreciate it," Ellis added wearily, "if you could keep this to yourselves."

"None of my business," Zev said. "But Briar's got a real mad-on for you. If this is some secret he can use against you, he will. He strikes me as an arsehole that way."

"And most other ways," grumbled the woman to his left.

Zev grunted in agreement.

"You speak English," Randall breathed. His anger slowly faded to irritation. He couldn't really blame them for wanting to stay out of Briar's way, though he wasn't sure Briar was as bad as Zev made him out to be. Not *that* sure. Briar's behaviour lately had put that idea to the test, but if it really was some combination of the Blood Moon with Randall's presence...

"You claim an Alpha's gift comes from being in love, yeah?" Randall frowned.

"Ah, he told you?" Zev grinned, white teeth a quick flash in the dark. "Yeah. It does."

"How do you know?" Randall glanced to the pack, then back to Zev. "Why are you so sure?"

Zev flexed his shoulders and straightened his back. "You're human-born, ain't't'cha?"

"Yeah, of cour-" Randall broke off.

That wasn't a question any shifter he knew ever had to ask.

"Holy shit," he breathed. "Your mum was a shifter?"

"Mum and dad. Still are, but they're out Ilford way." He turned and picked out a woman behind him, pointing to her. "That's my sister Ameera, and that-" his finger swung toward a man shorter than himself, "-is my brother, Hasan." He turned to Randall. "When two wolf shifters mate, their children are always wolf shifters. It's when they start mixing with humans that it becomes unpredictable. Human-borns can come from one shifter parent, or a grandparent, or as a total damn surprise if the interbreeding came so long ago nobody knows who it was."

"Oh my god." Randall stared. He couldn't help it. "That's amazing! You have-" Tears welled up in his eyes.

They had family who understood. They knew who and what they were, and always had. They'd been *raised* as shifters, by parents who had been raised the same way. The oral tradition alone was invaluable! The stories, the knowledge they had, their experience...

"Randall?" Ellis said softly. He rubbed Randall's arm to comfort him.

"'S fine." Randall rubbed at his eyes and sniffed. "Just, uh. It's all a bit weird."

Zev smiled sadly. "We've got some lost cubs. I understand what you are going through, and I'm sorry. We saved who we could, but we've been further east than this most of the time."

"You're expanding?"

"Fact of life." Zev shrugged. "We need space just like anyone else. The more of us, the more space. Sooner or later we'll break into smaller packs. That's nature, nothing to fear."

Randall rubbed his forearm. "I'd really like to talk some time. Learn more about what you know, if that's okay?"

Zev smiled to him. "I think that would be good for you, yes."

Ellis' head snapped around and he held a hand up. "Five people," he whispered. "At the gate." He paused, then nodded. "Briar and the others."

Randall grimaced. "We should go. If he's after you he'll be pissed off to find you here."

"We're getting somewhere, though," Ellis answered. He faced Randall again. "This is important. We should at least see if Briar's willing to talk."

Zev's fingers drifted to his baton, but he didn't pull it out. "I agree," he said softly.

"We did invite them," Ellis added. "If we clear off they'll be convinced it was a trap."

Zev sighed. "Most likely. The man's a fool, but a sharp one. He can leap to stupid conclusions with prodigious speed."

Randall's heart sank. "I know what conclusion he'll leap to here." At Zev's raised brow he added "You're all loaded for bear."

"They keep bringing knives," Zev reasoned.

"Yeah." Randall's nails dug into his palms. "But I told him

to come unarmed this evening. He's going to see you lot and think we've screwed him."

"They're almost here," Ellis hissed.

Randall could hear them now: the crackle of tearing undergrowth and the snap of dry stems. They didn't speak, didn't argue among themselves. Were they under control at last? Calm? Because they wouldn't be when they got here and saw Zev's lot bristling with gear.

He knew *exactly* what conclusion Briar was about to leap to.

Zev hissed something in Bangla and every armed shifter hurried back to the trees to be swallowed by the darkness.

"It would be better for everyone," Zev whispered to Randall, "if you would step up and lead your pack."

Randall stared at him. "You're mad."

Zev snorted. "You and Ellis are in love. The moon knows it. You are the master of your own wolf, and you have the compassion to be master of theirs too. You should-" His gaze focused past Randall's shoulder and he shut his mouth.

"Well," said Briar. "You're all looking pretty fucking cozy."

THIRTY-FOUR

"YOU CAME," Randall said. It was redundant, he knew, but he had to say something to try and defuse things before the powder keg was fully lit.

"Oh yeah." Briar bared his teeth. "Can't have you lot gallivanting around behind my back, can I? Though it looks like you've already done it."

Ellis' hand slid to his wrist, and Briar snarled at the movement.

"He's just checking the time." Randall spoke quickly in case Briar decided it was something worth attacking for.

Ellis raised his hands slowly, one hand holding back the sleeve over his watch to show that was indeed what he had been doing. "Aye," he said softly. "And it occurs to me that you came late because that gives you a handy excuse, doesn't it?"

Randall watched in horror as Briar's expression shifted to triumphant.

"You did this deliberately," he realised.

Briar hadn't come to talk. He'd come late to 'catch' the 'traitors' collaborating together.

"You two have stabbed us in the back," Briar said. There was a grotesque calm to him. "It's about time you all-"

Zev's people emerged from the trees. They advanced slowly, weapons in hand. Hasan dipped to scoop up his abandoned chunk of gravestone.

Briar's glee turned Randall's stomach.

"Knives?" Briar howled with laughter. "Stones? What are you? *Children?*"

Briar's skin rippled and his dark fur pushed through. His body twisted and warped, gaining mass, growing in every way. His clothes tore and seams ripped apart.

"No," Randall whimpered. "Oh, god no."

Briar wasn't taking his wolf shape.

He was going to war.

The Alpha's monstrous body towered over everyone present. Claws sprouted from his fingers which were as long and sharp as the knives Zev's pack carried. His massive head bore jaws large and powerful enough to bite the door off a taxi, and the bright yellow of his eyes conveyed nothing more than sheer malevolence.

Briar threw back his head and howled, and his pack shed their human skins at his command.

Ellis clutched Randall's arm in terror. "What's happening?" he hissed.

Randall couldn't find the words. *Shit. Shit's happening.*

Zev's people broke out of their own bodies. In a matter of seconds Randall and Ellis were the only human-shaped creatures remaining in the park. Everything that surrounded them was easily twice Randall's size.

Overhead the red moon hung low and large, an omen Randall wished he had listened to.

He didn't stand a chance of defending Ellis against them.

Not in this body. Hell, probably not in his own halfway body, but it was all he had.

"Get down," he snarled at Ellis.

He shucked his jacket and changed.

"Randall!" Ellis screamed.

Randall shoved Ellis toward the ground, his hand so massive now that it spanned the suddenly-small vampire's shoulders. Ellis fell face-first into the dirt, and Randall crouched over him to shield him with his body.

Ellis got his hands under himself and pushed his head up. Randall pressed down to keep him from getting off the ground, and started to drag him toward the crooked crypt, but Ellis grabbed at his arm instead. Then he froze as he clutched fur and muscle instead of cloth and skin.

"Urrrhhh," Randall rumbled. *Get down.*

Ellis nodded weakly and let go, then wedged himself up against the stone.

The air thrummed with howls and snarls, thuds and rips. Wood splintered and cracked. Randall hunkered over Ellis' prone body and raised his head to peek over the edge of the grave.

It was carnage.

The park was filled with monsters: massive, powerful creatures whose sole purpose was to bring death to their enemies. Randall only recognised a handful of them, and of those Briar towered head and shoulders above the rest.

Claws slashed through fur and flesh. Muscle and blood were sprayed across the night sky. He saw Nazim plough into a body and tear out a mass of intestine which trailed after his fist like string. Briar wrenched the arm off one of the monsters and wielded it like a club against the next, smacking her across the face with it even as it shrank back to a human limb. Blood streaked across Lara's pale fur, marking her with darkness.

Randall ducked his head and stared at Ellis' small, petrified body. He looked like prey.

Randall lowered his muzzle and sniffed the creature huddled beneath him, but it didn't smell of much other than the faded scents of toothpaste and soap. The look on its face was that of a predator, in spite of its evident fear. It looked hungry.

He looked hungry.

Randall groaned and struggled to remember. This was Ellis. His name was *Ellis*, and Randall loved him.

The scent of blood was thick. God, no wonder Ellis looked like a starving man at a buffet. He'd said he could detect the faintest trace of blood, and now the damn stuff was everywhere around them.

Shit.

What if Ellis couldn't control himself any more than the shifters busy trying to kill each other could?

Something slammed into his side, and Randall roared in fury. He rounded on the creature and recognised Jim.

Motherfucker! Jim had attacked him! All the other damn werewolves around and Jim had come for-

He'd come for Ellis.

Randall reared up and swung his claws at Jim's face with a ferocious roar. Jim sprang back and Randall's blow landed against his ribs instead to draw vicious wounds across them. His claws came away caked with blood and fur, and Jim launched himself at Randall.

This wasn't sustainable. If the shifters had gone at each other with batons and blades they'd heal quickly and be at it all night, but with teeth and claws death became the only possible outcome unless the fight ended fast. They healed too slowly from these wounds and there was plenty of time to compound one injury with another until even a shifter's body couldn't take it anymore.

Jim raked claws over Randall's side and Randall flung himself to the ground to prevent them getting into his abdomen, but Jim followed and landed on him like a freight train.

Randall elbowed him in the nose. Jim screamed, so Randall did it again, then rammed his knee into Jim's bollocks.

Jim's indignant squawk matched the wild look of outrage in his eyes, so Randall jabbed his knee in again, then shoved Jim aside and rolled out from under the curling body.

The pain wouldn't last. Jim would heal whatever damage Randall had done him, so Randall used the few seconds he'd bought to crouch back over Ellis. He snarled possessively and raised his hackles at Jim.

Try me. I dare you.

Try to take him from me.

Then something changed. There was a peculiar lull in the fighting. Randall didn't dare take his gaze off Jim, but Jim sensed it too, and turned away from him.

A mournful howl broke across the abandoned graveyard, and it was joined by two… three… five more. Then even more, the voices merging into a sorrowful song of loss that prickled Randall's skin.

Someone had died.

The howling changed. It mutated into something more. A song for the dead, and a cry for vengeance.

Randall stared at Ellis as the vampire tried to bury himself further against the unyielding stone.

This was it. Randall would lose everything he'd ever loved, and then if that wasn't enough, he'd lose himself too.

It would all be over soon.

THIRTY-FIVE

RANDALL SHRANK BACK to his human shape and placed a hand on Ellis' shoulder. "It's me," he breathed.

"Randall." Ellis grasped at his forearm, his relief only a momentary thing.

"I'm so sorry."

Ellis shook his head. "Stop them. Oh, god, there's so much blood. Stop them!"

"I can't!"

"You're an Alpha!" Ellis' grip tightened, and Randall caught sight of the tips of his fangs as he spoke.

"I'm not-"

"You are the *only* werewolf here in control of himself!" Ellis snarled. "You have to stop them! They're going to tear each other to pieces!" He turned his head, then groaned. "No."

The howls broke apart and the ground shook with the force of a charge. Randall risked a peek over the lip of the stone and saw the two packs rush toward each other for another go of it. Ellis was right: they were going to kill each other if nothing stopped them.

He couldn't do it. They wouldn't do as he said. He wasn't an Alpha.

His gaze fell to one of the bodies on the ground, still and torn.

Zev.

"Oh god," he whispered. Without their Alpha, Zev's pack would keep on until they were exhausted or dead.

He couldn't do it. But he wouldn't be able to look himself in the eye ever again if he didn't try.

Randall planted his hands on the crypt and vaulted up onto it. The stone chilled the soles of his bare feet, and as he stood he felt horribly exposed. Even as he raised himself up on the old stone the beasts towered over him.

He felt blood trickle down his side, a slow but inexorable river that reached his thigh before it dried and stuck to him like a stain.

"Everyone, listen," he said weakly.

Beneath the stampede, he caught a glimpse of Preeti's body, limp and tiny. Her naked human shape was-

Lost to him in the press of bodies.

"Preeti!" he screamed.

"Randall!" Ellis yelled up at him. "End this!"

He wasn't an Alpha. Oh *fuck*, what was he doing here? They were like dogs, fighting and yowling at each other in hatred and fear.

Like dogs.

They needed a diversion, something unexpected to capture their attention. With dogs he'd clap his hands or hiss at them, but that wouldn't work on intelligent, thinking, rational creatures.

There wasn't anything rational out there among the graves. Randall had felt it himself when Ellis had been beneath him - he'd almost forgotten who he was and why he was there, almost mistaken Ellis for something to be hunted and killed and eaten.

The moon was mocking him.

Why hadn't he taken Preeti's warnings seriously?

Randall cupped his hands and clapped so loudly that the sting hurt like hell. He clapped three times, paused, then clapped again.

"Listen to me!" He spoke with all the calm that he could muster.

He didn't shout. His voice was firm, but yelling was Briar's way and Briar's way had failed.

"Listen to me," he said again. He let his hands fall to his sides. "I know that you can hear me. I know that you can understand me. I know there have been losses." His throat closed and his eyes stung and he had to push past that or lose whatever ground he may have gained. "There will be more unless you do as I say. Listen to me."

Briar snarled and broke from the fighting. He limped toward the gate, blood flowing from several gaping wounds, and soon Nazim was on his heels.

What remained of Zev's pack started after them.

"No," Randall said firmly. "Stop."

Two did. They blinked at him.

"Stop," he said again, a little more loudly. "Wait here. Let them go."

A third turned toward him and bared fangs the size of fingers.

Randall raised his chin. "Calm," he stated. "You don't want to do this. You are people. You can choose to stop. Come here."

Two more stumbled to a halt, and the last raced onward toward the gravel, his fury far too strong for Randall to cut through with simple words. There had to be something else at play.

Randall had nothing left to do but guess at the shifter's identity. "Hasan!" he called. "If you go out onto the street you will be seen, and you will reveal us all, and that is *not* what your brother would have wanted."

Hasan faltered.

"Please. Come back here. What we do right now could help us heal, or it could destroy us all. If they want to run naked through the streets, let them, but at least they had the sense to change bodies first." Randall drew breath. "Let go, Hasan. Your pack needs you."

Ameera was the first to shrink back into her human shape. Tears made her eyes glossy and ran tracks down her cheeks. "He's right," she sobbed. "This isn't what Zev wanted. None of this."

Others slowly sank down from their monstrous forms. Fur receded, replaced by skin and blood.

Hasan snarled and raked at the ground, then turned back to Randall and shrank as he walked toward him.

Randall jumped off the grave and landed on something sharp. It cut into his foot and he hissed, then healed, and he approached Ameera as though she was a wounded animal. For all he knew she may well be, although she seemed to have little more than scratches. It didn't matter whether her skin was intact. She'd lost a brother.

And Randall had lost a sister.

He couldn't think about that now. He didn't dare squander whatever scrap of authority they'd invested in him. Instead he came to Ameera and offered her his arms.

She stared up at him, and then fell crying against his chest, and Randall held her.

Behind Ameera, Preeti's body gazed sightlessly up at the moon.

THEY HAD to bury the dead.

Nobody wanted to. They wanted time to mourn and to say goodbye, and Randall had to be the one to deny them their grief. He had to stand up in front of strangers and order them to dig graves and put their family in the mud because otherwise the corpses of people carved up by giant animals would draw too much attention.

Ellis sat hunched on the stone that had probably kept him alive the entire evening. His knees were pulled tight against his chest, and his arms were wrapped around them to keep them there. He'd heard every single heart until it stopped beating, and Randall couldn't spare one minute to comfort him.

This, then, was the burden of an Alpha.

After all the noise, the howling and screaming, they wouldn't be able to carry a single body out of here without getting caught, so smuggling eight out was impossible. The dead would have to rot in unmarked graves and maybe in a few years an anonymous tip-off could see their remains re-interred somewhere more decent, but for now the secrets their corpses held had to go away.

Wolves dug between the trees while human shapes scoured the park to collect every last shred of clothing. Keys, phones, wallets and anything else that could identify the bodies were stripped from the material and gathered together in a pile by Ellis' side, which the vampire studiously ignored.

Randall helped carry the bodies to their final resting places. Those he knew were outnumbered by those he didn't.

"I'm sorry," he whispered as they lay Zev into the cold ground. All of his knowledge and experience lay with him, wasted.

Randall brushed tears from his eyes and fetched Jim's wretched body. The man hadn't been Randall's friend, but he wouldn't ever have wished this on him.

"Police," Ellis said quietly.

Randall glanced over to him. "How far?"

"Hard to say. Five minutes? Six? Depends on if they know to come straight here."

Randall's jaw flexed at the inference. Humans might have placed calls to complain about noise, but Briar or Nazim might have put in a tip-off and named the park itself.

"All right." He gestured to the wolves. "Bury, quickly. We're out of time."

They kicked mud over the bodies fast, and Randall went back to fetch Preeti.

She was so light. So fragile.

This woman had saved his mum's life. She'd saved Kieran's, too. She'd helped Randall find the job that he loved, and she'd intervened whenever the pack's bullying grew too much to bear.

She should have been their Alpha, and instead he was putting her into the dirt like rubbish to be ashamed of.

"Randall." Ellis' voice was soft. He hadn't moved from his seat, yet he knew.

Randall didn't doubt that Ellis could hear his crying.

Ameera placed her hand on Randall's shoulder. "We must hurry," she reminded him softly.

Randall gathered his wits and hurried to the grave that awaited the body in his arms, and he lay it down as though afraid of waking her.

"Three minutes," Ellis said. "At best."

Randall hurried to help push dirt and other detritus over the evidence, and then he gestured to the pile on the crypt. "Everyone take something and go."

Ellis tilted his head toward Randall as the shifters rushed over to grab whatever they could. "You have to go with them," he said flatly.

"I have to get you home," Randall said. There was no way the vampire could travel safely from here without someone to guide him. He had no dog, no stick, and he didn't know his way around.

"You have to lead your pack," Ellis countered.

Randall froze.

"Randall, these people need you. The moon's still up there, isn't it?"

"Yes, but-"

"Go with them. They need you. You have to protect them now."

Ameera clenched her jaw. "We need an Alpha," she agreed, her voice raw.

"And that's you, Randall. One minute now. Go while you still can."

"What about you?" Randall insisted.

"I can't run with wolves, petal. Take them to safety."

Randall wanted to argue. Ellis was being ridiculous. Briar's pack never ran through the streets in their wolf shapes, not in numbers. It was too risky.

He looked around at the shifters, all waiting for his next command. Not a single one of them had a scrap of clothing left on them. They'd have to be wolves to escape this without getting arrested.

Ellis knew they were naked. He knew they had to shift to get away. That was what he'd meant. He couldn't run with wolves.

Randall snarled in frustration and leaned in to kiss Ellis' cheek. "I will find you," he insisted.

"I'll be all right. Go."

Randall turned away and fell to all fours, and the other shifters around him did the same. They took what they could carry between their jaws, and ran through the park as the screaming of the police sirens reached his ears.

THIRTY-SIX

Everything reeked of blood. Ellis' fangs refused to retreat even though he hadn't been hungry earlier. But then there had been fighting, and the blood...

It dug into his brain, into his stomach. There was too much of it. Too much, and it was too fresh, and it had been all that he could do to stay on the ground where Randall had shoved him.

It terrified him. Through all the carnage, through the stuttering halts to heartbeats to the sickening rattles of final breaths, Ellis had grown fixated on the blood.

He wanted it. He needed it.

Just a little.

Nobody would notice.

By the time Randall cleared the pack out of the park, the driving need had begun to ebb, but he couldn't get his fangs to retreat. The smell lingered, seductive and wet.

The sirens niggled at him.

Ellis jerked his head up and listened. They'd come soon. They'd come, and if they entered the park he didn't know what he'd do, or if he'd be able to stop himself if a fresh, warm body came as close as Randall had done moments ago.

Jesus, poor Randall. People he'd known all his adult life had died, all because Ellis had insisted there could be a diplomatic answer. What a bloody idiot he'd been. He didn't know a damn thing about shifters and he'd thought that if Randall was so quickly and easily calmed in spite of all his superstitious-seeming fear about the moon, the rest of them could be too. Not that Ellis had been ready to use quite the same methods, but he'd at least hoped that Preeti was indeed an Alpha and her latent talent could be put to use.

Too late now.

He unfurled his legs and slowly lowered himself off the crypt. The squeak of the gate was his only navigational aid, and he began to walk toward it. Each step was a nightmare. The undergrowth was like so many grasping hands and it clung to his shoes and the legs of his trousers. Then he found why Randall had steered him in a zig-zag on the way here when he banged his shin hard against a gravestone.

"Fuck!" He clamped his mouth shut and rubbed at his leg.

Briar had escaped. He'd heard him run off like the bloody coward that he was. His steps had been uneven, so he'd been injured. If he was so injured that he couldn't walk properly when he left then there was most likely blood, and Briar would have been able to see and avoid all these stupid sodding lumps of stone in Ellis' path.

He breathed in.

There were two blood trails near him. They called to him, like sirens on a distant shore. He staggered toward them and hit two more gravestones on the way, but then he was on the trails and following them. He fell twice, but that just brought him closer to the blood, and when he scrambled back to his feet it led him on until he reached gravel, and then the gate itself.

Sirens screamed past, the echoes of them reverberating off the buildings and drilling into Ellis' brain. *God*, they hurt! He stood and prayed that they hadn't seen him, then moments later he slipped free of the gate and stalked away up the street. One hand trailed along the railing until he reached a wall, and then dragged over the wall too. The brickwork was new, and the mortar didn't crumble under his touch. He walked, arm outstretched, as fast as he dared. He felt brick give way to wood, then the glass of windows. More brick. A door.

The blood trail crossed the street, but Ellis didn't. If he followed the shifters they'd take great pleasure in tearing him apart and the only way he could defend himself was to kill his attacker.

Assuming they didn't kill him first.

Slowly, reluctantly, his fangs began to withdraw. His gums itched with the movement, then he was in control again.

In control, but completely lost.

JAY FOUND HIM. He always did.

Ellis sank into the back of the cab while Jay gave the driver his address. He was exhausted both physically and emotionally, and wished he could sleep.

"You scared the living daylights out of me," Jay whispered. "Where's Randall?"

"I don't know." Ellis closed his eyes and tried to forget everything he'd heard tonight. "He's okay. He's not hurt. But he had to go."

Jay sucked air through his teeth. "He left you?"

"I made him do it, Jay. I'll explain when we get home." He sighed. "I'm sorry to wake you in the middle of the night."

"As if I could sleep anyway." Jay huffed.

Ellis nodded grimly.

He'd made it all the way to Mile End Road by the time Jay got to him. It had been harrowing. He'd crossed small streets and tripped up steep kerbs, always heading away from that damnable gate's metal squeals. The sirens had driven back and forth before they cut out, but that didn't mean the police had left the area, just that they'd stopped the racket to avoid waking the entire borough. When Ellis found a street with a wide pavement he had stopped by the kerb and texted Jay, then waited around half an hour before his assistant pulled up beside him and hauled him into the taxi. Every passing car, every set of footfalls, every little creak or heartbeat or drunkard had set his nerves on edge. Would this be the police? Was it Briar? A vampire? A mugger?

The car dropped them near Ellis' flat. Jay paid, then escorted him inside and up the stairs.

"You should get back to Han," Ellis mumbled.

"Not until I know what happened." Jay steered him into the flat and closed the door.

Ellis heard the click of the lights, and he reached for the wall to orient himself, then headed for his living room. He just about managed to kick his shoes off before he curled up on the sofa. "They fought," he said wearily. "Some died. Preeti died."

Jay held his breath, then blurted, "Oh my god."

Ellis drew his legs up to his chest and hugged them. He explained what had happened. Everything from their arrival and the conversation with Zev, to Briar's return and what had led from that. He tried not to be too detailed, but that didn't stop the memories welling up inside him, and he clung tighter to his knees.

"Oh, sweetie." Jay's words were little more than a sigh. "Take some time off. I can handle the gallery. Christy's a quick learner, we'll be fine, okay? But you and Randall, you need to be there for each other, so don't you dare show up at the office tomorrow."

"What about your Star Wars marathon?" Ellis tried to lighten the tone.

"Your office may well smell of popcorn by Monday. Is there anything I can do?"

Ellis shook his head. "I don't think so. Go home, and tell Han I'm sorry." Han had to be sick of hearing how sorry Ellis was by now, surely. "Tell him I'll make it up to him, I promise."

"He might hold you to that." Jay squeezed his shoulder. "Go have a hot bath and some sleep. I'll text you in the afternoon to make sure Randall came by, and if he hasn't I'll find him and smack him into next week."

"Thank you, Jay. I don't know what I'd do without you."

"Hookers and blow," Jay quipped. "All night every night. I ruin your fun."

Ellis mustered a weak half-smile, and Jay fussed over him some more before he finally turned the light off and left Ellis to his own devices.

The problem with his own devices, it soon transpired, was that they were incredibly detailed, and most unforgiving.

THIRTY-SEVEN

RANDALL HADN'T the time to mourn. Not yet. Ellis had been right: Zev's pack needed him.

They ran east until they were well into Newham. It wasn't an area Randall knew all that well, so he was dependent on the others' knowledge. They sprinted through one park and into another, past houses and parked cars, darting from shadow to shadow in a long line to try and avoid attention. When they found a copse of trees to take human form in, the pack was distraught and angry. The moon still rode them hard, and Randall stayed with them until dawn to listen to their heartache, comfort them in their loss. He had to push his own grief aside and see these strangers through until dawn, and even then he couldn't leave them. They were naked in the middle of a public park with a school nearby, and Randall had to organise a way for each and every one of them to get home.

Some had families to go to, others lived alone. Randall sat them down to work out who lived closest, who was able to take someone home with them and find clothes, and which order and direction they should all leave the park in. Those who looked more wolfen he tried to pair with those who could be mistaken for a dog, and he urged everyone to muddy themselves up to hide their markings. The injured ones were to keep their wounds close to their chaperone's side lest some kind member of the public see injured animals and call the RSPCA.

With the plan in place, he exchanged phone numbers, then sent every last one on their way before he allowed himself to go. And once he did, where could he go? He didn't dare go to his own flat for long: without a functioning bathroom it was all but uninhabitable, and Briar would show up there sooner or later.

He wondered whether Ellis would take him in. That would be a bit weird, wouldn't it? They'd been seeing each other a few weeks and if this Alpha nonsense were true they did genuinely love each other, but still it'd be crazy.

He couldn't go to his mum, not in this state. She'd want to know what had upset him so much, and he couldn't tell her.

In the end he ran all the way to Ellis' flat. He couldn't stop off home first because he'd need to swap to his human shape to use his keys, and a naked man at the door to a block of flats wouldn't be well received.

He ran, with his phone, keys and wallet in his mouth. Every few streets he'd drop something - usually the bloody phone - and have to stop and pick it all up again. He needed doggy panniers. He'd suggested them to clients whose dogs needed to feel like they were working, but right now they'd be bloody useful. His phone screen had already cracked after landing on its corner.

Randall took a circuitous route to avoid the rush-hour traffic. Even the Thames Path was busy with pedestrians and cyclists, so for most of his route he was stuck darting behind bushes or sprinting across streets. It must have taken him well over an hour, and by the time he reached the old building which housed Ellis' flat he felt like he was overheating.

He leaped up to hit the button for Ellis' flat with his nose, then pressed it several more times before realising that Ellis couldn't use the intercom.

Please open the door. Please. I know it's early, I know it's daylight, but please just open it…

Nothing.

Could Ellis hear the street from his flat? He heard the police from several minutes away, he had heard the footsteps of a vampire from around a street corner… Randall nosed the button a couple more times in the hope that Ellis couldn't possibly sleep through the racket, then put his belongings down on the doorstep and yipped.

It's me. It's me, I'm here.

The door clicked.

He turned the handle with his jaws, used his flank to push the door open, and grabbed up his stuff once he'd backed halfway into the lobby. After bolting up the stairs as fast as he could, he scrabbled at Ellis' door, and it opened.

He dropped everything, shut the door with his arse, and ran straight to Tiberius' water bowl.

ELLIS LET him in and they'd shared a restless sleep, then showered. The vampire dug out a first aid kit from the bathroom and Randall had dressed his own wounds. They would take a few days to heal properly, and he had no idea whether they would leave scars. Sticking gauze over them was the best he could do.

They lay in bed after, mostly quiet. Ellis held him and gave him time, and Randall appreciated the peace.

"I'm glad you came," Ellis whispered after a while.

Randall didn't know what to say to that. He couldn't admit that he'd been forced to choose Ellis' flat, that he had nowhere else to go. That wasn't the right answer. He couldn't give a happy answer filled with cheer, either.

So instead he asked, "Are you okay?"

"Oh, you tempt me." Ellis' answer was wistful.

"How's that?"

"My natural inclination is to say yes." Ellis' brow creased. "But I'd rather not lie to you. How's about yourself?"

Randall swallowed. "Not a hundred percent," he admitted.

Ellis nodded. "Whatever you need, petal, whatever I can give you, it's yours." He tilted his head to face Randall. His pale gaze missed eye contact by a fraction.

"I don't know what I need." Randall moved slightly. He could pretend Ellis saw him now.

"Do you have a place to live?"

Randall laughed weakly. "I don't know. My bathroom's a wreck, Briar knows where I live-"

"Then stay here." Ellis tipped his head again.

"Don't you think it'd be a bit fast?"

Ellis' features relaxed into a weary half-smile. "I love you, Randall. And I know full well that you love me. Stay here, even if it's just until you get your bathroom fixed and your life back on track. Give yourself time to cope with everything, eh?"

"I do love you," Randall agreed.

Once it had seemed that admitting those feelings would be the end of him, as though daring to open himself up to Ellis would lead to some kind of inevitable pain when Ellis abandoned him. He'd seen what losing dad had done to mum and he never wanted to go through the bitter, empty loneliness of her crying in the night when she thought the boys were asleep.

Now it was as though refusing to accept how he felt would inflict more hurt than just growing a pair and owning his feelings. There were problems in the world far larger than whether or not he could say three words to the most amazing man he had ever met. He had responsibilities now. He was a *leader*, for god's sake. He had to be the best Alpha that he could be, because the lives and well-being and happiness of Zev's pack, their families, their friends, and even strangers they met on the street were in Randall's hands now.

What kind of leader was afraid of love?

"Then stay," Ellis murmured. "Stay and find your feet."

It would mean he had to trek back and forth across the city, but he could do that. He would have to introduce himself to the members of the pack who hadn't been there last night, and get to know even those who were. He had to get them all comfortable with his presence and leadership by the next full moon, and nature wouldn't move that deadline no matter how nicely he asked. He would see if clients preferred him to visit them at their homes, and find another location for those who insisted they come to him.

He'd make sure the pack was okay. He'd get back to work. Every morning he'd wake up beside Ellis, and every night he'd fall asleep in his arms.

Randall smiled hesitantly. "Thanks. But, uh. Just one thing."

Ellis' eyebrows climbed. "What's that?"

"I haven't got any clothes here."

Ellis blinked, then laughed. "Then we'd best get you some, hadn't we? Unless you want to stay indoors all the time. Which I wouldn't say no to."

"You wouldn't?" Randall watched him.

"Oh, aye." Ellis rolled toward him and snaked limbs around his body. He pressed against Randall like a cat in heat and nibbled his ear in a way that made Randall's worries melt away. "I can think of worse things to share my life with than you, naked…"

Randall pressed against Ellis' lithe frame and held him close. "You're a dirty bastard, Ellis O'Neill."

"You bet your arse I am." Ellis traced his palm over Randall's ribs and took care to avoid the patch of gauze. "Christ, you're a beauty."

"Well coming from you, I'll take that as a compliment." Randall settled his cheek to Ellis' shoulder.

Ellis held him in his arms as they dozed, and Randall felt safe at last. He had space; time to breathe, to think, to cope.

He was home.

EPILOGUE

CHARLES REGARDED the young cretin across the expanse of his office. He didn't like them to come any closer than just inside the door, and so almost every visitor had to wait there without ever receiving the offer of a seat. That suited him nicely and kept them in their place all at the same time.

"Speak," he commanded.

"It's about O'Neill."

Charles had no interest in the fool's melodrama, so he threaded power through his words and said, "Tell me."

"He crossed my territory the other night without permission," the boy obliged, unable to stop himself. "He had a human with him, a black man. He said he was travelling on official business, but I've checked. The Council never requested him, and he wasn't there." The youth's features sagged into some small hope that the news had been worth Charles' time, coupled with a little disappointment - likely that Charles hadn't allowed him to spool it out to make himself sound more important.

"Where was the dog?"

The vampire shook his head. "He didn't have it with him. Just the human."

"Describe this human to me."

Charles listened as his visitor prattled on. The boy could use some training in observation skills, because the description largely consisted of "black", "short", and "twenty or thirty". The rest was drivel about what the man had worn and yet still lacked the finer detail of what clothes may have revealed. "Jeans" could have been five pounds or two hundred, and this wastrel couldn't tell the difference.

Still. The boy's lack of intelligence was partly what made him so useful.

"You may go," he cut in when it seemed there was no end in sight. "Tell no-one that you were here."

"Yes, sir."

He listened as the vulgar creature left his property. Best to be certain that the help was long gone before his business for the evening really got underway.

It came soon enough. The familiar sound of a finely-tuned but large engine stopped outside the house. There was a scuffle, and a heartbeat like that of a frightened deer among calmer, more placid notes.

Everything ran like clockwork. His Thralls dragged the young woman into his office. They, mere humans in the pursuit of their duties, were allowed further inside than anyone but a Constable or Councillor, and they pushed Charles' guest down into the chair across from his desk. She kicked and made plaintive, muffled noises from beneath the bag over her head.

"Christy Ryan, isn't it?" Charles said. "Diminutive of Christine, I presume?"

She paused, her limbs akimbo, body pinned to the chair by the hands of three of his biggest oafs. "Mmph?"

"Sit up straight, Miss Ryan, and don't move. Don't speak until I ask you a question, and even then only to answer what I ask of you."

His power coiled from his lips like poison, and she was contaminated by it immediately. She straightened herself in her seat even as her chest rose and fell in panic.

Charles flicked a glance to the Thralls, who pulled the bag from her head and retreated to the door.

Christy Ryan wasn't an unattractive girl, but she didn't do a great deal to aid her cause by burying herself in cheap, shapeless clothes and having her hair back in a messy ponytail. Her perfume was unpleasant; it smelled of chemicals and little else. Her eyes were quite pretty, though: hazel, with a corona of green around the irises. She might scrub up well, as the saying went.

The look of sheer bloody terror on her face was mildly off-putting.

"Do relax," he ordered. "Now, Christine. You have recently taken employment at the O'Neill Gallery, is that correct?"

"Yes," she said.

"Wonderful. You and I are going to become well-acquainted, I can tell." He placed his elbows on the arms of his high-backed leather chair and leaned back against it. "Tell me what you know of Mr. O'Neill's movements. I want to know everything that you know: who he has seen; who his customers are; who his friends and staff are. You will tell me everything that you know, won't you?"

Of course she would. What choice did she have?

TOOTH & CLAW

Blind Man's Wolf

Blood Moon Rising

Balance of Power

Monsters Within

Mirror Flower, Water Moon

———

Visit https://ravenswordpress.com to discover more about the characters and world of Tooth & Claw, and to sign up to the newsletter.

Join the Discord server at https://ravenswordpress.com/discord.

INHERITANCE

Laurence Riley has too many problems, and his uncontrolled psychic powers are just the tip of the iceberg. But when he accidentally summons a god, his only hope for survival might be another wild talent: the enigmatic and aloof British earl, Quentin d'Arcy.

Lose yourself in a world like no other in this award-winning series.

RAVENSWORDPRESS.COM

ACKNOWLEDGMENTS

Blood Moon Rising made me cry, and I hope it made you cry too, because I'm just that kinda gal.

Huge thanks to everyone who helped this book happen! You know who you are!

If you'd like to get sneak peeks of upcoming releases, why not join my Discord server? You can find it here:

ravenswordpress.com/discord

Love,

Amelia Faulkner, London UK, August 2018.

ABOUT THE AUTHOR

Raised on a steady diet of Star Trek and Doctor Who, Amelia Faulkner stood no chance in not becoming a grade-A geek. They have sat on the board of the British Fantasy Society, contributed fiction and fluff to various published roleplaying games, and written non-fiction for SciFiNow and SFX Magazines. For every positive there is an equal and opposite negative, and Amelia is forced to admit that they love Wild Wild West.

In their spare time they enjoy travel, photography, walking their Corgi, and trying to convince their friends to replay the Pathfinder Adventure Card Game with all the Goblins decks.

RAVENSWORDPRESS.COM